Praise for Vanessa Hannam

The Hostage Prince

Vanessa Hannam has built a sumptuous fictional edifice that combines history with imaginative fiction. An enthralling tale of divided loyalties, personal integrity, greed, lust and chivalry, *The Hostage Prince* is teeming with fully realised, memorable characters who linger in the mind long after reading, in particular the protagonist, Lady Elisabeth Anne, whose beauty and spiritual strength bring about the happy denouement. A remarkable achievement.

Shusha Guppy, author of *The Blindfold Horse*

There is a charm and integrity about this novel of the English Civil War that keeps you reading. The author has done her homework, and is thoroughly in love with her subject. If you want an old fashioned (in the best sense) historical novel, then you need not look any further.

Elizabeth Buchan, author of *Revenge of the Middle Aged Woman*

I truly loved this book and can genuinely recommend it without a trace of hesitation… Particularly the heroine, Lizzie – beautiful, intelligent, independent minded and strong headed – with whom the reader and hero fall in love at first sight. Vanessa uses the story to good effect to write about social, political and religious issues raised by the Civil War with rare insight and balance.

Peregrine Worsthorne, *Country Life*

A Rose in Winter

A novel written with passion and relish. Rich in historical detail and feel for the period, it is hugely enjoyable.'

Elizabeth Buchan

Vanessa manages to weave a superb tale of love, drama and deceit into high politics... A real page turner.

Stanley Johnson

The book has a lot to say about balanced love and intelligent marriage, and imparts to its readers much more than a history lesson.

William Radice

Division Belle
A passion for music, the strains of political life and sense of a woman's ability to cope with loss all provide a wealth of inspiration for Vanessa Hannam's novels.

Country Life

Change of Key
As an opera singer, I was astounded at the insight of this book into a very difficult and rarely understood way of life. I was, at once, gripped by the colourful characters and storyline, but it was the little details that brought it so vividly into focus – I did not want it to end.

Valerie Masterdon

SUMMER'S GRACE

SUMMER'S GRACE

To darling Nairn

from

VANESSA HANNAM

Vanessa with Love

x

QUARTET

First published in 2016 by Quartet Books Limited
A member of the Namara Group
27 Goodge Street, London W1T 2LD
Copyright © Vanessa Hannam 2016
The right of Vanessa Hannam
to be identified as the author of this work
has been asserted by her in accordance with the
Copyright, Designs and Patents Act, 1988.

A catalogue record for this book
is available from the British Library
ISBN 978 0 7043 7421 8

Typeset by Josh Bryson
Printed and bound in Great Britain by
T J International Ltd, Padstow, Cornwall

In loving memory of Maria Attallah

"There are no keys for there are no doors. Here it is – Life – not locked away from us, but all around us."

Kahlil Gibran

PROLOGUE

PORTSMOUTH HARBOUR, JULY 1740

'That stink would turn a hardened stomach,' said one of the two burly oarsmen as they approached the first ship, rowing furiously against the tide. As they got nearer the smell was familiar to them: it was of death and decay, festering food and rotting flesh. They were bringing provisions to the great ships bobbing on the high tide, some of which were strangely silent. The two men in their small open supply boat looked apprehensive as they stowed the oars and came alongside the enormous Centurion; the largest in a flotilla of nine heavily armed vessels comprising the squadron that was to be bound for the South Seas. The ships loomed impressively but eerily devoid of commotion. The arriving men would have expected a hive of activity; carpenters and sailors working, to repair masts, decks and the slimy hulks where all manner of sea creatures and weeds had made a home. To the unfamiliar eye the ships appeared top heavy, a maze of masts and spars rising to a great height from elegantly built cabins in what looked like hastily added afterthoughts. Intricate carvings and ornate bow windows looked glaringly out of place on what was, after all, a warship. 'The first gale and this lot will go,' sneered the bigger oarsman.

'Is this a ghost ship? How do we get this lot on board if there is nobody to help?' called up the smaller of the two. 'There's not a man jack here.'

'Ahoy there,' they yelled in unison, 'anyone aboard?'

A scruffy, emaciated sailor peered down at them from the great height of the vessel.

'Load it, I will let down the pulley. But where to put it? We are alive with rats and lice. Two men died yesterday but a decent burial will have to wait till the Commodore comes,' came the desultory reply.

More of the crew appeared and soon the deck was strewn with sacks and kegs of the things that were supposed to keep the sailors alive for the next few months. But who were these men, the visitors wondered, as they observed the motley collection that had begun to assemble? Some of them looked like invalids and several were minus a limb; one or two of them had the air of a man who waits only for a timely end and cares nothing for the manner of it. The rest were a ragtag of boys and men pressganged from the streets of Portsmouth, and some were the flotsam that worked the boats in the rivers and docks of London, judging by their accent. Now they were trapped in an uncertain fate, as they had been contained on board for almost nine months with no news of the actual voyage while the Admiralty dithered and prevaricated. It was fear of being shot and a daily pint of brandy that kept them there, as well as the fact that none of them could swim: the ships stood back just far enough from shore to prevent a man from jumping.

When the two men had supervised the loading of the cargo of salt beef, sea biscuits already infested with the weevil, and, of course, the rum, the sailors began to lower it into the hold. They had to cover their mouths and noses with the kerchiefs they kept about their necks to avoid not only the stench but swarms of flies, which assaulted them in an angry cloud. The place seemed to heave in the dim light, so much so that the visitors wondered if it were the motion of the ship on the water, or if their eyes deceived them.

'It's the lice,' said the sailor who seemed to be in charge, having seen the expression of horror on the visitors faces. 'They are already breeding and no man can sleep a night without the biting and the nibbling; one of the dead men had his feet nibbled off as he slept and we haven't even got to sea yet. Course he came with some of this other rabble let out of Newgate Prison. The poor devils thought it was a gift from heaven but now they find themselves in a worse hell.'

'My god, let's get off this hulk before we catch the ague,' said the bigger man. 'Lets dump this lot wherever we can … it's not for us to worry about these poor devils. One bite of this filth and they will die very quick, it rots the guts does this stuff.'

Later in the comforting surroundings of the alehouse on the quay, the two men discussed the sad state of the King's navy. Neither of them were particularly surprised at what they had witnessed, since they had experience of the way sailors were regarded. They were viewed as no more important than the wretched animals also taken on long sea voyages.

'Take man's dignity and you take his soul,' the bigger man added firmly.

'I was there when they loaded the horses for France,' said the other. 'Animals know when death awaits them. I lived on a farm before I came to London and it's the eyes, they have that look about them. Those poor blighters today, they know it's the last they will see of the land they were born in.'

'True enough,' the bigger man replied. 'But it's the wives and children that I think of, left in rags and filth, starving on the steps of the Admiralty while the great Lordships hold their fancy kerchiefs to their greedy noses, and get them shovelled out of the way like sacks of rubbish.' He paused before continuing. 'Don't mind telling you, things have got to change or the poor will rise and those fine gentlemen and their great ladies will be sent to hell; but truth to tell there are some that are speaking for the common man these days, and that Walpole is the one that should watch his back on dark nights.'

'He has the King's ear they say, but soon things will change,' his friend replied. 'This is a prime minister who does not know how the men and women of England suffer and how we feel about our King since the poor Queen, God bless her, departed this life and left a father and son who fight like rats in a sack. I feel it in my bones, time for a new generation to stand up and make themselves heard.'

This new generation were that moment ascending the grand steps which led to the forbidding facade of the Admiralty headquarters. There were two of them; Commodore Anson walking ahead of his companion who followed with an aura of deference. Both had their hair neatly tied back with black ribbon and were smartly dressed in what passed for naval uniform. Anson had with him a bag of coins, and he stood quietly among the supplicant press of emaciated women and children, who had little to decently cover themselves with on that drab May day when rain came down in a thin mist.

He handed the bag to his companion, instructing him to distribute the contents. The crowd did not push forward but assembled in an orderly manner, taking the coins quietly, and some of the poor women attempted what might pass for a little curtsy.

'You see the basic dignity of a human being is in danger here, rob a man of that and he has no soul, treat people like animals and animals they will become,' the Commodore said. 'This will be a mighty last voyage and on it I will gather all that I can to reshape this navy. It is what made England great but now it is a shameful thing, a refuge for old men who have no moral compass. I tell you, it is the compass that must guide us; be it on the sea or in our souls, the compass is all.' With that he slapped his companion on the back and they approached the Admiralty office, Mr Anson's boots clacking purposefully towards the door where they were announced inside.

Behind the imposing desk sat the First Lord of the Admiralty, Sir John Norris, aged eighty, and Sir Charles, aged seventy-three, an officer long retired but on the Admiralty board. Both men wore full periwigs and their wrinkled prune faces were incongruously framed in the silver silken locks. Neither smiled or got up. Truthfully, neither of them could, as they were troubled by gout and suffering from the health problems associated with too much port. The atmosphere was decidedly chilly and there was an intentionally awkward silence while the old men waited for the Commodore to say something. But the Commodore audaciously did not and as the clock ticked loudly a full five minutes of silence ensued. Eventually Sir Charles broke it, as the Commodore knew he would.

'So what is it this time, Mr Anson?' he began querulously. 'Complaints about the soap or the down in the pillows? My God man, is it sailors you are taking on the voyage or a lot of lily livered girls?'

Anson's companion stood to one side in respectful silence as his superior began to speak.

'Well, my Lord,' replied the Commodore evenly, 'I have just been delivered one hundred and seventy men from the Chelsea Hospital, the most decrepit of the Chelsea Pensioners, many of them suffering from infected old wounds and other chronic incapacitating illnesses and some of them over seventy years of age. I should imagine what healthy men we do have amongst these poor devils, or amongst the prisoners from Newgate and young lads pressed from the streets, will need all the nursing skills available and as much soap as they can get their hands on.'

Sir Charles regarded the Commodore with distaste. This was the kind of man he disliked. The Commodore was a man who had started life at sea and was hardened to it. He had moved through the ranks, joining the navy aged fourteen as a volunteer on a gunship called the *Ruby*, and had soon been on the successful voyage during which they captured the *Porto Bello*, a Spanish treasure ship, off the coast of South America. He was, as a result, already a rich man. He did not look his forty-two years of age and had an air of quiet confidence about him that the elderly, moribund Sir Charles found arrogant and challenging.

Sir John had also stiffened when the Commodore referred to the age of the pensioners on board, recognising a not-so-subtle comparison with Their Lordships' decrepitude. But he did not quite share Sir Charles's obstructive attitude to the Commodore. It was Sir John who had first spotted the man's leadership qualities and promoted him to the rank of lieutenant at the age of nineteen. However, with an old man's jealousy, he thought Anson had risen a little too high. It was time to put a reef in his sail.

'Upon my word, Mr Anson, you must think the King's navy has money and men to spare to do more for such a venture as this,' he said slowly, regarding the younger man through narrowed eyes.

'Well, Sir John,' said the Commodore, with a lightness that further annoyed both men, as of course it was meant to. 'There is the need to discover many things about navigation and the prevention of the diseases that carry away most of the men Your Lordships laughingly refer to as the King's navy... A navy, as we will call it then, survives on its provisions as indeed an army marches on its stomach. I do make sailors of even the most wretched of men, and it is my intention to show that we can indeed have a navy that will be respected and productive.

'To start with there is the matter of longitude. Did you know, My Lords, that men had this knowledge centuries ago and yet the proper use of it defeats us still. If Your Lordships would only consider how many men would be saved if you would advance the money for the last minute adjustments to Mr Harrison's clock. Depending on its durability, it could transform navigation as we know it.'

'Oh yes, the contraption you took on the *Centurion* to Lisbon,' said Sir Charles in a bored voice. He lent back a little in the high-backed chair, which gave him a magisterial air. The Commodore could not suppress a slight smile as the chair and Sir Charles both creaked with a noise sounding suspiciously like something else.

Sir John interceded quickly. 'That must have been at least four years ago.' He looked around furtively. He tapped his fingers and spoke quietly. 'Surely we would have more evidence of its success by now if it were as revolutionary as you claim.'

'The problem is that Your Lordships have failed to express an interest in it,' said the Commodore flatly.

The Commodore knew perfectly well that it was the twenty thousand pound prize money to solve the problem of longitude which loomed in Their Lordships' minds. It was an enormous fortune and some of their own cronies were chasing that particular star. The idea was pure genius, so simple in its basic concept: a clock that set itself to Greenwich Time in London at noon. If accurate it would tell you how far you were from London at that exact second, so your precise position could be found wherever you were. And midnight locally meant you were half way round the world.

'One hundred and eighty degrees longitude. That would be half my voyage completed, but I fear it will not be the case,' said the Commodore.

'So then why are we not presented with the finished clock, if it is so simple?' asked Sir John sarcastically.

The Commodore paused. He knew well this was a waste of breath, but he answered eventually as Their Lordships' gaze wandered distractedly, Sir Charles's aged hand tapping a quill pen on the highly polished desk in a slow, stuttering rhythm.

'Mr Harrison has not quite perfected the final touches, which would enable the piece to keep accurate time in treacherous seas – for instance when rounding Cape Horn at what will now be an intemperate time,' the Commodore said coldly.

Of course he knew full well there was a multiplicity of reasons why he would not get the clock in time. The board probably did not want such a jewel to fall into the hands of the Spanish, with whom the English were at war. And the board were thinking of many ways of retaining the prize money. Anson also knew, sadly, that Harrison probably had perfected the instrument by now but was guarding it from the men who wanted to take the credit for his work.

Sir Charles had decided to bring the meeting to a close, saying there was nothing more they were prepared to do for the venture. But there was still one matter he wanted to address and his reasons were not entirely altruistic.

'Before you leave us there is one thing,' he said slowly.

The Commodore recognised this as a dismissal but of course he asked what this one thing might be.

'The *Neustra di Covadonga*, the Manila Galleon?' said Sir Charles slowly.

'Yes the great galleon,' answered the Commodore with a slight smile. 'We will get it, but I fear it will cost us dear.

Now, with all the delays, yet again the seas will not be as I would have preferred. This circumnavigation of the globe is fraught with challenges; it is a voyage into the unknown. If we survive the Horn, which, as I have already explained, will be hazardous, we will winter in China.' He paused for effect. 'Perhaps in Macau.' he suggested, wondering if Their Lordships had ever even heard of the place. 'We will search for the galleon in the Pacific on our return journey.'

'Search for the galleon in the Pacific if you will but you will be in the doldrums; you will encounter the Great Pizarro's squadron. You young men have your dreams, but it is a question of turning them into reality,' snorted Sir Charles with more than his usual scepticism.

The Commodore was used to this, and was quite comfortable with the idea of being a 'young' man at forty-two. He considered that Sir Charles was being sarcastic, so he spiked his guns on both counts with his usual studied calm.

'Young I am not, My Lord, but experienced yes, and I am well tested, I would say. I never expect a man on my ship to do anything I would or could not do myself. The men know this, and this earns their loyalty and respect.'

He paused for a moment and drew his chair closer, looking with unnerving directness at the old men who were, in his opinion, no longer fit for purpose.

'Hum,' said Sir John.

'Pizarro will be tired,' the Commodore went on, unabashed. 'His men will be exhausted. We will be good as new, having wintered and repaired in Macau. His ship, the *Galleon*, will be easy prey, and yes, I will find it and I will bring you back the biggest, indeed the greatest, prize of the oceans. The long voyage between Acapulco and Manila will have weakened the Spaniards. We will return by the Cape of Good Hope, and each man shall have his portion. That is the navy I dream of, Your Lordships.'

'What do you mean by that?' asked Sir Charles warily.

'I mean, Sir, that I will pay the widows the share their men would have got. If men have perished their families will get it from my portion.'

When the Commodore had gone, the old men did not laugh and smile smugly as they so often did. Each knew they had been privy to the wind of change. Anson would come back and with him would come a very different navy. One they had fought to resist. But they had probably lost the battle.

CHAPTER ONE

PORTSMOUTH,
SEPTEMBER 1740

They huddled together: the mother, the father, the two boys whose heads now came to their mother's shoulder, and Grace. She was a tall girl, towering above her siblings as their father clasped them all to his stiff blue uniform with gold epaulets on its shoulders. There were so many components to the scent Grace breathed in as she stood there that day: the new cloth, the tang of the sea, the faint aroma of animals as they were herded towards the waiting ship. There was strongest of all the pomade her father used on his thick fair hair which, bleached by his years at sea, was tied back in a bright blue satin ribbon, the one her mother had worn on the day of their wedding sixteen years ago.

'My precious family,' Matthew rasped as he held them so tightly that the boys in the base of the human pyramid could hardly breathe. Grace's mother Margaret knew she must not weep, it would not help, and, besides, looking about, she noticed that most of the men boarding the rest of the ships in the flotilla had nobody to wave a kerchief for them. They looked bedraggled and thin and most of them old or disabled.

'What kind of men are these, husband?' she whispered into his ear. 'They look fit for a shroud and who could call them "topmen"? They can hardly get up the plank to the ship, let alone go up aloft.'

Captain Matthew Lively stood back, putting distance between them to answer her directly, and spoke in a businesslike manner, addressing his whole family. He knew that Margaret was used to goodbyes; after all, she had bought into a life as the wife of a sailor. But whereas he was fired with the spirit of adventure and the dream of prize money beyond imagination, she would be left on the windswept quayside with nothing but uncertainty and foreboding.

'Wife, children,' he said gravely, 'this is one of the most exciting voyages in naval history. I am proud to be on the flagship the *Centurion* serving under the great Commodore Anson.'

One of the sick looking men who were being marched to the ship had heard Matthew's words and called out to them. 'Well I for one will not be coming back, so I am looking forward to heaven if heaven it may be,' said the man without a tremor in his voice. Then he turned and marched with his one-legged limp towards the boat which was to take him to the ship.

The man's remark, called out so flippantly, caused Margaret to have one of those rarest of moments when a realisation flashes into the mind and nothing will ever be quite the same again. This would never happen again to her, this farewell, on a windswept quayside. Matthew could think what he liked, but if and when he returned she would be a different, hardened woman. But she still had her fantasies, and in her mind's eye she even saw a glimpse of another figure, one who would be to her as Matthew could have been. She had loved Matthew with all her soul but the love he returned was of a different nature. His dreams were of adventure, they did not incorporate the small things of which happiness is made. It struck Margaret that there was a selfishness in the choices he had made. It was she who would have to steer a very different kind of ship. Aboard it were her three children and she suddenly felt very alone, and abandoned. Then the small voice of hope tweaked in the back of her mind. She would make something of her life without him; this was about survival. It was as if a door had been opened into a room she had never entered, but which had always been there waiting for her.

'Wife, children,' Matthew repeated solemnly, 'we don't listen to that kind of talk. The Commodore knows the journey well; there is no safer pair of hands for a man to trust in. This is a great flotilla and when I wave to you we will be on our first step to a great adventure. It is the biggest flotilla ever to set sail on such an undertaking. Why, just look at it! The *Gloucester*, the *Pearl*, the *Severn*, and the great supply ship the *Wager*, which is filled with all a man can need, supplies that will last us for years if needs be.' He faltered, seeing the alarm on his wife's face, and crossed himself. 'Pray God we will be home before they run out.'

'But father, you will be rounding Cape Horn,' gulped Samuel, the younger son. 'I have looked it up on the map, as you showed me how. It is dangerous and how do you know the ships are strong enough or that your water will not be sour by then?'

'Do not be fearful, Samuel,' answered Matthew reassuringly. 'Just look at those ships, my boy, beautifully fitted and in perfect order. New sails, new rigging. We are as well-equipped as any man could hope for. And as for the water, we sail firstly to the Isle of Wight, to St Helen's bay to fill up the water casks; it is the freshest, sweetest water, which would last for ten years or more, so there is no need to worry about that.'

'Do you think we are stupid?' Margaret burst out suddenly. 'Do you think we wives have not got to hear about the Commodore's battle with your fine Admiralty over the filthy sheets sent on board crawling with vermin, the mattresses stuffed with sweepings from the poultry house floors and the feathers with the flesh and bones still attached?' Margaret felt a rising anger as she allowed herself to think of the low value the men who ran the Admiralty had for these brave men who were to sail in the name of the King. *Were they fools, these men, or, more likely, villains?*

Matthew knew full well that the two old men who ran the Admiralty were in their dotage and had lost their grip on the reality of what would be required of these ships and the men who sailed them. It was their petty wrangling that had delayed the departure of the fleet by at least two months. Now they would be setting off at a most dangerous time, hitting equinoxial gales and rounding the Horn at its worst. But he knew he must reassure his family as best he could, despite having many doubts himself about the venture.

He thought about the hasty addition of the new quarters, created from storage space for the proliferation of officers' cabins. As a result of this adjustment the ships lay low in the water and the portholes caulked up. This would encourage disease through the lack of air. The Commodore was known for the attention he gave to ensuring healthy conditions for his men and the rows with the naval board had been numerous, even over a request for soap to wash the filthy sheets, but to little avail in this case. Then there was the engagement of invalids from the naval hospital, in a bid to avoid paying their pensions. Everybody knew most of them would die before they hit the Atlantic – that is, those who had not managed to desert before the ships sailed. These men were joined by the terrified, resentful men and boys pressed from the back streets of God knows where, most of whom had never seen a ship.

'Now, family, you stand to attention and listen to me, Captain Matthew Lively,' he said with a touch of humour. 'I can see the Commodore approaching and he will have this lot brushed into shape before they know it. He is the best officer the navy has ever had, an officer who will never ask a man or boy to do anything he could or would not do himself. He has already been aloft inspecting every rope and sail. He could navigate through the most fearsome of seas and he cares for his men. You'll be hard-pressed to find a man who would not lay down his life for him when this voyage is ended, you have my word on it.'

The family turned to greet the great Commodore himself. He was accompanied by the beautiful dark lady whom everyone knew was the Commodore's close friend, and some would say his paramour. She was, even at first glance, a great lady, standing apart, and she bore herself with an exotic style that commanded respect. A small dark boy followed behind her, lifting the train of her intricate black lace gown, which would otherwise have trailed along the mire of the ground that she tripped over with dainty elegance.

Margaret thought the Commodore was a fine looking man by any standards, but despite the new uniform and heavy gold embroidery, nothing could disguise a certain earthy quality there was to him. It was said that in far off South Carolina where he had spent some considerable time, 'he had an eye for the ladies'. He had spent many years at sea and romance was one thing, but undertaking this voyage ... well? She wondered about this. He was old now for such challenges. She had calculated him to be at least forty and his many triumphs must have taken their toll. He was heavily tanned and his face was deeply lined. His dark kindly eyes, large well-formed nose and full lips made an attractive impression and were instantly engaging. A ready smile hovered on his face, rather as if he would read humour into the direst of circumstances. His companion, on the other hand, was unfathomable and strangely out of place on the busy quayside, buzzing with the rough hue of life. Margaret gazed with fascination as the Commodore presented her.

'Mr Lively, Mrs Lively may I introduce Donna Consuelo Gonzalez,' he said with evident pride.

'So, Mrs Lively,' the mysterious woman said warmly with a faint accent. The family bobbed a greeting as the woman went on with a dazzling smile. 'This is your lovely family, how delightful.'

Matthew smiled proudly as the Commodore's companion, about whom there had of course been many rumours, was introduced to his children. He thought her a woman of unusual charm and kindness as she took each hand in turn, beginning tactfully with Rupert his youngest son, now just twelve but with, as his mother often said, 'a small body, big brain'.

'And you, Master Rupert, you have a scholarship to the Mercer's school, I believe. You are to be congratulated,' the woman said in a rich mellifluous voice. The boy looked with awe at Donna Consuelo and could not utter a word.

'And this is Samuel,' interjected Margaret quickly, for she felt very keenly her eldest son's lack of brains, although of brawn he had plenty. It was, she thought, always Rupert who came in for approbation.

'My and what a fine lad,' came the strong voice of the Commodore as he ruffled Samuel's hair. 'And I dare say you will be following in your father's footsteps. In fact you are of an age already I expect. You wouldn't be the first father and son on the same ship... Ask your mother and we will have you aloft in a flash,' the Commodore quipped. Matthew caught the furious look his wife darted at him and put his arm firmly about Samuel's shoulders. The conversation was interrupted by a commotion and loud voices and all eyes were drawn to a small boat approaching the quay, rowed by four smartly dressed sailors and an officer. The craft drew up some steps adjacent to where the group were standing and the officer saluted as he saw the Commodore and Captain Lively. A strong incoming tide made the water choppy against the quayside walls as the Commodore broke away to enquire what was going on and Consuelo followed with the Livelys. In the boat, prone and lifeless, were two young boys about the same age as Samuel. Their heads hung unceremoniously into the bilges of the boat, murky water sloshing about their noses and mouths.

Margaret let out a cry, 'for God's sake, they are drowning! Get their heads up! They will drown, they can't breathe!'

'Stay back, madam, this is no place for you to be and it's too late for the poor lads, I am afraid,' said the Commodore.

'What does he mean, too late, father?' cried Grace, her bonnet falling back from her ashen face. 'Get them out, do something.'

The officer in the boat signalled to the men and the boys were manhandled out of the bobbing boat and dumped on the quay. Suddenly the bright sunny day laden with brave promise became grey and silent. The Commodore removed his hat, likewise Captain Lively. The last thing he wanted his family to see as he set off for this voyage was a scene such as this. Before he could say anything the officer spoke.

'They jumped, terrified they were, and it proves our point, sir, that it is a bad day for the navy when lads such as these are pressed, taken from their mothers when there is not yet a hair on their faces.'

'What do you mean they jumped?' said Grace in a shrill voice, and Matthew Lively flushed with embarrassment at the directness of his women.

'Why didn't they swim for it?' chipped in Rupert, encouraged by the forthright remarks his mother had made previously.

'Sailors can't swim by and large. Country boys like this have never seen the sea, but sometimes the terror of what they see on board is so great that they lose their minds and jump,' said the officer.

One of the men tasked with rowing the ghastly cargo to shore stood very close now and nudged the bodies with his foot. 'See, young mistress, he is dead now; nothing to be done.'

'Wretches, the pair of them,' chipped in another of the sailors, a weasel-faced man with skin covered in warts. 'Scum that's what they was like,' he persisted. 'Not even the guts of a girl. The birch, that's the only way.'

'Silence, bosun, I will have none of that talk here. Show some respect. There are women and children present and there will be no brutality on my ships. Do I make myself clear?' thundered the voice of the Commodore.

'Why didn't you try to save them?' Grace shrieked.

'For what?' said the wart-covered sailor quickly. 'They would have been flogged within an inch and nothing left of them. It breaks men, you see.' The man closed his eyes as if to shut out a terrible vision. 'That kind on flogging, you wouldn't want it for any creature; deserters are better left to drown. It's not a bad death, miss,' he added by way of consolation.

Matthew Lively was a hardened sailor, he would never be anything else and a man has to become used to death if he wants a life at sea. This was not shocking to him, he had seen it many times and much worse, but one of the reasons he had chosen to serve the Commodore with such loyalty and admiration was because of the man's vision of a new and humane service. He knew the Commodore disliked pressed men and invalids, and no better leader could there be. Matthew could tell that he was deeply disturbed by the sight of the dead boys lying cold and unmourned on the hard grey stone. And, as if reading Matthew's thoughts, the Commodore spoke again.

'Ladies, we should withdraw from here, this is man's work. You men, I want to see some respect for these young lads. We will take them out to the ship and give them a decent sailor's burial in the ocean that claimed them. Word must be got to the families that their sons died bravely. We don't want to ruin lives if we can help it. Let their people receive the news with pride that they lost their lads in service to their country, and God rest their souls.'

Grace had been watching the figures of the drowned boys in silent horror. Responding to her impulsive nature, which had often got her into trouble, she went to the boy nearest to her before the Commodore could guide them from the spectacle, and knelt beside the boy's head. Her mother put out a restraining hand, but Grace shrugged it off and with great speed she ripped her new shawl from her shoulders and bundled it up. Lifting gently, she put it under one of the boy's heads, which flopped sideways. Then, to a gasp from the crowd now gathered, the boy opened his eyes and vomited a jet of murky sea water. His whole body convulsed into life amidst cries from the people who pressed closer.

'It is a miracle!' declared an awestruck woman in the crowd.

The first thing the boy saw as the life flowed back into him was the face of Grace looking down at him from above, tears coursing along her cheeks. 'Am I in heaven?' he rasped. Matthew knelt down beside the pair and lifted the boy to a sitting position, as the crowd moved forward.

Before she could think what she was saying, Grace found herself whispering in his ear urgently: 'For God's sake get up and run ... run for your life!'

Her father heard her and his eyes met hers, his face inscrutable. He nodded almost imperceptibly. The boy stood up and fixed Grace with a look she would never forget. Every feature of hers was sealed in his mind forever. There is sometimes a second in which a man can save his life, literally the chance of a lifetime, that is all he has, and she could not be sure he would take it, or have the strength to take it. But as the crowd pushed in still further, the boy darted to his feet and ran between their legs, behind the women's skirts as Consuelo's little dark page nimbly blocked the path of one quick witted sailor. Among the throng of people that encircled him there were none who would have stopped him, not even the Commodore, except the bosun, whose heart shrivelled bitterly as he saw the boy fly like a trapped bird from a cage. Bosun thought of a moment long ago when he'd had the choice to make his own escape. He had made the wrong decision and embarked on a journey from which there was no turning back. As for the boy, he did not look back, not even once.

CHAPTER TWO

A JOURNEY FROM PORTSMOUTH TO LONDON

'Well, my dear, it is settled then,' Consuelo had said firmly. 'You will be coming with me in my coach. We will take you directly to your door.'

At first Margaret had demurred. She was not sure how wise it would be to get so close to the Commodore's lady, but the boys had whooped excitedly at the prospect and Grace had squeezed her mother's hand encouragingly, relieved at the idea of not having to travel on the public stage coach and share the journey with a selection of people like the ones they had travelled with before. There had been a woman with a bad cold who had coughed and sneezed all over Grace and wiped her nose on a grimy sleeve. And another passenger had returned from the break on the journey at Guildford with a bottle of rum, glugging at it until he fell into somnolent slumber, lolling onto her mother's new bonnet, crushing the feathers and dribbling onto the sleeve of her gown.

On the way down, they'd been forced to spend the night at an inn near the harbour, as it was an early sailing to catch the tide. None of them had slept and Margaret had felt the first pricks of bed bugs and fleas. She was aware that on their return she would be obliged to remove the whole family's clothing and they would all be subjected to what the children knew as 'Mama's War' on crawling creatures.

So Margaret had, in the end, accepted gratefully and now they were comfortably seated in Donna Consuelo's coach, a delightful picnic spread out on their laps with fine linen napkins and silver goblets.

Donna Consuelo was observing the family with interest. She was a woman with a history so very different from anything she had thus far encountered in England. She had long ago made a decision not to talk to people about her story; their eyes would glaze over and they might offer some polite inanities, but she found that people generally preferred to talk about themselves and found her a sympathetic listener. She had a sharp eye and was an unusually acute judge of situations and characters, something the Commodore had found beguiling. But she was still baffled by the blurred lines of hierarchal snobbery which pervaded the English psyche. Although of noble birth, she had found herself not quite accepted by the inner circle of English aristocracy, so she floated serenely on the outside of it, occasionally bursting through with her beauty, wit and charm and above all money – only to find that sooner or later a shutter went down, as if her strange foreign extraction might contaminate in some way. Take for example Pepe, her little page: he occupied a place in her heart that was unique and she adored him intensely, but, because he was a mulatto, his closeness to her was something she had already perceived as inappropriate in this strange country where children of mixed race were an oddity.

Now she watched this very English family with the piercing dark eyes that had captivated the Commodore many years before. The girl struck her as the most interesting, with something unpredictable about her. Consuelo had been very moved by the way Grace had lain down her obviously new scarf beneath the head of the young sailor, and also noticed that Rupert had quietly retrieved it when all the fuss had died down. Consuelo had whipped it away from him and handed it to her maid Jane telling her to get it rinsed in clean water at once. She presumed the scarf was flapping away somewhere on top of the coach where Jane now sat making eyes at John the driver, with the little page happily between them. Normally Jane would travel inside, but today it was so bright and sunny she had asked to be outside with the young man.

Consuelo watched Grace carefully and had asked her a few innocent questions; but the girl was taking her time in responding, with a slightly nervous look about her, and Consuelo was not quite sure whether this was shyness or something more complicated.

In fact, Grace was in awe of the exotic Consuelo and intrigued by the way the little dark page had tired of the open air and slid in through the window like an acrobat. He now sat close to his mistress, fallen against her bosom in an easy slumber. Grace was transfixed by the fan of black lustrous lashes on his cheeks and the cherubic fullness of his lips. Occasionally Consuelo put a gentle arm about him as the coach swayed.

Soon they all descended into sleepy silence, during which Consuelo had a chance to observe the girl admiringly. She decided that Grace had definite potential, with her unusually bright blue eyes set in a somewhat unfashionably sun kissed face and framed by an unruly cloud of tawny hair, which changed from blond to a reddish colour as the light caught it. She concluded that the girl must spend a lot of time in the open without the modesty of an obligatory bonnet. She had also noticed that Mrs Lively had the coarse hands of a woman familiar with hard domestic work, but that came as no surprise as the pay for middle ranking naval officers was a scandal. By contrast the girl's hands were fine and delicate and she kept them still and modestly folded in her lap. On her right little finger she wore a handsome ring with a single pink stone, which looked to Consuelo like a pink sapphire. The ring was strangely incongruous in a family that was clearly struggling to keep up appearances.

'So don't be shy, my dear. Tell me about yourself, Grace,' said Consuelo, when it became clear that the rest of the coach had fallen into a deep sleep.

'I am lucky, Ma'am. My parents allow me to do the thing I am best at,' answered the girl, 'although it is neither fashionable, nor considered appropriate for a young lady. I sometimes feel very guilty because my mother has to work so hard while I have the luxury of doing the thing at which I am best.'

'Come, Grace,' said Mrs Lively, waking suddenly and flushing with embarrassment, feeling that her daughter was being *far* too frank with Donna Consuelo and revealing too much about their straitened circumstances. 'Donna Consuelo,' she went on, 'does not want to hear about these things.'

'Well, she obviously does, Mama, or she wouldn't have asked, would she?' piped in Rupert, who had also wakened and never liked to be left out of a conversation. Always showing a singular disregard for social semantics and niceties, he was eager to continue, but his mother soon put a stop to that.

'Rupert, hold your tongue. If your father was here he would box your ears,' cried Mrs Lively, beginning to feel quite desperate at the behaviour of her extraordinary children.

'Well he is not here, Mama,' offered Rupert with a grin, 'and even if he was, which he hardly ever is, he would never box anyone's ears. He always says he sees too much of that sort of thing on board ship.'

'Well, Mrs Lively, you certainly have a family who live up to their name – most charming and delightful,' said Consuelo, smiling broadly. 'But none of you have told me yet what it is that keeps Grace so absorbed?'

'She is a musician,' explained Rupert. 'People say she sings like a nightingale and mother has got her a harpsichord and she is a genius. That's why she wears mother's ring – to remind her to keep her hands out of rough work in case she injures them.'

'So, Grace, where did you learn your music?' asked Consuelo.

'My father plays the fiddle and our grandfather was a ship's doctor but he also made instruments,' replied Grace, warming to the subject and whipping off her bonnet, which she had been longing to do, as it was decidedly hot in the coach despite the open window. Consuelo nodded, indicating she wished to hear more and deriving great pleasure from seeing the young girl opposite begin to come out of herself. To Consuelo Grace seemed the embodiment of youth and hope, but she was also still no more than a child on the cusp of life. She was certainly going to be a beauty, Consuelo thought, but there was something a little wayward about her and, as if to confirm this impression, Grace's hair now sprang into life, free from the constriction of the bonnet, and tumbled about her shoulders.

Consuelo was put in mind of a painting she had seen in the Catholic Cathedral Santa Domingo Carolina when she was a child; taken back for a moment to those days when she did not know the path her life would take, she began to feel a great sympathy for Margaret Lively. In one way Consuelo knew as well as any woman that when a man becomes fired up with the spirit of adventure, nothing can stop him; he seldom turns his head to the life he has left behind, until, that is, death looks him in the face and he calls, as they always do, for his mother. But how she envied Margaret Lively these wonderful children, the life they gave her, a reason for getting up in the morning even though things were obviously hard. She was bound by a routine of care that contrasted with Consuelo's own. Consuelo came out of her reverie as

Grace continued to explain the family's musical bent and her grandfather's craftsmanship.

'He made the fiddle my father takes with him wherever he goes, and father says it is his consolation at sea when they are on a long stretch and a man can get bored.'

'Well, that is wonderful! I would love to hear you play, my dear. Perhaps we can arrange something?' said Consuelo. 'I have a close friend, Mr Handel, who has found great favour with the King and often plays at court where a singer called Susannah Maria Cibber is making a great name for herself. Mr Handel writes serious music for her because she made her name singing in a kind of musical play called *The Beggar's Opera*, which has been the rage in high circles but is not a fit thing for a serious young woman.'

'Well, that would be very nice,' exclaimed Margaret, not thinking this was a serious suggestion, but nevertheless gratified by the interest and to some extent reassured that Donna Consuelo disapproved of vulgar entertainments. She had heard mention of the work written by John Gaye and instinctively felt it was somehow improper. To her relief the conversation took a different tone.

'You will meet our grandfather. He lives beside us and when father goes off we see a lot of him,' chipped in Rupert. 'He looks after us when father is away.'

This brought Margaret down to earth again. She followed Consuelo's gaze to her daughter and realised that Grace would be a woman by the time she saw her father again and that both the boys would be launching themselves into the adult world... With the exception of Matthew's father there would be no man to help her steady her children as they took on the slings and arrows of life. For a moment her spirit failed her. If it were not for her father in law she did not know how she would survive. It was not a woman's world. A tear began to trickle down her cheek.

Her tears were observed by Consuelo, who was momentarily glad of the trials she had encountered at such an early age. She fell to thinking about a time long ago when she knew nothing of what was to follow, of the losses and consolations. She had been dreading saying goodbye to her protector but here among her new friends for some reason she felt a flicker of pleasurable anticipation.

Chapter Three

Holly Farm,
Clapham Common

'Oh, my heavens, the lad has let the geese into the front garden!' exclaimed Margaret as the coach swung to a halt. It was late now, at least ten o'clock, but the bright moon illuminated the common and the houses that overlooked it. On the far side were several mansions with sweeping drives, but here, in the woodland beside a small lake, upon which the moon glistened, were a group of more modest houses. By far the most attractive of these was Holly Farm, which nestled behind a hedge of vigorous holly trees through which could be seen the flashing white of geese disturbed by the coach's arrival.

It had been decided that the great Consuelo would stay the night in the house and Margaret was quickly out of the coach to alert Alice, the maid who often complained of 'luggin and draggin', a sobriquet by which she was sometimes referred to.

A lantern appeared at once, but it was not Alice, rather an elderly man who hastened his step to welcome them. The boys were the first to run to him and he enfolded them in a tight embrace. Eventually they stood aside to make room for Margaret who clung to the old gentleman as he held her warmly. Margaret felt tears prick at her eyes and said a quick prayer of thanks that at least the world still offered them the gentle support of their home and those loved ones who remained.

Consuelo watched from the coach as the driver and her maid came to help their mistress down. She noted with pleasure the emotional exchange between Margaret, her children and the old gentleman. Margaret turned towards Consuelo as if suddenly reminded of her presence and watched her carefully alight from the rickety coach steps.

'Oh I am sorry, where are our manners?' she exclaimed hurriedly. 'This is Donna Consuelo Gonzalez,' she went on with an air of importance. 'She has kindly given us a ride in her coach and will be spending the night with us. This is my father in law, Doctor Algernon Lively.'

Consuelo took the old gentleman's outstretched hand and observed a firm and purposeful grip as she negotiated the uneven ground to the gate.

He gave her an elegant bow, holding up the lamp as the party made their way along a wide stone path leading to a pillared stone porch and an open front door in which stood a smiling Alice. A warm, inviting light shone from behind her, silhouetting her wide skirts and hastily donned mobcap.

'Oh, Mam, I have been so worried about you, and there is ham and warm ale waiting and I banked up the fires when I heard the coach,' cried the girl.

'Alice, we have a guest. The Lady Consuelo.' Margaret had decided that for the likes of Luggin' and Draggin' the name Donna Gonzalez would be very foreign and so Consuelo had been renamed. Consuelo was well accustomed with the English, whom she had long ago concluded had an insular indifference to all things foreign.

They entered the house to a whirl of activity: two large dogs came leaping from what Consuelo assumed must be the kitchen area, a chicken squawked as Alice shooed it from the house and a burly lad appeared to carry in the baggage, whilst Alice hissed instructions. Consuelo was taken up a winding staircase with barley bannisters to a little gallery which led

29

on to her room. Every footfall creaked on the old wooden floor with the sighs of a thousand stories and a strong scent of lavender and polish wafted as she entered the bedroom where Alice was banking up a fire in a duck's nest grate.

There was a four-poster bed with muslin curtains and sparkling white linen pillows. An old iron washstand with a flowery ewer and bowl stood in the corner by a window, covered in thick curtains which fell to the floor in puddles. The room had a cosy air and Consuelo longed to fall on the bed and sleep, but through the door came the enticing smell of wood fire, ale and spices and she realised she was very hungry. She made her way downstairs.

She felt strangely at home as she entered the room where the family was gathered and had a presentiment: The Lively family had taken her in and she had a hunch that from then on their battles were her battles and that their joy would also be hers.

Pepe was right behind Consuelo, nervously peeping round her skirts and still as uncertain about this new development as the younger members of the Lively family. Unlike her boys, Margaret knew exactly what manner of woman the charming Lady Consuelo was. Word had got round the naval community. The Commodore was held in such high regard that his exotic lady friend was afforded great respect, and even Alice felt her chest would burst with pride at being able to serve the great lady; she would tell all her friends in the village and add a little to the story for good measure. Jane, Consuelo's maid, stood snootily by the door as the boy Pepe took Consuelo's hand and whispered something.

'Pepe is hungry. Do you think you could find something for him to eat?' Consuelo said, turning to Alice.

Alice had a penchant for little boys and immediately ruffled his unruly curls, having already decided to feed him fresh custard tarts. She swept him off to the kitchen.

Meanwhile, Consuelo was led to the seat offered on the right of the old doctor Algernon, who sat at the top of the table. A merry fire and many lamps and candles gave the room a festive air. The boys stood up hurriedly, as did Algernon. Consuelo noticed they were being waited upon by a young lad dressed in what was decidedly rough clothing. His hands shook uncontrollably for he had never seen such a lady as this in his life. He was amazed by the size of her skirts and the swishing of silk as she moved. The air around her was heavy with her perfume. He wanted to touch the thick coils of black hair wound about her head like serpents and was equally transfixed by the flash of the whitest teeth he had ever seen as she smiled to thank him. He sneaked a look over her shoulder at a magnificent bosom bursting from the frothy lace of her dress. He almost fainted from the exposure to something so heady and far removed from the rough and tumble of the girls on the common.

'Get to it, lad,' came Alice's voice in a hiss. 'A cat can look at a queen but not you this fine lady. Stop gawping like the idiot you are.'

The lad Tom was not the only man who looked with pleasure upon the visitor. Algernon felt ten years younger and smiled at her indulgently as he set about carving a large succulent ham with surgical precision. Consuelo had a deal of experience with men, but she still received his attentions with pleasure; he was a distinguished old man who displayed a bearing and had manners that spoke of a higher birth than his circumstances might have indicated. Talking to him above the hubbub of the boys and the strangely intimate dialogue between Alice and Margaret, she found out that he had been a ship's surgeon on many important ventures and still had close contact with the Admiralty, constantly badgering them about the conditions for sailors in the decrepit Georgian navy. She learned that he lived nearby to the Livelys and that the delightful, if rustic, Holly House was the farmhouse to the Lively family mansion, which was now let out by Algernon's elder brother to a grandee who used it as a weekend retreat from London.

'I have often regretted it. As a younger son choosing to be a doctor I was never in a position to intervene, my dear,' he explained ruefully. 'But one of these days these strapping grandsons will make do and perhaps one of them will be able to raise a family quiver of Livelys there again. Matthew, my son, will always be a sailor and no woman will ever be able to tame him...' He hesitated, darting a look towards Margaret as if to check that she could not hear what he was saying. 'Even if he got the prize money that sailor's dream of,' he went on, 'it is a poisoned chalice I tell you, it does not bring contentment... A man should be happy to stay at home with a woman such as Margaret.' He glanced at his daughter-in-law affectionately. 'She comes from a sound farming family you know, what would she be doing with a fleet of servants and an idle life among the teacups?'

'I come from a nation of settlers, Doctor Lively, so I should warn you I understand men like your son Captain Lively,' said Consuelo, lowering her fiery dark eyes mysteriously to great effect. '*You* may have guessed that my attachment to the Commodore is a close one,' she went on. 'He is one of those men of vision who see a world beyond teacups, as you say. It is lucky the world produces men such as this, for without...' She hesitated and Algernon lent forward with rapt attention. 'You see, I owe the Commodore my life.' Consuelo's voice shook and the delightful lilt of her speech became more pronounced. The table had become silent and all now listened intently to their visitor.

Margaret was at a loss as to whether to encourage the family to listen to what, after a glass of Algernon's strong wine, had brought a flush to Consuelo's cheeks. Pre-empting her hesitation Algernon poured some wine into Margaret's glass.

'The great Commodore saved your life?' said Algernon.

The question hung in the air for a second before the expectant silence was interrupted by a scream from the kitchen area, and a cacophony of sound coming from outside the window. Tom, the lad who had been in the kitchen with the dirty dishes, burst into the room.

'Mam, Your Ladyships and esteemed doctor,' he exclaimed, 'there is a hue and cry; the constable has caught a knave stealing Her Ladyship's horses – he was not alone and the villains had a musket. We must all go … the village are out all a-crying and shouting… The thieves will be taken to the lock house if we can get them there…'

Algernon was on his feet at once, spilling his glass of wine over the white cloth. 'Get me the sword in the hall and Captain Lively's piece from the chest and you boys come on. We all have to protect our homes and you women, you stay where you are.'

Consuelo paled visibly as the pandemonium brought back terrible memories of just such a night in another happy family dining room. She remembered the screams of women, flames leaping and catching the rich curtains, the helpless attempts of her parents to throw water on the fires, the sound of muskets firing and the pitiful pleading of the mulatto servants; the terrible cry that would ring in her ears for ever: 'My baby, spare her! Please kill me!' Then, as real as if it were yesterday, the horrible laughter and the most anguished sound she would ever hear: a long gurgling scream and the shriek of a tiny baby like a small trapped animal. The fetid breath on her mouth and the tearing of clothes and then the thing, which, try as she might, she could never erase from her horrific memories, only soften with the cool, strong

33

voice of George Anson; George Anson her protector, who was now far away on a stormy sea calling to his men with that same voice, filling them with resolve and banishing fear.

She would always remember the naval officer barking orders to a troupe of armed men who obeyed without question. She recalled as if it were yesterday the low sobbing of women, her father gasping, his breathing laboured from a wound in his chest. And then the smoke as men ripped the hangings from the windows and walls and beat out the flames, amidst the cries of the intruders, now dispatched without ceremony.

Then her mind returned to the present, as Algernon's voice cut through the vivid nightmare of the past, reassuring and confident.

'My dear lady, you must not distress yourself, these villains are soon dealt with. We will all join forces, as we always do, and administer our own law enforcement. Every man and boy responds with any weapon we can lay his hands on. Believe me we make short shrift of these sorts of men. It's a rough justice, I am afraid, but no less than they deserve, trying to rob a person of what is rightfully theirs.'

Alice returned from the fray full of the satisfactory outcome of the incident. There had been no need for Algernon to join the younger men. 'Two bedraggled boys who looked as if they hadn't eaten for a month,' she announced. 'To be sure Doctor Lively,' she went on, 'I felt sorry for them, they were probably no more than fifteen. They are on their way to the lock up and will most probably be hung for their trouble.'

'Come, come, girl,' responded Algernon quickly, 'don't waste your sympathy on those boys. They would slit your throat as soon as look at you, and Her Ladyship's fine horses would have been cut into pieces for meat in hours. They have no idea of the value of things, let alone a human life.'

Suddenly there was a movement in the shadows and Pepe emerged beside Consuelo's chair. Algernon noticed the way she put her arm about him and ruffled his hair, muttering words of reassurance in some strange patois that Algernon could not identify.

He was a great believer in the maxim that everything happens for a reason, and he tried to think why this beautiful bird of paradise had been dropped into the midst of their quiet, ordinary lives. And then he saw the face of his granddaughter Grace in the flickering firelight. She was watching Consuelo enthralled, as if she could see into another world and Algernon knew that a mysterious door had been opened by this visitor. There was indeed a life outside this contained, orderly home which obediently waited for the return, or not, of a father who had that same fire in his eyes.

Chapter Four

Holly Farm,
THE NEXT DAY

The following morning Consuelo's maid, Jane, came downstairs looking alarmed, her cap in disarray and brow puckered with concern.

'Is anything wrong?' enquired Margaret, who had been about since first light. She and Alice still had much to do; the cow had to be milked and the pigs fed the kitchen slops from the previous night. The chickens had started a cacophony of squawking. The kitchen stable door was half open and three geese heads peered over the top making a queer purring noise. Tom the boy was preparing the long table in the dining room for breakfast, a farewell to their distinguished visitor. Margaret bustled and Alice hummed; it was a scene of pastoral domestic bliss, one which Jane was not used to, since she had been plucked from poverty and elevated to Consuelo's rather undomesticated household with its city ways.

'My lady is unwell, madam, it is an ague. This is something she had when she was a child in those foreign parts,' said Jane. 'Can you go to her? I fear we will not be able to travel this day.'

'I will go at once,' said Margaret, wiping her hands on her apron and throwing it aside. She went quickly up the staircase and found Consuelo looking flushed and lying back on the pillows.

'My dear lady, you look ill. Your girl says you have a fever. I will bring some cool water and get Alice to tend to you, because I fancy that girl of yours will not be a good nurse, and as for you setting off for the city today, I will not hear of it. No, you will stay here until you are better and that little lad of yours better take off those fancy clothes and get to it with a bit of help in the kitchens.'

Margaret knew about these 'returning' fevers since Matthew had them sometimes. The fever would run its course and the patient would shake and sweat it out and be left weak as a kitten. From what the feckless girl Jane had said, she soon assessed that the patient's sickness was not a danger to the household.

'Mrs Lively, I am so grateful to you,' said Consuelo pitifully, raising a languid hand to her brow. Consuelo was a woman who had many people around her who professed to serve her with loyalty and devotion, but, truthfully, the departure of George Anson had left her feeling alone and vulnerable. Despite her undoubted beauty and wealth she had no children and she was far from her roots and her family. This gesture of kindness from Margaret Lively and the welcome she had offered in her home was to Consuelo very effecting.

Margaret was increasingly worried about Consuelo and realised she would be hard pressed to care for her guest. She had an idea. 'How would you like it if I took that maid of yours under my wing for few days and gave her some lessons in practical housekeeping? For example, I could take all your fine linen and undergarments and teach her how to see that they are done correctly,' she suggested in her usual direct way.

Normally, of course, such a suggestion might easily cause offence but Margaret Lively was a woman who saw things as they were and it was impossible to be put-out by her easy manner.

'Mrs Lively, I would be so grateful to you. Jane is rather untrained, just a town girl who has never been taught, and I myself do not have the experience to take this on. We have managed after a fashion, and Mr Anson always had his naval men about him who kept things immaculate, as they must on board a great ship. But now he is gone, well…' Consuelo's voice trembled a little. Margaret noticed this but quickly bustled about the room, making notes in her mind's eye as to what she should do first to put the sick woman's surroundings in order.

'I will come back with Jane, Lady Consuelo, and put her to work, and you, boy, you will come with me,' said Margaret to the child Pepe who had been lurking behind Consuelo's travel chest, his eyes wide with concern. He made no move to do as he was bidden. Consuelo spoke to him in her language and the boy came obediently to Margaret and took her outstretched hand. The two left the room and Consuelo fell back on her pillows and cried quietly.

Grace had been in the room for some time, sitting quietly by the bed, watching the sleeping woman and memorising every little detail: her beautiful manicured hands, the jewelled rings on her fingers, a delicate lace sleeve, the long lashes on an alabaster cheek, the thick lustrous hair bound in braids finished with satin ribbon. A faint smell of some sort of exotic perfume hung in the air suffusing all the garments that Margaret had gathered to take downstairs to the wash house, where protesting and sulky Jane was being given a lesson on linen care. Beside the bed was a small, exquisite painting of the Madonna and Child set in a travelling-frame and a rosary made from smooth stones which Grace could not identify. During the time Grace had been looking at Consuelo, something had been taking form in her consciousness. It was a picture of a life far removed from her simple existence in Clapham, somewhere, in another kind of world, where people walked and talked with elegance and beauty, where they ate from silver dishes and drank from fine glass and swept about on floors polished by anonymous servants. The women wore huge dresses and their dainty hands rested on their skirts. Men would walk slowly across these floors and give the ladies long, voluptuous bows. In this world a man would take Grace's dainty hand, touch it lightly with his lips and lead her to an open harpsichord. Then she would sit with a swish of skirts and a page would stand beside her and turn the pages of the music as the audience of glittering people nodded and sighed in appreciation; the ladies would click their fans and eye the men with secret looks whilst the men looked at the girl at the piano and vowed undying love for her.

Such, of course, are the dreams of young girls and seldom do they have the chance to turn them into reality. But a new reality was there for Grace, dancing in the light from the autumn morning as shadows of trees soon to lose their leaves moved in a last celebratory moment before the stark winter winds changed the landscape. It was there in the fragrance of Consuelo's perfume, the cascade of silks tumbling from her boxes, in her rounded breasts rising slowly as she breathed and in the faint smile on her lips which spoke of many things Grace had not yet savoured.

Grace's reverie was interrupted when a small black head came round the door, its craned neck as sinuous as a snake. A pair of wide black eyes fixed on her.

'Me come,' said the child hesitantly. 'Me love Lady Con,' he went on. 'Me bring her flower, she love flower. Captain bring her flowers, many flowers, he put them on pillow while she sleep. Me do this now and then she better; you see...'

39

Grace smiled and nodded, holding out her hand to the child. For some reason she knew her mother would not approve, but the child had touched her heart, and she knew as if by osmosis that the connection between the child and Consuelo was far more than what was to be expected between a privileged woman and a little dark skinned page. The child ran to Grace and held out his hand in which he had some of her mother's late roses. He had wound the stalks with strands of long grass and made half a dozen little nosegays. The child stood against her knees. He was wearing some of her brother's old clothes and his hair smelt of wood chippings, flecks of which bobbed up and down in his thick black curls. The child put the flowers on his mistress's pillow. She stirred in her sleep and awoke to see Grace picking the chippings out of the boy's hair as tenderly as a mother.

'I have a plan, Mrs Lively,' said Consuelo. They were sitting in the front parlour in the full morning sun. Prior to Consuelo's arrival the room had been shut up and seldom used, as Margaret found little time to pursue the activities commensurate with a front parlour, but Consuelo had need of somewhere to sit as she recovered from her fever and got her strength back. She had taken great pleasure in helping Margaret resurrect the room and then with a stroke of genius she had suggested moving the little harpsichord there from the steamy corner of the kitchen where Grace had previously practised.

Now life at the farmhouse had become more elegant and tea was taken in the parlour in the afternoon with old Mrs Lively's porcelain cups. These had not seen the light of day since Margaret had been given them by her mother on her wedding day.

The strange thing about all this was that Margaret realised that there was no reason why she should not have enjoyed such things before. It was merely a matter of organisation. Even Alice had got out her best apron. Margaret had begun to see that there were such things in life as aspirations and no reason why she should not have them.

Mirroring this theme, Consuelo told Margaret about the proposition she had to make.

'Mrs Lively, I have been thinking about your daughter Grace,' she began.

'Oh?' said Margaret, looking up from her sewing. The table beside her was strewn with patches of assorted materials, the fragments, a potted family history, cut from many long-discarded items which had seen births, deaths and loves, some resolved and some not. She was making a patchwork coverlet, which would take many months, even years, and was something she imagined she would give to Grace proudly on her bridal day. There was a symmetry about this, which chimed with the hopes she had for Grace. She had often begun to wonder if her daughter could do more than marry the son of a local family and raise a bevy of children with no hope of real betterment.

'Yes, you see I would like to take Grace to town and let her live with me while I polish her up, so to speak,' said Consuelo in a matter of fact way. If English had been her mother tongue she would have realised that the words she used were too direct and might be taken amiss, but Margaret was a plain speaking woman herself and did not indulge in delicate niceties. Consuelo sensed this and continued unabashed. 'This will give her a chance to set her sights on a good match and at the same time continue with her undoubted skill as a musician. I know Mr Handel, you see, and her voice would be a very pleasing vehicle for his music. Never fear, Mrs Lively, she would always be respectable and carefully chaperoned,' Consuelo added.

'And how would this all happen?' asked Margaret tentatively.

'I would take her to court,' replied Consuelo. 'The old King likes a new face and I could prepare her for it. I have an entrée. Of course I would pay for all the expenditure; I have no children and it would be a pleasure to me.'

Margaret was taken completely unawares by the suggestion; it had never occurred to her for one moment that Grace could be offered such an opportunity, but at the same time she was worried. After all, she did not know anything about the court. Her quiet life in Clapham had never given her any cause to think about the life in that world. Of course, Matthew had met the King when he went with the Commodore to talk about the great voyage. He had described him as an affable, intelligent man. But since the death of the Queen, rumour had it that the court was not as it should be. The King had at least two mistresses and there was a lifelong enmity between him and the Prince of Wales.

'It is very kind of you, Lady Consuelo, but I need time to think about such a step,' said Margaret cautiously, 'and besides I would have to ask Grace what her feelings were.' Margaret cast a nervous look in Consuelo's direction, suddenly concerned that the matter might already have been discussed with Grace without her knowledge.

Consuelo had an instinctive way of reading people's thoughts and picked this up at once.

'You will understand I have not mentioned this to Grace. It would have been quite wrong to do such a thing without discussing it with you,' said Consuelo, taking Margaret by surprise.

The conversation was interrupted by Alice who had arrived with afternoon tea followed by Grace who was clutching a sheaf of music. It was their new custom to sit there while Grace entertained them with her playing and this she did now most beautifully.

Margaret watched her child carefully, seeing her in a new light. She found that she already thought of her in very different surroundings, beguiling the world at court with her beauty and talent. Of course her mind was made up; she would let Grace go. Who could possibly stand in the way of such an opportunity? But she was more than a little aware of a certain quality in her daughter, which might or might not serve her well in this new life she had been offered. It was the same quality as her father: a wild daring which, of course, had driven him to the life at sea, where risks were a part of life. Margaret had an ominous feeling about this latest trip though. A man only has so many lives and Matthew had few left to play with. To have to worry about a husband and a daughter would be hard indeed, but Grace had wings and Margaret knew she would always use them to fly, just as her father did. Consuelo would be a good guardian of her daughter's wilful soul.

Chapter Five

Madeira,
November 1740

'Confound those westerly winds,' said Matthew Lively. 'There is no chance of getting to the Horn at a favourable time now.'

'Aye, sir, if we don't reach the southern latitudes by January, I don't fancy this old hulk surviving those seas,' replied the master of the *Wager*, Mr Clark.

'The Commodore will be cursing those old fools at the Admiralty,' said Matthew. 'The delays have cost us dearly and look at this lot, Mr Clark. Still not a sailor among them. The poor souls who still lie in their hammocks... It feels like we are running a hospital not a ship of war.'

'Beats me why the Commodore took them on, old men with quavery voices from the veterans' hospital. They know they will never see home again. I don't know how some of them have lasted this long,' said Mr Clark. 'But the cry of land has got them going. I think it would be a kindness to take them ashore, Mr Lively, let them see a bit of life before they die. One thing is sure: they will not desert. They are sailors and stay loyal unlike some of the other dogs who will have to be watched with your pistol at the ready.'

The *Wager* was an old Indiaman, a ship that had conveyed goods for trade but only when the winds and tides had combined with the clement season. No amount of paint could cover her age or strange wide construction and she had just two stories which gave her a flat, lazy air that would not strike fear into the heart of any attacker. All the men knew this and despite the constant practice of firing cannons on their long journey, which had taken forty days instead of twelve, they still had little confidence in the old ship. Matthew Lively had been dismayed when the Commodore had billeted him to the *Wager* instead of the flag ship *Centurion*, but the Commodore, in his deceptively mild way, had pointed out that his skills were very necessary on the large, cumbersome ship, which held the lifeblood of the great voyage in its sealed hulk. Matthew had watched the loading of the mysterious cargoes, including many fine luxury items which, it was claimed, would be a means of barter in the far flung places they were to visit where supplies would have to be found. That cargo was sealed tight below and woe betide any sailor who tried to get into it. They would be shot at once and every man knew it.

'Well, there's one thing I know,' said Mr Cousins. 'When we do find some wind, the *Wager* – God save her – will be struggling to keep up with the rest of the fleet, and as for beating to wind and tactically avoiding the enemy we shall most surely find we are a sitting duck, Mr Lively, a sitting duck with no feathers.'

They were only just beginning their voyage but the crew, such as it was, had already suffered a series of problems. It had been plain sailing until they reached the Bay of Biscay when the sea had started to foam and the old ship had begun to groan and creak. The mast had tipped to forty degrees and the invalids in their hammocks were the most fortunate as they rolled with the ship. This glimpse into what was in store was a mere trifle to the hardened sailors, but the pressed men began to vomit and some to pray for death, anything to escape the torture of nausea. The fleet managed to stay together, but sometimes hidden from sight as the ships sunk into troughs as large as houses. Most of the men had never seen the like and this was when Mr Cousins, the bosun, a rough and ready fellow with a sharp temper but a gift for making jokes and lifting even the most dismal of scenes, was called upon to at least attempt to cheer up the men around him. The captain had shown signs of ill health himself and it had fallen to Matthew to step in and impart some discipline.

Now they were in glorious calm and it was time for some floggings. The poor wretches had known full well just what they were in for. Matthew hated the punishments, but he knew that they were essential to establish an unquestioning discipline amongst the men, which would save lives. It was all or nothing at sea; each man's role was vital and one small lapse – a worn sheet which would snap under sail and set the sail free to flap and tear – could mean they all perished. Today there were to be a hundred lashes for a worn looking young fellow who had eaten another man's salt pork, which he had concealed in a carefully sewn pocket in his hammock. He had been starved of rations since discovery of the crime, and there was little sympathy for him amongst his fellow men.

The ship's company was assembled and a bright cloudless sky shone beatifically upon the deck of the *Wager* as the bedraggled offender was led from the dark hold into the light. The crew were at their smartest, each man washed, spruced and standing to attention while the officers in their leghorn hats and braided coats eyed them beadily to see if any should look fainthearted at the boy's punishment.

The culprit was no more than a lad, taken from his family business of cobbling in Portsmouth. His parents were mild people who'd never had cause to beat their children and none had ever gone hungry. His mother grew vegetables in the back garden behind the small house and the boy had grown used to a rich and varied diet, with meat from the sleek black pigs his father kept and eggs as big as a child's fist. The boy grieved for the family stolen from him when he had never done a bad thing to man nor beast. His resentment knew no bounds and the hunger for decent food had driven him to the depths. He had begun to show the first signs of scurvy, and sores had started appearing on his legs and extremities, but of course the boy had no idea of the connection between them and his craving for mother's fresh cabbage and crisp apples. He dreamed of them in the short nights when he was not on watch, confronting the endless sea, which he feared would eventually claim him. None of the other men seemed to be interested in the miserable lad, and stealing the pork had been more of a gesture of rebellion than anything. He stood now in the bright sun and looked miserably at the scene before him. He began to tremble and to his shame a trickle of urine came down his leg onto the pristine deck, scrubbed to the whiteness of the finest marble.

For the boy there was a sense of unreality about it. He was a simple lad and there he was with a hundred pairs of eyes upon him. Even the invalids had risen and emerged into the light to witness the spectacle. A burly seaman, stripped to the waist, stood to attention, holding the vicious cat of nine tails and the sweet sound of pipes and drums began. Then rough hands lashed him to the wheel of the great ship.

The first lash of the whip brought unimaginable pain. The boy's eyes felt at as if they would bolt from his head and his body shut down; he no longer had a brain, just a heart and a pair of lungs. He was nothing but a burning mass of pain and horror; it was as if he had been immersed in a boiling cauldron in hell. Then came another and another.

Someone stepped forward with a gag and put it in his mouth as he began to scream in the high pitched voice of the boy he really was. Not a man hardened to the ways of the world, he was a gentle creature who at this moment would have been prepared to give up all that he had ever had in life

47

to put an end to his agony. He called for his mother in his heart. He called for his father; he called for God, but there was nothing and he fell insensible.

As for the men who watched the spectacle, there were not many who did not feel for the boy. The flesh on his back would forever bear the scars of this day but the sailors knew that they were as nothing compared to the hardening of his heart and soul. It was of course a rite of passage which must be traversed if the boy were to survive the challenges of what was to follow; hardship beyond the imagination of most men and little glory save for the prize money which was a long way from this place.

Although Matthew was an ocean away in many respects – for him there was glory to be had and pride in a ship which had a compliment of loyal sailors with a thirst for adventure – he made a note to keep an eye out for the boy, who was, after all, the same age as his eldest son. This time would be crucial for the boy, he knew. Would he take the chance, in fact his only chance, of entering the brotherhood of seafarers, fresh as he was to the brutal law of the ship? Or would he lurk quietly, harbouring a resentment that would separate him from his fellow men and probably cost him his life?

'Get the water and take him below,' Matthew ordered without a flicker of the concern he felt. Even the salt sting of the seawater on the flayed flesh of the boy failed to revive him from the blissful escape into unconsciousness. The man who threw the water at the wounds did it with care; he knew that a rougher hand would have torn the hanging strips of flesh but he thought the lad had been punished enough. Matthew cast a quick look at the blood soaked deck and noted the hasty clearing up operation. As the boy's blood was swished through the gunnel, he pondered the fact that the sight of blood still turned his stomach.

'A job done, men,' he said, 'and may every man learn his duty.'

The cry of 'land!' brought all hands to the deck. Forty days at sea in the North Atlantic and they had arrived at the island of Madeira. Matthew looked at the great ship as they sailed into the harbour. She belied the low opinion of her master: her decks were scrubbed, her white sails dazzling in the morning sun and her crew smartened up and drumming the arrival. She ambled gracefully in the slight swell like a fine lady wearing her Sunday best, her skirts swaying as she moved, confident and unabashed, past her rivals. The fleet made a magnificent spectacle and there was not a man among them, even those who had been pressed and were resentful, who did not feel roused by the adrenalin, the shiver of pride and above all by the thing that only a sailor can describe: the smell of land. The officers were the first to be taken ashore.

The city of Funchal had laid on a warm reception and, much as a woman forgets the pains of labour, the tired men forgot the hardships of the voyage, brushed their hair, shaved their beards, put on clean kerchiefs and went ashore with honour. They drank with rather less honour, except for the officers who had to keep the men in check and look to the good housekeeping upon which they would all depend.

George Anson was what was called a 'ladies' man', but even the charms of Funchal could not allay the fears he had about the delays. He knew that waiting another year was not an option; uncharted waters lay ahead. He took this opportunity to write a very long letter to his beloved Consuelo. He spared her his concerns and spoke much of the loyalty of his men, but he did tell her that most of the invalids from the naval hospital had already succumbed and remarked wryly that it was a convenient way to dispose of the elderly pensioners, a plan which could not possibly be the intentions of Their Lordships at the Admiralty.

CHAPTER SIX

CONSUELO'S TOWN HOUSE,
ST JAMES'S SQUARE

'So, my dear, the first thing we must do is order you the dress,' said Consuelo. The weather had turned cold and the large house in St James's Square was freezing compared to the cosy farmhouse in Clapham, where Alice's diligent attention to the fires always kept the place warm and snug.

There was a magnificent fireplace in the spacious double drawing room that looked over the square, but Consuelo's maid Jane felt herself too elevated to attend to duties of this kind. For a moment Grace had an urge to attend to it herself and go down to the nether regions of the kitchens in the dark basement to get coal, which seemed to be the preferred fuel in the house. Even the scuttle, which now stood empty, did not shine as the ones at home. She wondered just how Consuelo managed in the large house with so few attendants, and was mindful to ask her.

'The dress you must have is the mantua. It is really the most ridiculous garment, and purgatory to wear. I have seen women topple over from the weight of the metallic supports in the skirts,' said Consuelo. 'But they invest all their money in such a thing. The skirts could hide a couple of children and they must be embroidered with jewels and fine silks; as for the metal hoops under the skirts, they are a menace. It makes it most difficult to relieve oneself. There are special receptacles available to put under the skirt without having to lift it. You must always have one available and your maid must carry it, preferably in a little velvet bag,' added Consuelo with a twinkle.

It was of course for this reason that the wearer of such a garment had a draughty gap in the now fashionable French knickers that had once been considered so licentious. This was just one of many things Grace found strange but, having been raised with her mother's punctilious housekeeping and attention to cleanliness, the most challenging thing for Grace to accept was the slovenly servants and ill kept house in St James's Square.

She had also ventured out once or twice when the so-called cook had gone to do some shopping, but even the smell of the meat she had bought had turned Grace's stomach, and the milk, carried on the milk maids' shoulders in open buckets on a yoke, had all manner of filth dropped into it. The day before she had found a piece of fingernail in the posset Jane had produced before they retired. Grace saw that the linen was grimy and grey looking; it had been sent out to a foul wash house, from whence it came back looking greyer than when it went. Grace had inspected the lower floors and found there was an outside washhouse where the copper had never been lit, and there were filthy washboards and rusty irons.

An air of idleness pervaded the house and Grace, who had become extremely fond of the beautiful Consuelo, made up her mind to mention all this in the gentlest way she could think of. But when the opportunity revealed itself she lost all semblance of subtlety and came straight to the point in a manner that her mother had warned her many times would not be thought to be ladylike.

Nonetheless, the moment had come. It was the mention of bodily functions that persuaded her. Such arrangements in the potentially elegant house were loathsome to Grace.

It seemed expected that such things should be done in a receptacle in the bedchamber from where, if you were lucky, one of the grubby maids would take it and empty it through a trap door into a vile smelling place in the basement. But in fact Grace had seen that the open window was the chosen route for such disposals.

'Lady Consuelo,' Grace began loudly, when the two were alone in the upstairs salon again.

'Yes, my dear? Whatever you are going to say is, I would guess, of some importance, since you look most business like. Pray what can it be?' Consuelo was seated by the miserable fire, an exotic shawl about her shoulders, looking through some designs for the dress she had described to Grace. There was something vaguely distracted about her. There was a bright green parrot in the room in a large brass cage, who called out occasionally with a series of oaths more suited to a low tavern than a refined drawing room. One such oath came out before Grace could speak and Consuelo stifled a laugh.

'Oh, my dear, how I miss him!' Consuelo suddenly blurted. 'Hearing such words as that wicked fellow says puts me in mind of him so ... I ...' and with that she burst into grievous sobs.

Automatically Grace went to her and put a comforting hand on Consuelo's own. For Grace it unearthed memories of her father, whose life was in the Commodore's hands. Or perhaps, she pondered, it was the other way around. In any event the feelings engulfed both women and, while Grace felt she could express things she had never been able to with her own mother, Consuelo continued to give voice to her sense of abandonment.

'You see, my dear child, there are so many things I miss about the Commodore. Just look at this house, which is filthy now that his sailors have gone; they did everything, you see. The Commodore was a very organised person and the house was run like a ship. We even had the ship's cook and I found most generally that those men were better at such things than the idle girls I have now, who are all pilfering and cheating. I have seen the foul way they do things. Where I come from such things would not be tolerated. I come from a country where domestic order both inside and out were highly prized … but here I rarely like to venture outside for the filth.'

'But what did you do when the Commodore was here?' Grace ventured.

'He handled it all. We always had an escort, and I went with him often to court where the old King was pleased to see us. But the court is not the same since the Queen died and though there is of course a rival court with the Prince of Wales, one does have to choose because the father and son hate each other.'

Grace had been thinking hard and something had occurred to her.

'My lady, why do you not send for servants from your own country? They would most surely be better as they know what sort of person you are and, with respect, they will treat you as a lady of importance. And have you seen all the poor creatures who have served in the navy on the streets? Let us offer them work. The house needs a thorough clean and things need to be as my own mother has them. I could oversee them for you and at least then I could feel I was of some greater use to you.'

Consuelo felt as if she had been rescued at last. She had been hiding how abandoned she felt now that her protector had gone, and it was beginning to dawn on her that most of the high-life was about illusion. She could have the fine house and the trappings and take her beautiful charge to court and show her off, but what she needed was authority. She should create her own little court about her. Grace's plan began to blossom like a young tree finding its summer foliage.

'As a matter of fact,' said Consuelo slowly, 'I have already sent for two of my loyal personal servants, but it will be a few weeks before they are here. I sent word on a trading vessel, which left three weeks ago. I expect a reply through the diplomatic bag quite soon. But I wanted them to arrive at a house which was in good order and not one such as this has become.'

'I have an idea, Lady Consuelo,' Grace blurted suddenly. 'Let us go to the naval hospital in Chelsea, where there are many experienced veterans, men who would be more than capable of running a tight ship here. You will be a good judge of some of the poor souls who would be diligent and grateful to have a chance to do some honest work.'

Consuelo clapped her hands joyfully. 'Oh, what a wonderful idea, child! The Commodore even suggested this himself before he left. Let us plan to go as soon as possible.' She rang the bell that hung on a silk tassel beside the dying fire and, spurred on by the hope of restoring some sort of order in her life, spoke with greater authority when Jane responded to the summons. Jane hovered in the doorway, wiping her hands on an apron that had acquired the same patina as all the rest of the linen in the house.

'Jane, will you come inside the room please?' said Consuelo, in a tone that surprised Jane, who had become accustomed to lethargy since the Commodore and his men had left. She had mixed feelings about his departure since she knew in her heart that the Lady Consuelo would recover herself at some point and demand a return to the regime that the Commodore's naval life expected.

Jane slouched into the room, giving Grace a look of dislike, something Grace had little experience of having been so protected under her mother's wing. Since she had come to live with Consuelo, things were different and she had seen that there was a life beckoning to her that would require a very different approach.

One of the Commodore's officers had found Jane. She came from a family near Stafford where the Commodore lived with his brother in a charming house called Shugborough, which he had begun to build onto as his fortunes continued to improve. The girl had been the daughter of one of the outside servants and had come to London where she was at first pleased to have so great an opportunity. While the Commodore was there and the house was run with a firm hand, she had been eager to learn and Consuelo had been very happy with her, even promoting her to be Consuelo's own personal servant. But since the Commodore had left, Jane had become lazy and belligerent. Consuelo had been quite unable to understand this and it had only just occurred to her that the girl probably considered Consuelo a fallen woman with no protector.

Mindful of this and emboldened by the presence of Grace, who was now her ward whilst she lived under her roof, Consuelo suddenly retrieved her former confidence. After all, she had plenty of money and assets at home in the Americas which rendered her a substantial heiress.

'Jane,' she began briskly. 'Miss Lively is now my ward and therefore her future is of great interest to the Commodore whom your brother now serves. I propose to introduce Miss Lively to the court next month, when the seasonal celebrations begin. We will of course be doing a deal of entertaining here and the house is to be completely reorganied.'

Jane straightened and fixed Grace with a narrow look. She thought quickly, for she was not unintelligent and could see that she must either enter into this new regime with enthusiasm or travel back to Stafford and hope to find a husband. But she had taken a shine to the boy who was the footman on Lady Consuelo's coach. She quickly calculated that she must dissemble at once. Truthfully she did not really like either Lady Consuelo or Grace, whom she thought of as not quite belonging to the likes of kings and queens. She had little experience of the world and did not appreciate that in high circles things were more complex than with country people. She would of course soon find out that the fact that Consuelo had no husband did not impede her acceptance in society as long as she had the money to pay for it, and that respectability came in many clothes. Nor did she yet appreciate that the Commodore was a powerful man and nobody knew when he would return. Be it this year or next he would settle any scores that had been incurred by disrespect to the Lady Consuelo, or indeed the daughter of one of his most respected officers. But there was a vague feeling in the air this morning, which made her straighten her cap and listen intently.

'Whatever I can do, my lady, for you and Miss Lively...' she said quietly.

'I will be getting a steward as soon as possible and then of course a housekeeper and cook. I have sent for some of my servants from the Americas. Tomorrow we shall be going to the retired sailor's hospital to find competent men who would be glad of a position in a good house.' This last point Consuelo made very sternly and Jane knew exactly what she meant.

'So I am giving you a chance to show me what you can do and we will start to clean up the house with that lazy lot of people you have now,' Consuelo continued. 'I will call them to the hall downstairs and tell them that, until a steward comes, you are to be in control and I want you to listen to Miss Lively, who knows about household management. Listen to her in all things. We have much to do so now let us begin.'

Grace gave Jane a formal smile and observed it was not returned. Consuelo caught her eye and nodded briefly.

CHAPTER SEVEN

ST JAMES'S SQUARE, DECEMBER 1740

The great day had finally come. Consuelo had put her house in perfect order with Grace's help. The dress had been delivered the previous day and the household assembled to see the transformation of the girl who had got her hands dirty just to show them how it should be done. Consuelo had had concerns about this approach at the beginning because she wondered just how the distance which must exist between those who serve and those who are served could be preserved. But she soon noticed that Grace had more about her than she'd originally observed. Grace's pupils had quickly realised that, although the girl could do all the things that they were expected to do, there was a line they must not cross. Yes, there was a familiarity there, accompanied by sweat and fatigue, but at the same time Grace, or Miss Lively as they called her, was a ruthless taskmaster.

Two girls had already failed to live up to Miss Lively's standards and been sent packing. But despite this, or perhaps because of it, by and large they had all begun to take a pride in the household and had great respect for Grace, so much so that she had, without encouragement or suggestion, been promoted to the title of My Lady. There was a hierarchical snobbery to this, since the household in St James's Square was of great interest to the local community both above and below stairs. Consuelo was a mystery, but the Commodore had been greatly respected due to his rumoured connections to the court and the ear of the King. But the household had kept itself to itself, and no amount of approaches had ever revealed anything other than stony silence. Now though the servants were not so discrete and it was their desire to promote the status of their employer and themselves with it. Grace, or Lady Grace as she had become, was alleged to be the daughter of some wealthy Lordship who had passed way, leaving the Commodore's Duchess (daughter of the King of Portugal, no less...) as her guardian.

At first Jane had tried her best to demote the rank and history of her young mistress, but soon her brain had begun to wake up to the fact that her mistress's future was very much linked to her own. The girl had never before in her life worked out just what loyalty was, that life having commenced in a dog-eat-dog world where you took what you could, when you could. Any thought of reward gained by means other than grafting and complaining was quite alien to her. But things had subtly changed. In a word she had started to love, not just the life she could now live but, in a wary fashion, the young girl who had given her the chance. She loved the new frocks she had, with a special one for Sunday best. She loved the food she ate, which was carefully selected by Grace from providers who knew they would be discovered if they dyed the stale meat or watered the wine and ale. And the milk was fresh, brought in from the countryside, from a fat cow with long eyelashes and a shining body, whose udders were washed in clean water by spotless milkmaids. She had been with Grace to the farm and watched as the girl held up the eggs in the market to see if they had become dense with age. The fact is Jane felt different and she wanted to be better in every way. She had even prayed to God to keep her on the path of this lightness she had found. But most of all she loved Grace. This was the first time she had loved anybody in her life.

'Jane, I know you will be there, keeping an eye on me,' said Grace as they watched the two seamstresses unpack the dress that had been made for Grace to wear to court. Consuelo had ordered a dressmaker's dummy that stood in Grace's elegant bedchamber, which overlooked the gardens at the back of the house. Winter had set in with a vengeance and the trees were covered in frost. There were fires burning in all the grates and Jane constantly kept an eye on them, giving orders to the girl who had been engaged to keep the scuttles full of coal and sweep the numerous hearths, the only source of heat in the great house.

Grace was relieved that her introduction to court wearing the ridiculous dress was in the winter; she could hardly imagine the unbearable heat of such a garment in high summer. She had practised in the large drawing room for weeks, wearing the under skirt and perfecting the gliding step that made the vast creation sail. She had even tried the emergency arrangements for relieving herself and it had made her blush. But no, Consuelo was not having any of that, informing Grace that a woman can have no secrets from her maid. The stiff whalebone hoops were about to be removed from the dummy and Grace was to step into them. It had taken two of them to get this part of the garment in a position where Grace could step into it. It lay on the floor now, concertinaed and waiting for the wearer to stand still so that it could be raised above her hips, where it was fastened to the corset that nipped in the waist and pushed the breasts high on the chest.

Grace could already hardly breathe from her nerves but worse was to come. The women laid the vast skirts, embroidered with silver thread, on the bed and then they solemnly put them over Grace's head. Immediately she felt as if she were being dragged to the floor.

'Now for the bodice,' said the seamstress reverently, and after much lacing and tugging Grace was dressed.

The theme was to be artful but simplistic. Grace's hair was coiled around a string of pearls and with a fine dusting of powder on her nose and a plain velvet ribbon about her neck she was ready. Consuelo stood back to admire her ward. 'A vision of elegance,' she said. 'But first we must see if you have remembered everything I have told you about the strange world at court. As I have explained, the King lives simply but his court would not have it so … games are played but the King's great solace is in the music of Mr Handel, who in turn owes the King a great deal: the popularity of his work is partly due to the monarch's support. Apparently, he has taken possession of a great new harpsichord made by a most talented young man and we are to be given a first performance. In an ideal world, my dear, I would hope that you might be able to sing for the King. I know your sight-reading skills are excellent so it is possible that this might happen. I have mentioned to Lord John Hervey that you would indeed be prepared to do this.'

'Who is Lord Hervey again? I have forgotten,' said Grace nervously.

'He has the King's ear and is an advisor to His Majesty, but he is also the court gossip and the dearest friend of the King's favourite mistress Amalie Marianne Sophie Wendt, whose married name is Wallmoden,' Consuelo explained.

'So how shall I recognise the King's mistress?' asked Grace, beginning to realise that all this information was only the start of a challenging journey.

'She is plump and placid, she has fine black eyes and excellent hair which she dresses naturally; which is a nice change since many of the court ladies are nearly bald under their wigs because of the years they have spent burning and teasing what God gave them. It was Lord Hervey who persuaded Amalie to come to England to be with the King, who had been dallying too much in Hanover the better to enjoy her charms. The remarkable thing is that it had been the Queen who wanted it; she was a far sighted woman who had known that a contented husband is a most desirable thing.'

Grace thought, for a moment, about the simplicity of her parent's relationship, but then she reminded herself that all men are unfaithful to their woman. However much they love them, there is always another pull. In her father's case it was the sea and the call of adventure ... but he always came home ... but then one day perhaps he would not; and what then?

'Why should women always be the ones to compromise?' asked Grace of her new and dearest friend Consuelo, whom she had begun to love like her own mother.

'Well, my dear, I have often asked myself this, and the answer is that a clever woman will appear to do so but will in fact be building her own fortress within herself; in a sense her own castle where she will guard the treasure she accumulates. I think of you as a daughter,' she went on, 'and it is not often that I have seen such a lovely young woman who wields so much power by the very force of her nature and yet is so delightfully unaware of it.' Consuelo looked fondly at Grace, who radiated an innocent beauty in her finery. She did not for a moment underestimate the mendacity of the world into which she was soon to put this delicate bloom. But she determined to arm her protégée with the necessary wisdom to take what was good from her new life and guard against the corruptive forces which always surrounded the court and its hangers on.

'So the King's mistress is accepted in the royal household?' said Grace quizzically.

'The Royal mistresses are very much respected in these circles; in fact, the King has two of them. The other one is Lady Deloraine, who is to be rather pitied. She is an intelligent woman and came to the King's notice when she was governess to his daughters. People harbour a great resentment of her and I suspect the lady will be the victim of her own fecklessness. Our prime minister, Lord Walpole, counselled them not to waste their time worrying about the lady since "people must wear old gloves until they get new ones." They both have a pension and an income for life. Amalie moved directly into her predecessor's rather damp apartments in Kensington Palace.'

Grace thought on this as Consuelo continued to tell her about the people she was about to meet, but it all began to wash over her and the only two she was really interested in were the King and Mr Handel. She had a picture of them in her mind: they were of similar age, now both in their sixties, which to a young girl like Grace was very old indeed. She wondered if they would be like her grandfather, Algernon. She had of course seen many images of the King and expected him to be portly and bewigged. It seemed incongruous that there was all this talk of his mistresses; old men should not be interested in such things in her opinion.

'I see I have lost your attention, my dear,' Consuelo's voice cut through her reverie. 'I have told you quite enough to arm you for this great event so let us depart – but one more thing, never be separated from your maid; it is she who will guard your honour, because there are many in the rivalrous clamour of the court who would besmirch it.'

Jane was now bedecked in her best frock with added frills on the corsage and an apron so white that it dazzled the eye on that chilly winter morning. But not so much, she thought, as her young mistress's beauty. Jane was experiencing a strange feeling, it was how she imagined a young boy might feel when going to into battle. She was part of the big scheme of things, and it was empowering. She had begun to get through a day without thinking of her own individual needs; it was as if she were liberated from the life she had led, with its limited horizons. To see the King of England with her own eyes in the great royal palace, it was beyond anything she could have imagined and she had to catch her breath just to make sure it was real.

Grace was going through similar emotions as they set off in the coach. Jane had smoothed out the voluminous skirts as the footman closed the door and Pepe was as usual attached to his mistress, clutching a silken purse strung to the cuff of his jacket. In it were Consuelo's smelling salts and a little gold flask of rum elaborately initialled *G.A.*

'Be ready with the medicine, friend, we are going to need it, and watch Lady Grace like the little imp that you are,' whispered Consuelo to Pepe in Spanish as the horses lunged forward into the crowded streets.

CHAPTER EIGHT

KENSINGTON PALACE

Peter felt awkward in the lace cravat he was wearing for the first time. He felt perspiration coming down the back of his neck, and knew it would soon be coming off his forehead. He got out the kerchief his mother had put in the pocket of his fine new velvet jacket and quickly mopped his brow. He wiped his hands and clasped them in front of him while Mr Handel walked slowly towards the harpsichord. Due to Mr Handel's infirmity, the normal custom of a bare room with no seating, so that nobody could sit down in the King's presence, had been abandoned. Chairs had been arranged and these were gratefully perceived by the assembled company, who hoped this might be the start of a new custom. Perhaps at last they would be relieved of the tedium of long hours standing in uncomfortable clothes and shoes. The room became silent and everyone remained on their feet until the King was seated on an elaborate chair higher than the rest.

A footman pulled out the seat ready for the celebrated Mr Handel to sit in. The old composer sat down heavily and there was a creak as he gently eased forward. Not a sound could be heard as the old man flexed his bony hands together and raised his head a little, his eyes half closed. He slowly lowered his hands to the keyboard and with a subtle stroking movement, he played the first notes. He had no need to introduce the music; his works were deeply rooted in the culture surrounding the elderly King's court.

For the young man, of course, it was the sound the instrument made that mattered most. He watched the old man's face intently and saw a distinct smile playing on his lips. There was a nod of approval from the King as Mr Handel turned his head towards him and opened his eyes to send a message of approbation.

The work came to an end and the room stayed cautiously silent. Then all eyes were upon Peter Zuliekom. The King rose to his feet and beckoned to him. Peter felt as if he were in a dream as he walked hesitantly towards the smiling monarch whilst the room broke into a rapturous applause. The boy shivered despite the new jacket and the warmth of the room, full of so many people with their fine clothes and powdered faces, all of whom were deeply moved by what they had heard.

'My boy, we are experiencing a great moment,' said the King in his strange, accented way. 'Mr Handel, this is the young man who made this fine instrument.'

Peter bowed to them both and the two old men, strangely alike to look at, welcomed him. They recognised that he had his whole life before him but felt no jealousy and wanted to celebrate the next generation, affording Peter every chance to prove himself.

As Peter rose from his rather imperfect bow, something strange occurred. The moment was heavenly enough as it was but what happened next was surreal. Glancing beyond the King's shoulder, he saw a face in the midst of the crowd that he recognised with glorious clarity; it was angelic, it was the face which had looked into his when God himself had intervened that autumn day on the Portsmouth docks and given him back the life that had been wrenched from him. The story of how he had come to be in such a wretched state flashed before him. He had been on his way home to his parents' house a month previously with samples of wood for the cabinets he was making with his father. They were in the first stages of fashioning a keyboard instrument of a revolutionary design and he had not heard the thump of feet behind him before the sack was put over his head and he was dragged away to captivity. It was a long month until he was able to hold his mother in his bearlike hug again. Upon his return she had dropped the pan she was holding and fallen to her knees praising God for the miracle, asking what angel had been at work for them... And now here was that very angel in the room with Peter at the time – the precise second – when all his efforts and the history of family endeavour and skill were being enjoyed by the King of England and the greatest musical genius, whom Peter believed was also blessed by God. He remembered something his father had once said to him: 'Coincidence is God's way of remaining anonymous.'

But angels are ever pursued by demons. The evil hunter must be quiet and stealthy and a figure had been watching all this unnoticed from his vantage point at the far doorway. Sir Hartley Slinkwell disliked music except as a vehicle for his own ambition and furtherance of lust. He had been examining Grace carefully; the shadowy concealment of the thick brocade curtains draped in the doorway gave him a perfect anonymity from which to observe his latest prey. She was obviously fresh from the country and her bloom, like the velvety down on a ripe peach, was untouched. He had ventured a few discreet enquiries and learned that she was the ward of the exotic Consuelo Gonzalez, the great Commodore Anson's whore. Although, looking at Consuelo now he could see that the word was not entirely appropriate; the court was treating her with considerable deference, and she had a bearing which spoke of confidence and good breeding – probably far superior to Sir Hartley's own. His rakish good looks were already beginning to show signs of deterioration. He had a pronounced retroussé nose and his lips were rather too full. He was not overly tall, but he had a swaggering manner, which gave him an air of importance. Some pointed out, behind his back of course, that his grandfather had made his fortune – which Sir Hartley was busily squandering – from slavery and had bought his title from Charles II in return for a donation to one of the King's projects that provided care for sick sailors.

Sir Hartley was a rare case as a human being in that he had no moral compass whatsoever. Even the most evil men have some small chip in their carapace, which allows for moments of compassion. But Sir Hartley … no, it was not that he had a heart of stone, he just did not have one at all, and that made him all the more dangerous. And he was owed many favours at court. He had a dossier on many of those men and women in high places who were assembled in the room; the room into which the latest delicious little morsel had just wandered like a tiny mouse scuttling past a half sleeping cat. The feral Sir Hartley narrowed his eyes and gave a sigh as he visualised the exquisite conquest.

The room remained silent, waiting for the King to speak. It had fallen upon Lord Hervey to be the equerry for this occasion and enforce the strict protocol, which meant that nobody was allowed to address His Majesty without introduction.

'Your Majesty, may I present a young lady who has, by all accounts, an excellent singing voice and may I venture to suggest, if Mr Handel is willing that is, that she gives us a rendition of one of the maestro's arias.'

Grace stepped forward and gave a shaky curtsy, not as polished as the ones she had so carefully practised at St James's Square, but pretty enough to please the old King greatly. He had an eye for a pretty girl and one who was proficient enough to be presented to him in such circumstances was worthy of his time and attention.

'We will have to ask Mr Handel about that,' said the King kindly. He could see that Grace had something folded in a little silk bag and suspected she had come prepared. He could also see that she was extremely nervous and was greatly overwhelmed by the occasion. The King was shorter than most of the men in the room and, given his liking for good food, especially sweet puddings and chocolate, had become decidedly paunchy. His late wife had tried to keep this in check, but as she herself had put on a considerable amount of weight by the time she died, it was a losing battle. As Grace looked at him she found it hard to believe that he had indeed fought in a battle, leading his troops bravely from the front. None of this was evident in the man before her, but when he gazed intently at her with slightly protuberant china blue eyes, she saw a flash of the man he had been.

The King was known for his rather irascible temper, but it was also said that he was 'quick to anger, quick to forgive', which was somewhat at odds with the on-going spat he had with his elder son. Despite this, he had a surprising empathy with young people, which was often remarked upon, particularly because his family history was one of continued domestic strife. His own father had openly disliked him and history had repeated itself with his eldest son. They were not on speaking terms and there was a rival court that was publically at war with Kensington Palace. So much so that the prime minister, Mr Walpole, feared this antagonism was not only a danger to the monarchy but also to the very peace of the country. The population expected an example from its royal family, as Walpole had often lamented. Such dysfunctional petty rivalry in high places was bad for collective morale.

The King stared soulfully at Grace. Some people who did not know him well might have thought this staring contained some sort of lustful intent, but those who were more familiar with the monarch knew it was one of His Majesty's 'absences'. He had seen something in Grace that reminded him of the only recollection he had of his mother, who had a similar look. This of course set him on the doleful path of regret. In his mind's eye, he saw the receding picture of his mother being sent into exile for doing what his father had always done; she had fallen in love with another, hardly surprising since his father was a blatant lecher who had paraded endless mistresses before her. But for the unforgiving Hanoverian George I, sauce was for the goose alone. Separation, exile and murder were the price his wife paid for her affair with the handsome lover whose remains had never been found. The anguish and loneliness the King had suffered as a child was something he had vowed not to repeat with his own family. However, fate had it otherwise. His beloved wife had given him tolerance and happiness, and now she lay dead, her passing horrible in its suffering; and there was no comfort to be had from his son, the heir apparent. He doubted the rift could ever be repaired. He continued to ponder all this as the room waited, until Lord Hervey cleared his throat loudly.

'Do you have something prepared, my dear?' interjected Mr Handel. 'Is that it in your purse.'

'Yes,' replied Grace, taking the folded paper from her bag and handing the work to Mr Handel.

'Ah, "Acis and Galatea", a most fitting choice; let us proceed, we have no need of the music, do we?' he said firmly.

The room settled down with a murmur and a rustle of skirts, and Grace sang like the dove described in the music; 'As when the dove laments her love all on the naked spray, when he returns no more she mourns but loves the live long

70

day.' The simplicity of her delivery set all hearts sighing and none more so than Peter the harpsichord's maker. For him there would be no other event in his life that could ever surpass this moment. All the doves in heaven could sing a heavenly chorus, it would not be as beautiful as this.

Of course Grace was completely unaware of the effect she was having. She did what young ladies should do and blushed prettily. The old King was enchanted. He graciously took her hand and turned to address the room.

'And who do we have to thank for this young lady's arrival here?' he asked.

'If I may,' said Lord Hervey moving deftly to Grace's side. 'It was the Lady Consuelo who brought Miss Lively to my attention. She is Consuelo's ward here in town.'

Consuelo stepped forward and made a low curtsey to the King. She used her large, beautifully painted fan to great effect, gently fluttering it as she rose, in a sign of modesty, the fan remaining in front of her mouth. A glimpse of her fiery eyes held the King in thrall, particularly so as Consuelo was of a slighter build and shorter than the other court ladies. He thought her a wonderful creature and not for the first time envied his friend George Anson the licence he had had to import this bird of paradise from foreign climes. If he had been a few years younger he might have suggested a liaison with the Commodore's lady, who he knew was living in splendour in Saint James's Square, but a voice of caution would even then have warned him that George Anson was not a man to be trifled with, and would not view sharing his amour with the King as an honour. But then there was the fan! How subtle and clever, he thought. It said many things, and the dark eyes were alluring but a warning!

'My dear lady, your ward is a most delightful addition to us and must talk with Mr Handel, whilst we shall mingle for a brief moment, and then I will retire and let the ladies

71

and gentlemen amuse themselves as they wish.' He turned abruptly and signalled to Lord Hervey, who gave a brief clap of his hands. The room, which had been straining to hear everything the King said to the Lady Consuelo, burst into a clamour of chatter, painted faces and bewigged heads nodding like a flock of magpies.

Grace stood rather awkwardly; she was not at all sure what she was supposed to do next, and then she was saved by Mr Handel who, having stood up briefly by the King, looked towards her and spoke.

'Come, young lady, let us see if we can give this fine new instrument an opportunity to excel. Are your keyboard skills as proficient as your singing?' He inclined his head towards one of Lord Hervey's minions who immediately produced a small gold chair. 'My new oratorio is called "Imeneo". I have it here, my dear child, for four hands; do you think we might attempt this together?'

Grace's heart was pounding in her chest as the great man spread the music out on the ornate stand. She perused the notes quickly and saw they were marked allegro, with falling cadences from the beginning. Before she could say anything, Mr Handel suggested she take the top part. She looked up wildly. Surely Consuelo would come forward and spare her, but she did not. The only pair of eyes that locked with hers belonged to the young man who had made the harpsichord. He was standing at the other end of his instrument. She held him in her gaze and he nodded. She had a curious feeling of bravado, as if she had gained some kind of force beyond that of which she was herself capable. Without a word she smiled at Mr Handel and poised her small hands above the keys. As musicians alone understand, the room disappeared entirely. In her mind she was in a pleasant garden in Athens. The notes in the music echoed majestically in the hearts of all who beheld her.

When they had finished Mr Handel patted her hand softly. 'Excellent, excellent,' he said quietly. 'You see, many a fine voice is paraded for me, but the voice is not enough. They may sing as beautifully as nightingales, but they are not musicians. They can be as nothing if they do not know the soul of music, the complex construction of notes; it is through the keyboard that all is revealed. It is then that I can see the truth and integrity that make the moment a message from God. The greatest ambition I could have is to write a work which will bring God to the hearts of men and women for generations to come.'

He turned as if to get up and move towards the door; he was tired and he no longer had the heart for grand affairs, preferring to work and then to hear his music in his small house in Brook Street where he gathered the most talented musicians in London. But then of course it all came together in a great building like this. Mr Handel was always on the lookout for new talent. 'Young lady, I think I have it right … Grace?' He paused for thought. 'Yes, definitely. Grace: a most suitable name. I will invite you to my house; I will ask permission from your parents and you may bring your "muzzer", you do have a mother, don't you?' he asked in the gruff way he often addressed people, his accent still evident, despite the fact that he had been in London for almost thirty years.

'My mother lives in the country, sir,' said Grace, 'and my father is on the flagship of the Commodore Anson's voyage.'

'Then I shall ask your chaperone, Miss…?'

'Donna Gonzalez,' interjected Consuelo's voice as she came towards them.

Mr Handel had observed that the fine lady who laid claim to the young singer was a handsome woman of influence and position. He could not help but admire her magnificent breasts and captivating dark eyes. The room was hot and he disliked small talk of any sort, but this woman was unusual and he recalled vaguely that he had encountered her before. Suddenly he remembered. She was the great and dashing Commodore Anson's 'lady', about whom there had been so much discussion, with many jealous tongues wagging about her arrival in society, her living openly with the brave and rich naval officer. All this appealed to Mr Handel; it was the stuff of love and passion, the stuff of the Gods, upon which he based so much of his work. He felt a ripple of excitement.

'Madam, may I send my man to invite both you and your young charge to my house one evening? It would be an honour. The Commodore would, I am sure, consider it a suitable engagement in his absence. A tempestuous sea, madam, is so often in the back of my mind as I compose. The Gods feared the sea and I feel for you during the Commodore's absence, but we look for great things from men such as him.' Mr Handel did not wait for a reply but left the room, his man appearing as if by magic and clearing a path through the gossiping courtiers.

Several people had been listening carefully to the encounter, but the most attentive were Peter Zuliekom, and Sir Hartley Slinkwell. There were, of course, some who had been genuinely moved by the girl's prowess and courage but there were also some who would like to take that gift in its bloom and defile it. One of those was Sir Hartley. He had decided he would affect a swift introduction.

Standing with Sir Hartley was one of the court gentlemen who knew rather more about him than most people. This gentleman leant towards Sir Hartley and spoke in a low confidential voice:

'Be careful, Hartley, this little prize is not worth the risk. That fellow Anson will be back one day and there are spies everywhere. They work quietly, and a man can find himself assigned to the Thames one dark evening with no questions asked. The Commodore looks out for his men, and cares for their families, you heard the girl say that her father was one of Anson's officers. Lay a hand on the girl and he will know; news travels fast these days with the King following the voyage with a passion.'

'The King … fiddle sticks,' said Sir Hartley. 'He is an old man who likes to play cards at night with his fat mistress.'

'You know, Hartley, for such an ambitious man with no fear of God, a man who is as ruthless as you are, you are a fool. You underestimate the King, as do many people – at their peril. If it were not for him, Anson would never have got the money for his voyage. The King has vision. As we speak he is still at war with the Admiralty, those old fools, some of whom have never even sailed a ship… It is the King who will have bullied them to find the money for that poor man Harrison, who will now be able to finish his longitude clock. It will transform the seas. These people are powerful, Hartley.'

'You are beginning to bore me, my friend,' scoffed Sir Hartley. 'The air hereabouts is full of sermon, I do not care for it. Watch me and you will see how I charm them … it is the woman Consuelo I will address first: the tree first, you see, and then pluck the little fruit. Yes, snap it off and devour it.' He laughed lecherously and the gentleman shuddered. He had known Hartley since they were boys and had seen him become the man he was; sometimes he got tricked into thinking he was not quite as villainous as he seemed but then the shaft of light this conjecture brought would disappear as if a cloud had obscured the sun.

'Hartley you disgust me,' said the gentleman. 'I tell you, when you are in danger there are few who will come forward to speak for you.'

'Yes, this may be true, but you will, my friend, you will because you are a fool. Whereas if it were you, well…' Sir Hartley laughed.

'Have a care with the woman,' cautioned the man, 'you may have met your match. See the little half breed she has at her skirts, well it is a creature of the occult I think, small and clever, easily concealed, fearless, and her, well she comes from a place where things are different. She is rich, and money can buy many things. And the fellow Anson, he did not become the wealthy man he is without a ruthless streak. Be careful, my friend.'

Hartley turned on his heel and made his way purposefully through the throng towards Grace. Consuelo did not see him coming, but suddenly there he was, nudging between her and Grace, a gesture of breath-taking rudeness in the ritualistic court.

'I am looking at an angel. May I present myself?' oozed Sir Hartley, commencing an elaborate bow.

Grace's eyes had widened; she did not know how to reply and she was aware that people were looking at them. A deep blush crept up her neck. Before she could stammer a response, Consuelo's voice interceded like a clarion as she snapped her fan shut and tapped Sir Hartley firmly on the shoulder with it.

'No you may not present yourself to my ward, sir,' she announced smartly. 'I am the young lady's chaperone, and if you wish to be introduced you will first present yourself to me.'

Sir Hartley turned elegantly to confront Consuelo. He had been rather annoyed by his friend's warnings about her. He was a contrary, not to say arrogant, man and disliked being told anything by anyone at all. He knew he was being watched, but he had made a swift rather risky calculation. By deliberately bypassing Consuelo, he made sure that she would notice him and of course take instant exception to him; then, having offended the target, he would set about overtly charming her; consequently the older woman would be thrown off the scent and would think that perhaps it was she who was the object of his desires. This was a convoluted approach, but he had found that it usually worked.

Eye contact was the first step in the game and he had to admit they were a very fine pair of eyes, but all women, he had worked out, were vain creatures. He would flatter and cajole her.

'Madam, please forgive me. I can assure you that no disrespect was intended. I was looking carefully to see who was going to escort her home,' said Sir Hartley suavely.

'Can you think that Miss Grace Lively would be left to her own devices? The answer is no, sir!' said Consuelo coldly, quickly looking over her shoulder with a rather unnerving nod. At once Pepe came darting through the crowd from where he had been watching with Jane. 'Pepe, take my train, will you?' said Consuelo, as was her custom. She had a small train behind her dress and with the attendant Pepe this always drew admiring glances. Grace meanwhile gazed down; she had begun to wish she were anywhere at all but here.

'Grace, it is time for us to leave. Jane will go ahead and fetch our capes and word will be sent to our coach. I can think of no reason to stay.'

Grace had never seen this side of Consuelo before; she simply could not understand how anyone could be quite so rude. And although she did not like the look of Sir Hartley, with his ridiculous painted face and white powdered wig, she had not actually heard him say anything that could cause such offence.

'Oh, madam, but there is a reason,' said Sir Hartley quickly, 'I have still not been introduced to the delightful young lady who sang so beautifully.' He realised that he was about to lose his prey so he had better pounce quickly.

'Miss Lively, may I present myself to both you and your guardian, Sir Hartley Slinkwell at your service.' He gave a little bow and observed that Grace was looking alarmed. 'Now let me guess, you have been brought up in the country; you must find all this rather forbidding,' he said soothingly.

'Oh I do, sir,' replied Grace rather quickly in a surprisingly childish voice.

'Ladies, may I do you the honour of at least escorting you both down the magnificent staircase? Miss Lively, if your guardian has not already explained to you, this palace has an interesting history. If you look upwards before we get to the staircase you will see the most agreeable paintings, which are in the new palladian fashion, brought from Italy by Mr Kent who completed all the decorations here in rather a naturalistic style. But then art must imitate nature in all things,' he said in a voice loaded as usual with innuendo. 'Do you like the country, madam?' enquired Sir Hartley suddenly, as if they were the oldest friends in the world.

'Oh I do,' said Grace quickly, feeling that she was on safe ground, talking about the countryside.

'Of course we all like the English countryside,' said Consuelo, alarmed at the ease with which this man had engaged them in conversation against her will.

'Well, madam, I personally find the countryside can be a false friend. It does not speak to you and has no humour. This is why I enjoy the country idylls portrayed in Mr Kent's work, which I propose to show you as we leave. One can look at them whilst not living in them.'

'As for false friends, you, I expect, are familiar with them! And as for talking, there are times when one would be better without it! Come, Grace, we are leaving. I am sure you see the humour in that do you not, sir?' shot Consuelo with a vehemence which caused a flutter of fans around them, for there was no such thing as being alone in the court; a hundred eyes and ears watched and listened.

Grace was aghast; she had never heard such verbal unpleasantness between people. There was a kind of rough plain speaking in Clapham when things displeased anyone, but all this was delivered with such attention to detail. It was a kind of lethal verbal dance which, as far as Grace was concerned, was completely pointless. She didn't like Sir Hartley much, with his attitude, painted face and high heels, but then everyone in the room appeared entirely false. She didn't like this other Consuelo much either. The only real thing was Mr Handel's music and, oh yes, there was one other thing … the young man who had made the harpsichord. He had been watching her all evening and she would very much have liked to talk to him, but that, it seemed, was not possible. He stood out with his ordinary hair and commonplace clothes; he was obviously someone who was supposed to remain in the background, only to be brought out when needed, like a piece of cake from a high shelf in the store cupboard.

Suddenly they found themselves on the great staircase and Sir Hartley doggedly kept up a low babble about the palace which Consuelo, however reluctantly, seemed to be listening to.

'Life, my dear lady, is about jealousy and envy,' came Sir Hartley's voice, 'but you see, it is sheer tenacity which overrides everything else.'

'How true,' shot back Consuelo as they took delivery of their cloaks and started to make their way down the staircase. She had to admit Sir Hartley was persistent and could not easily be shaken.

He pressed on in what became an enthralling account of the paintings on their route. 'You see before you this great masterpiece, an impression of people's faces peeping through windows onto fictitious rooftops. Each face is based upon one of the royal servants who are now committed to posterity. You see, they are in a magnificent architectural setting. When you look up you will have the sense that they are all looking down at you from high above.'

Consuelo and Grace obediently looked upwards, and as a result Grace missed her footing, but there was Sir Hartley at her elbow, averting disaster. As he gripped her arm, Grace had a feeling of revulsion laced with something forbidden, but at the same time compelling.

Somehow Consuelo did not notice this event and against her better nature engaged in the dialogue.

'I have seen this idea before in the Quirinal Palace in Rome when I went with my parents to meet his holiness the Pope,' she said, thus giving her adversary a closer look at her auspicious lineage. This was not lost upon him but he went on with his running commentary.

'As we proceed you will see darker forces at work,' he explained. 'The paraphernalia of war and conquest, suits of armour; Britannia looks upon the empty star of a Roman head and sea horses dance between them.'

'The colours are so bright,' said Grace, 'and the blue is as none I have ever seen.'

There was now an attentive group of listeners and Sir Hartley played up to them magnificently. 'How perceptive, Miss Lively. There you have the great paint row which lost Sir James Thornhill, the darling of the aristocracy, the commission for this great work and of course the rest of the palace – which I will show you another time, with the Lady Consuelo's permission of course.'

'Perhaps,' said Consuelo coldly.

'Well, Thornhill, who had been more or less promised the project by His Majesty, sent in an estimate for the work which set the royal head in a spin. Meanwhile William Kent, an outsider trained abroad, quietly submitted an alternative plan. It was of course for half the money and although His

Majesty rather ambivalently let him start in the copular room, Kent's success meant Sir James never lived it down.'

'You mean he lost the commission completely?' asked Grace.

'Yes he did,' replied Sir Hartley. 'But a man who has come to take his position in life for granted does not retire easily. He tried all sorts of ways to discredit the inspired Mr Kent, even suggesting that he had used inferior paint for the ravishing blue, which was contracted to be made from the best lapis lazuli all the way from Afghanistan. Thornhill accused him of using the cheaper Prussian blue made from cornflowers or copper.'

'And was it true?' asked Grace.

'No, my dear, it was not. To imagine the finished painting is all part of the skill of a paint maker; he must have the knowledge of an alchemist, not unlike an expert poisoner. I have studied the art of a druggist and such things are not a mystery to me. I was present when the blue was examined by one of the King's experts, Sir Thomas Hewitt. It is beyond doubt that Kent used only the finest of materials.'

Consuelo heard many cautious voices in the back of her head as the coach made its way to St James's Square; the word 'poisoner' lingered uncomfortably in her mind.

Chapter Nine

On board the *Centurion*, the South Atlantic

'Mark my words, Mr Lively, it is idleness which is the great enemy at sea. That and the lack of attention to the preparation of a ship with the men's health in mind.'

Matthew had transferred from the *Wager* onto the *Centurion* when they left Funchal on Madeira. The Commodore often changed men about; it was a reminder that they were a squadron and no man or ship could adopt an independent path. Carpenters, the most skilled of whom were on the *Centurion*, would often be dispatched to sister ships to carry out repairs. This was often necessary in rough seas, and the loss of a carpenter on one of these exercises would be a disaster. This was one of Matthew's responsibilities now, along with looking after the interests of the expert sail makers. It was these craftsmen who would be the saving of the expedition.

Matthew Lively and George Anson were alone in the Commodore's private cabin. They had between them a good bottle of the famous Madeira sherry, which to them was preferable to the ration of rum that kept the men going – that is to say the ones who were not sick of the dreadful ague which had begun to affect them. The only thing was to placate the men with grog and pray for a fair wind and favourable current.

'It will come as no surprise to you,' said the Commodore, as he lay back in his throne-like chair and held his glass up to be illuminated by the large cabin porthole, 'that I have always known that blocking the portholes below decks would create a hotbed for infection in these infernal tropical waters.'

As he spoke, a warm but clement breeze came through the open port and stirred the charts on the table, in stark contrast to the fetid quarters of the men below, where natural light never penetrated. Some of the more robust men were now attempting to sluice down the decks with buckets of water winched from over the side. The two men in the Commodore's cabin were silent for moment, listening to a half-hearted rendition of an old seafaring song that floated on the air, melding with the regular slapping of the ocean on the old ship's hull.

'Sir John Narborough was a great man but his reported experience with the trade winds was most certainly amiss,' said the Commodore. 'I had expected more favourable help from them but we have made so little progress. I fear I see the first signs of the dreaded scurvy below decks. It is the lack of fresh provisions and there is little I can do for the men.' The Commodore spoke flatly. He had expected challenges, some worse than others, but, truthfully, this disease was the very thing he had dreaded most and such a slow passage would mean that already they were a month late in the year for the dangerous rounding of Cape Horn.

'The scurvy is the undoing of many a voyage, sir,' agreed Captain Lively. 'Even the famed Sir John Narborough said as much to the late King when he came to meet him on his return from the great voyage. He would be shocked to see that we have made so little progress. Had we had the clock in working order, I think we would have made the Horn before this, sir.' For a moment there was silence as the men thought about the implications of this and the doddering old pen pushers at the Admiralty.

'I can feel an unnatural calm… There must be something more sinister behind it,' said Matthew, looking out towards the sharp, elliptical light that came from under a sudden bank of heavy cloud. A dark premonition hovered uncertainly in his mind. Suddenly a gust of wind came as if from nowhere and took the great ship as she heaved to, sending decanters, glasses and pens clattering to the edge of the tables where they shuddered to a halt.

'I knew it,' exclaimed the Commodore, rising to his feet, 'this will be a great and terrible storm and the men are already weakened. To the deck, my friend; the sails must be reefed to the sticks.'

There was a flash of lightning as a fiery bolt shot across the sky, engulfing them all in an orange light. It was fearsome to behold and followed at once by a deafening roll of thunder. Matthew had never seen anything of the sort before and he recognised that they were to be visited by further terrors.

On deck the men stood apprehensively, not knowing what to expect. It was as if a dreadful portent had been sent from above. The sun still shone weirdly under a descending canopy of black cloud in the glowering sky.

'All you top men aloft at once!' ordered the Commodore. 'And, Lieutenant Scrubs, secure the ship. All hands on deck, batten down the hatches and get the men ready at the pumps, we are in for a brute of a storm!'

The men got to their stations at once but few of them believed there was reason for such alarm, until, that was, the skies opened with another massive crack of thunder and lightning which released torrential rain like stair rods. The old ship groaned as the wind took the sails before they'd had time to lock them down. The Commodore looked up and saw one of the lads struggling with a sail which flapped about him like a giant bat. He could see the boy would soon lose his grip and crash down to the deck and then that would be the end of him.

The Commodore wasted no time: good lads were hard to find. He was up the mast in a flash and with a steady hand pulled the boy in towards him, sail and all, and with great force released him from the tearing wind. Between them they secured the sail and he put a steady arm about the boy as they lowered themselves to the deck. The other men had heard of course that the Commodore had a reputation for never expecting any man to do what he could not do himself. But his fearless example was a double-edged sword on this occasion. A ferocious gust raised a mountainous sea from nowhere, and another of the sails flew out before the men could save it and hung from the end of the stack, filling with water and dragging the ship over at a dangerous angle. The impending catastrophe was obvious, but who would climb down the perilous boom to cut away the sail? One of the young lads had witnessed the Commodore's bravery and was out over the sea without properly attaching himself before anyone could stop him. He succeeded in cutting the sail and it lurched away on the crest of a huge wave, which towered above them as they plunged into the trough. The Commodore was by now at the wheel, down to his shirtsleeves, and with the help of Matthew they managed to bear away and avoid being pooped by the great mass of water. But the lad was nowhere to be seen.

This was the moment all sailors dreaded. They knew the lad could not be retrieved except by an act of God, which might lift him on another great wave and deposit him on the deck. Most of the crew had seen what had happened and for a short while they stood very still.

'Oh my God, this is a cruel life,' moaned one of the men.

'May the Lord in his mercy make it quick,' bawled another against the deafening roar of the sea.

'God spare him … there he is!' cried the other, pointing to a struggling figure on top of an enormous wave. The boy could see them all watching; many had left their posts to come to the heaving side. Some threw the odd bit of wood or even a bucket into the raging inferno in what they knew was a futile attempt to give the poor lad something to hang on to. Later some of them claimed they heard his cries.

In the meantime, the Commodore remained at the helm. Matthew was taking some of the strain as they kept the ship at an even keel. Now the sheets were down they were able to run with the wind, but were at the mercy of where it would take them as the ship reeled through the waves like a wild bucking horse.

It was a sight none of them would forget. For a moment the lad was there, but then he was receding as the force of the heavens took the ship and left him floundering; still thrashing through the cauldron to hang on to his life, which in his eyes was never so valuable as it was then. Each man was left with his own thoughts; there were no words that could ease the loss of the fine young lad. Most thought of their own families if they had them, and all knew that the lad would have called for his mother in his final moments.

Matthew thought of his own sons of course and lowered his head in a brief prayer; at least nobody could see that his eyes had welled up. This would be his last voyage he decided – if God spared him. For a second he visualised them all sitting by the big open fire at the farm. Perhaps Grace was playing her harpsichord … but there was no time for such thoughts. He felt someone beside him and saw one of the young midshipman, no more than thirteen years of age, standing there; the boy was trembling.

'So, young man, what is your name please? I cannot recall it.'

'Midshipman Bright,' said the boy in a high unbroken voice.

'Well, Midshipman Bright,' said Matthew, 'take the helm and then you can tell your mother that you have captained the finest ship in His Majesty's navy in the greatest ever storm and that the old ship took it like the great lady she is.'

'Aye aye,' said the boy in a firm, steady voice.

Chapter Ten

Holly Farm,
Christmas Eve 1740

'It will be like old times; do you think she will have changed much?' said Samuel to no one in particular, although the room was full of people busy with their own specific work. He was up on a pair of steps hanging thick branches of holly onto the dining room beams. Margaret had a huge basket of it at her feet and another with thick scarlet satin bows, which she had made the day before.

Alice could be heard berating Tom the kitchen boy for his lack of basting. He was supposed to be spooning a sweet sauce made of honey and lard onto a small pig on the spit, which was turning over the big open fire. He gave back as good as he got, complaining that cooking was a woman's job and he did not care for it.

'So, my pretty fellow, what else should you be doing I might ask?' replied Alice. 'You will think it fine enough when you come to eat it, won't you? Think of your poor family whose table would have been bare this Christmas if it weren't for Mrs Lively, what with your father losing his leg under that fat lady's carriage. Them is the sort of folk who don't care about the likes of us and Mrs Lively, like the good woman she is, God bless her, sent over a lovely bird from the kindness of her heart, so you, you wretch, will be having of two Christmas dinners, won't you? So stop your complaining before I box your ears again.'

'That is the trouble with Alice,' said Rupert quietly, 'she always gives a life history when just one quick sentence will do. Did you really send one of our geese to Tom's family?'

'I did,' replied Margaret, 'his father was a healthy man until he got run over and the coach didn't even stop. It left behind a family without food on the table – and with Tom's father about to set off on the great voyage. Heaven knows they have need of good carpenters at sea, but what use is a man without a leg on a boat in a rough and vicious sea? It's the likes of him that can save the ship but he would have to be able to go aloft as well as get down into the putrid depths of the ship where even the rats are loath to venture.'

The boys caught each other's eyes with a look that said, change the subject quickly, but they saw their mother brush away a tear and then shake her head quickly to dismiss the image. Of course many visions were flashing through her head, one very fanciful: that the door might open and in would walk Matthew, the man she loved, the man she had given her life to, the man whose children she would gather round her now as they celebrated the birth of their Lord, to whom she prayed each day to deliver Matthew home to them. She vowed there and then that she would never let her husband leave them again.

It was not long before Rupert, who had the sharpest ears, heard the clop of horses' shoes, enough to be drawing a fine carriage. Margaret ripped off her apron and Alice sped to the front door, which was only used on special occasions.

The coach came to a shuddering halt, the wheels skidding slightly on the ice that had already formed on this midwinter day.

Pepe was the first to alight, jumping out to let down the steps; then came Grace who ran to her mother in a flurry of thick velvet and fur trimmings; then a young man. He stood uncertainly, raising a hand to help the Lady Consuelo out of the coach. Grace broke away from her mother and, turning to the stranger, put a hand on his arm.

'Mama, this is Peter Zuliekom. May he share our Christmas with us?' Grace asked, knowing that her mother would say yes. 'He will leave soon to see his family who live in Portsmouth. He can take the packet coach from the common but it will not leave till tomorrow, and besides, he makes harpsichords and I know our instrument could do with some care.'

What could Margaret do? She would never deny a traveller, especially one who had arrived with the blessing of the great Lady Consuelo, in whom Margaret could already see there was a change in appearance. It was not Margaret's imagination, she was sure. It seemed to her that Consuelo faltered as she put her feet to the ground. And that was not all Margaret saw. One look at the young man and the way Grace looked at him was enough to tell her that this would not be the last time she would meet him.

But there was something else about him. It was as if she had seen him before, but in that moment she could not place him. He was tall and slender with a thick head of fairish hair that almost looked as if it had a fine dusting of wood shavings on it; he had a firm determined jaw and a set of dazzling teeth that were revealed readily with an open smile, which Margaret instantly thought a little too open. This was a young man who should learn to keep his thoughts a little concealed, the better to deal with the world, she thought. But it was the eyes that she noticed most. Margaret had always thought that it was the eyes that told you so much about the person, and these were a pair she would find it hard to forget.

It was cold and a thin covering of snow was beginning to settle. Grace and Consuelo's sweeping skirts and flimsy satin shoes caught the attention of Alice, who was not known for her forbearance.

'Mercy Miss Lively, you are in a lady's skirts! Before you know it you will be a gathering the goose droppings and taking them into the house. Better get your brothers to lift them for you as the little fella is doing with Her Ladyship's.'

And so the party made towards the house as the horses were led to the stable at the back; they too had memories of the farm and the generous feed of oats they had enjoyed on their last visit two months before. Consuelo was clearly fatigued even though the journey from St James's Square had taken no more than an hour; the horses had gone at a fine lick sensing a whiff of country air, which they were sadly deprived of in the smoke-filled city.

Inside, things were not quite as perfect as Alice would have liked.

'Her Ladyship's room is not quite ready,' Alice admitted. 'Where is the girl, the one who didn't like to get her hands dirty, she can get to and fire up the grate,' she added, looking round for a sign of Jane.

'Jane has gone to her family for Christmas,' said Grace quickly, 'she has become a wonderful help to us all, but I shall look after Lady Consuelo myself.'

'Not with them skirts, you won't,' retorted Alice.

Peter watched all this with a familiar affection; his mother had a maid like Alice, who ruled the roost in the same way. He could see there was no blurring of lines in this household. Each person had a place in the pecking order and they did the job allocated to them; nobody stood on their high horse; there simply wasn't time.

The discrepancy between the comforting life of the country people that Peter recognised in the Lively household and the life he had recently been introduced to at court was confusing.

He could not forget the voluptuous bosom of the fine lady that had been flaunted under his nose. She had looked upon the keys of the instrument he had made for her with a seemingly flagrant abandon which rankled when compared with the 'do not touch' coldness she had shown at a court reception later. The same pair of breasts had been paraded for the court gentlemen only and Peter had been ignored, invisible except for when needed.

'So tell us, what is it like to sing for the King?' asked Rupert later when the room glowed in the haze of mulled wine, blazing apple logs and the rich, earthy smell of garlands.

'It must be the same as singing for anyone else,' said Grace. 'That is what Mr Handel has shown me. Music comes from God, and he does not know the difference between a King and a shepherd.'

'That is well said, my dearest granddaughter, especially on this night when our lord was born in a stable,' commented Algernon, who was enjoying not only the return of Grace but another glimpse of Consuelo, albeit with a frisson of concern. With his doctor's eye, he observed something fading about her. The eyes were not as bright and her complexion was pale, with an odd flush like a little red spot in the centre of each cheek.

As for Consuelo, she was missing the attentions of her protector George Anson and even though Algernon was old enough to be her father, she could see that he was a man who still had a spark in him, a man who would still put up a good fight and more than a match for some of the idiotic fops who floated around smart society. She allowed herself to bring out some of her feminine wiles, smiling to him from under her rich lashes.

Algernon's old heart missed a beat. He looked into her eyes for a moment and he knew that he felt something like love for this woman, a love that was, in a strange way, returned. With this seal of intimacy he also saw something else. The little boy Pepe had popped up from somewhere under the table cloth and did not receive a tap on the head from his mistress. Instead he confidently stood up and Consuelo regarded him with a look that could be only one thing. It was the look a mother gives her child: indulgent, sweet and reassuring. The boy felt it too and on his way gave Consuelo's hand a little peck just where the lace sleeve stopped on the back of her palm.

So that was it, Algernon saw suddenly, this was her child, blood of her blood. The question was, though, how could this be so? Did George Anson know this? What strange union had made this child? Did this explain why Consuelo was living in a foreign land? Algernon could not help but be intrigued. And then, more pressingly, he considered what would become of such a child. Did he know that the hand he kissed so fleetingly, flesh he had touched many times, was of the mother who had cried out as he was pulled from her into the world.

In the blinking of an eye Consuelo saw that Algernon had perceived all of this; their eyes met and she gave him the slightest of nods and he returned it. It was sealed in the air.

Meanwhile, of course, all eyes were upon Grace and Peter Zuliekom; Margaret, especially, watched her daughter. For the first time she saw her as a woman and not a child, indeed a woman in love, though she probably did not know this herself, her mother decided.

Grace was sitting next to Peter and her looks towards him were bashful, but loaded nonetheless, and as is usually the case in a room where love is born, the air filled with a contagious feeling of happy excitement. Margaret watched the pair with their coy glances and breathless looks, and was quite sure she would be seeing a great deal of this young man.

For her part, Grace had watched the love games of the men and women during the short time she had spent at court, and she had learned that there it was not really about love at all but about sex and status. It was all a game to these people, she thought, they did what they pleased as long as they would not have to suffer the consequences. She had concluded that they were as careless as animals in the farmyard. She had seen many a strangely round beauty disappearing to the country and she had seen others coming back tightly corseted and fancy-free. She also knew the poor children born to these unfortunate women were farmed out to a world of anonymity and identity confusion.

So far Grace had managed to fend off the straying hands and sly remarks. Consuelo was recognised as a force to be reckoned with, but the word had got out that the beautiful Grace was not of noble birth. She felt different and however much she was dressed up as a fine lady, there were times when she wondered just what it was all for. She sometimes longed for home, with its smells of the country, the soft noses of the piglets and the hot breath of Adelaide the cow. Most of all, for all her quarrelling with Alice and her warring with Rupert and Samuel, she longed for her mother. It was the simplicity of life at home that was in her blood. But then she remembered the pride her family so obviously felt at her fine clothes and delicate hands and the vision they had of her being admired by the King himself. She was constantly reminded that she alone had been singled out to elevate herself and be a grand lady, able to scatter the spoils of her position and power.

Once again, these reflections came over her and she felt a frisson of foreboding. Then suddenly there was a strong male presence beside her. She was sitting in the cosy inglenook fireplace in the parlour while the family bustled about at their various duties. Consuelo had already retired to her bed, taken to her room by a solicitous Algernon who returned with a concerned expression on his face.

Peter came to sit next to Grace and suddenly the room was empty, the rest of them carrying on a lively banter in the kitchen. She felt his lips on hers, exploring and uncertain. Grace held back at first; despite those weeks at court she had never been kissed, and now all her body wanted to surrender to this moment, which roused in her the most delightful pleasure. Many things went through her head in a jumble. Why could she not respond to this wondrous thing in the simplest of ways? Would her mother not want this for her? Would people say it was a waste since fate had given her the chance of improvement? But one look at those wonderful eyes that now gazed into hers, one glimpse of those strong hands that were now gently exploring her breasts, the sweetness of the breath that now mingled with hers, convinced her that this was what she was meant for.

'Grace,' whispered the voice, hushed and breathless. 'I have wanted to kiss you ever since I saw you singing with Mr Handel but even long before that. You were the face that I saw when God gave me the chance of life after it had been taken from me. Do you not remember? Do you not remember the scarf?'

She drew back, shaking. 'The scarf, the scarf… I have it still.' Overcome, she leant towards him as she remembered the moment when she had said, 'Run … run for your life.' She gasped and sat very still looking directly at him whilst the revelation, which explained so much, swept over her. Then she felt the tears, tears of joy and amazement. What did it mean? How could she not have sensed it? Why had he said nothing for so long. Then it occurred to her that such restraint was a sign of strength, he had wanted the feelings she might have for him to be independent of that fateful moment. This was how Margaret found them.

'Grace, child, why are you weeping? What has happened to distress you so?'

The two looked up and Grace drew away from Peter, and closed her eyes for a moment as if recalling the past. She spoke quietly. 'Mother, this is the boy who lay as dead on the day father left for the great voyage, the one who came to life and ran,' she said in a matter of fact voice.

Margaret looked at Peter and the moment came back to life in her head. So that was it, she thought. That was the reason why her strange sixth sense had alerted her to something. But could this really be that urchin she had seen on the harbourside? He looked such a clever young man, and he was in favour with the court and well regarded in the highest circles – but of course it was his skill in the musical world that had elevated him. And what a charming sight they were... Then, in the sometimes unwelcome way she would glimpse the future, she feared that their love would not follow an uneventful path.

'Mrs Lively, I have never told Grace who I was, she had no idea, but how could I ever forget her? If I was to find favour with her it would be for reasons quite apart from that.'

It was almost too much for Grace to take in but now she recognised that it was more than Peter's skills and his undoubtedly handsome appearance that had made her heart race!

'When did you recognise me?' Grace asked him quietly.

'The very first instant when I saw you across the harpsichord: I could not think of anything else and when Mr Handel asked me to step forward to meet the King, I only had eyes for you, even though I had dreamed of the moment when His Majesty would praise me for my instrument.'

Algernon had come into the room. Of course Grace had told him of the incident at the time. He had congratulated her for acting bravely despite the presence of officers who, like the Commodore himself, and the hard-bitten sailors, were conditioned to savagery. It had taken a slip of a girl to cock a snook at the lot of them; and in the end all of them had seen her courage, which had allowed a spark of kindness and humanity to shine a light into their brutal world. It was a world Algernon had long ago grown to despise. He had found his own path, which, although it had not brought him high position and fancy rewards, gave him peace and wisdom.

'This calls for a celebration,' he said joyfully now. 'Call the boys, daughter. Was there ever a moment on a Christmas Eve so in keeping with the birth of our Lord?'

CHAPTER ELEVEN

HOLLY FARM,
CHRISTMAS DAY

The first thing Grace noticed when she woke in her old bed at home was the silence. No noise of horses, cries from the street or barking dogs. Just thick silence and something more: the odd tweet of a bird, but muffled as if the world was encased in gauze. The room was cold, so cold that she was reluctant to throw back the thick coverlet and put her feet to the floor. There were no thick curtains around the bed as she had had in St James's Square, only a sprigged cotton frill on the top of the old four-poster that creaked as she moved. The door opened gently and Alice came in with wood for the fire.

'Well happy Christmas, Miss Lively, just look out of the window. Nobody will be going anywhere today.'

Grace sat up and swung her feet to the knotted patchwork mat on the floor, lent for her thick woollen shawl and padded to the window. She had to rub a hole in the mist on the glass but then she had a peephole vision of winter wonderland. The trees outside bowed heavy with snow and icicles hung from the eaves. There were prints in the snow where foxes had sniffed their way to the chicken house as the hens clucked softly in their cocoon of animal heat. They knew instinctively that they would not be released today, but must wait for the pan of boiled peelings softened with mash to be pushed through the door and the voice of Alice who would come with the food. 'Now, ladies, how many eggs from my girls today?' she would say, talking in the strange purring tone that she kept for her beloved poultry.

'Miss Lively, you will catch your death with them bare feet. Put on your slippers,' fussed Alice, examining the beautiful embroidered mules. She held them to her chest for a brief moment and thought of the wonderful life which came with slippers such as these and how there was her little Grace living that life. Alice felt a kind of vicarious pleasure.

'So the coach won't be setting off today?' said Grace, thinking about the extra time with Peter this would allow. Alice knew exactly what all this was about. She was not sure at all that Grace should turn her back on the opportunity for a better life – but then was high society a better life? Alice wondered.

As Grace looked out of the window she saw Pepe in his silk breeches and velvet coat walking in the snow on the garden path. It was up to his knees and he was laughing.

'Alice, come and look at this,' she cried.

'I am going straight down, Miss Lively, to call that lad in and put him in some of Master Rupert's old clothes,' said Alice, flushing with disapproval. 'I am not having the neighbours seeing anything so ridiculous. It's about time that boy was given a chance to be an ordinary child instead of a pet dog. I am not standing for it! Airs and graces … begging your pardon, miss. If you see what I mean.'

She stomped out of the room, full of determination, and within seconds Grace heard her calling the boy in.

Later, when Grace went downstairs, there was no sign of anybody except Alice humming merrily, and her mother who was setting the table. The Christmas day meal would take place later, when the light began to fade and the family could draw the shutters and light the candles, stoke up the big fires and Algernon could start carving the enormous ham. Alice was busy in the still room where all the summer preserves were stored and where, on a thick slate shelf behind the fold of a hessian curtain, hid the 'forced' salads they would eat today: celeriac and celery, white and virginal as they sought the light. Then there were the preserves: fig and apple chutneys, a jelly made from the summer fruits in the garden, Alice's pigeon pie, pickled walnuts, broom buds and cucumbers, dried mulberries and quinces, a carrot pudding, and a neat's tongue pudding. The highlight of all this would be Margaret's plum cake served with syllabubs. This feast was the result of all the hard work they had put into preparing the food they had gathered in times of plenty and today was a celebration of it all.

There was a great deal of noise coming from outside the door: boys laughing and the gruff voice of a young man. Intrigued, Grace opened the front door and what a sight there was! There was Pepe, unrecognisable in thick country boy's clothes, her own two brothers in mufflers and bright coloured hats, and in charge of it all was Peter. They had shovelled a path through the thick snow and not a merrier picture could be imagined. Grace wished her life could be frozen at that minute; what more could any of them wish for in this single second? A robin came to complete the vision and sang his winter song, king of all he surveyed. All these young men had their dreams and hopes, so tender and at the mercy of life and the women who would cross their paths, be it mothers, lovers or sisters or just the ones who spun on the outer periphery. She had it in her power to influence these young men's hearts and at the thought of this her own stood still. Then she felt a shower of snow as Peter shook one of the holly trees on the path. She stood, her thoughts whirling, knowing that whatever happened, it would probably be alright in the end – but perhaps not in the way she imagined.

Later, when they were all sitting in the front parlour, Algernon began to tell them some of his old sea stories. There was an implicit understanding that all of them were affected in their own ways by the adventure taking place at sea. God knew where their loved ones were but somehow the quiet, sure voice of Algernon put some sort of order into their thoughts. It was not long before Margaret noticed to her astonishment that in the gentle fading light of the candles and the flickering fire, Consuelo's left hand was not folded in her lap where her other lay still and relaxed, but under the disguise of one of her flowing shawls, where she and Algernon were holding hands. She did not know what to make of this at all. Her mother-in-law had died so many years ago whilst Algernon was at sea on what was to be his last voyage and she had never thought that he might have eyes for another woman. Besides, how unexpected that the Commodore's lady should be thinking of him in this way.

What she did not know was that the reason for her father-in-law and Consuelo's attachment was more complicated than she imagined. Algernon knew something about Consuelo that she had forbidden him to divulge and for now she knew he would keep her secret and comfort her as much as he could. Meanwhile, Margaret, in her usual tactful way, decided to keep her observations to herself.

'Now is the time when we must all say a prayer for our men at sea,' said Algernon suddenly. This they did with bowed heads, each with their own thoughts, very far from the reality of the situation in the Atlantic.

'And now,' ventured Consuelo, 'please will you sing for us, Grace? After all, you have a skilled accompanist and we are lucky that the weather has kept him here so that we may show your family something of what pleased both the King and Mr Handel so well.'

They did not need much pressing, and were soon at the old harpsichord, billing and cooing like two turtledoves. While everyone was engrossed in this delightful sight, Algernon offered Consuelo his arm and they went back to the dining hall to another fire and a pair of seats discretely concealed. They sat down cosily and Algernon raised a matter that had been concerning him since Grace had disappeared to London. After all, the girl had no father to speak for her until Matthew's return, the fruition of which Algernon had realistic cause to doubt.

'My dear lady,' he said firmly to Consuelo, leaning towards her and looking earnestly into her large dark eyes, which were sparkling in the firelight. 'As we are quietly here and the family will be engaged elsewhere for some time, may I talk to you about my granddaughter?'

Consuelo had been half expecting this and was in fact only too glad to confide in Algernon, whom she had come to suspect was rather more than a retired naval doctor.

'Why, I would be glad to, Algernon,' she answered eagerly. 'Having Grace with me is both a joy and also a great responsibility, one which I take very seriously, as you should know.'

'Of that there can be no doubt,' Algernon reassured her. 'But the time has come when I must reveal something to you,' he said as he held up his hand in a comforting gesture, 'but only if you are prepared to listen to what I have to say in strict confidence. These are things my family know nothing about and I do not wish them to.'

'Of course,' replied Consuelo carefully. 'We both have our secrets it would seem, and I cannot imagine yours are anything but honourable.'

'Well, I will come straight out with it then,' said Algernon. 'I am not retired, you see; I run an establishment which rescues fallen women and girls from the iniquitous streets of

London. It is not far from here. We have midwives who can deliver the children of these hapless creatures and if they get into difficulties I am there. Often the mother dies and the child lives, which is the most terrible fate, but in the world there is still a pool of goodness and I have some great ladies who find a life for these poor babes. Sometimes they grow into splendid people, for no one can know what gifts they have inherited from their parents. As often as not, though, their mothers are too far gone with illness when they reach us: the terrible ravages of syphilis, and then the horrible effects of the mercury with which they are plied with the futile and false claim that it will cure them. Of course it does no such thing but makes their suffering worse.'

Consuelo listened silently. She thought of her own life and the secret she had told Algernon, which he had received with the mere nod of a chin and a soft smile of understanding.

'I know why you are telling me about this, Algernon, and now I must speak openly about my own son whom I took to my heart. If I think about what would have become of him ... it ...' Consuelo began to weep quite openly. This was the first time she had ever spoken so clearly to another human being about the ghastly events in her past. 'You see we should have known what might happen. I warned my father those poor slaves ... no, you would not have done those things to a horse or a dog. It made no difference that my father treated his slaves so well, that he never separated a mother from a child, that he would not use the slave hole, that they were never whipped and that the women were not allowed to be used for men's pleasure like animals. You see the other owners despised us for it. But when the uprising came they made no distinctions between any of us. We were all the cruel oppressors. There were so many scores to be settled, it was a night of retribution.'

Algernon took her hand, encouraging her to go on.

'I could not tell you which one of them gave me my son, there were so many of them, but I knew then that I would never be able to bear another child. How he found his life in me I do not know, but he did and he owes that life to George Anson.'

'I thought as much. You have done well to rescue your life, dear lady. It is easy to see why you are able to live as you do, far away from the place where these terrible things happened.'

'George came just in time, his men doused the flames but not much of the house was worth saving and it killed my father; he had loved his slaves and that is how he was repaid. Whichever one of them put his child in me, he cannot have been an evil man because my little boy is the gentlest of souls. I love him so very deeply, but he can never know the truth. He thinks his mother was a mulatto who died giving birth to him. But sometimes when he sits so near to me and presses against me there is something which goes beyond rational explanation.'

'And the Commodore protected you whilst you gave birth to the child?' asked Algernon gently.

'Yes he did, he was glad that the child lived. He had seen one of the slaves turning on an indoor servant who had a new baby, which she held to her breast in terror as they tore it from her, saying she was a white man's whore ... and they killed it. I will never forget her screams. They haunt me in my worst nightmares.'

'My dear, how you have suffered! It is well that people do not know any of this; when you walk in such darkness it colours the air around you.'

'You can understand now how coming here to be with George has given me a new life and I do not want to be tainted by the memories; but I have a great fortune and I want to share it, dear Algernon.'

'My dear lady, this shines out of you, your goodness; sometimes such suffering can bring wisdom.'

'I hope so,' said Consuelo wistfully. 'But I do not have the wisdom to know what will become of my son. I sometimes think he is like a pet monkey in London. He would be better living in the country, you know, where he could be a normal child. He has become wily and London is a bad place once you leave the gilded cage of the court and the kind of life that I am able to lead. I know George will return one day, but…'

She left the words hanging in the air and Algernon intuited that she was considering her own mortality. There were many things he needed to talk to her about.

'Would you like to come to see one of the sanctuaries where some of my poor women and babes live? I feel it is something I would like to share with you – and this brings me to the question of Grace.'

Empathy had developed between Algernon and Consuelo, which was far removed from the clean, simple life at Holly Farm. They were two people who had witnessed things that others could not even imagine. They had travelled down dark roads and neither of them would ever see the human condition except stripped naked of niceties. Algernon came straight out with it.

'I am not happy about Grace being in so terrible a place as London, even with your protection,' he said bluntly. 'There are forty-four thousand women who work in the evil trade of whoring, mostly the victims of circumstance, and usually they get started because they think it is just the once, maybe even in the mistaken idea that some man actually loves them. Grace would not be the first pure fruit that had been defiled in such a way. The court too is no stranger to vice, my dear.'

'I love Grace as my own,' replied Consuelo fervently. 'I do know something of what you speak, and I never let

105

Grace out of my sight,' she assured him. 'That is where Pepe has his uses! He is to some extent invisible in these circles and he hears and sees things that are very valuable. Grace is surrounded by protectors, I can assure you. Besides, George is a powerful man. He knows about Grace and that her father is one of his officers. I do not think she would be easily trifled with.'

'Believe me, some of these men are ruthless and they are also fearless since they have neither morality nor the wisdom to calculate the price of anything, except the spoils to be had from the ruination of so many human beings.'

Consuelo sat quietly; she was deep in thought making a decision. 'I would like to come with you to see this place.'

And so it was decided. Algernon wanted Consuelo to be aware of just what a den of iniquity Georgian London was. Grace's great beauty and talent made her even more of a prize for the evil men and women who preyed on young girls from whatever walk of life they came. He had a feeling that Consuelo had been shielded from the reality of all this. Seeing his granddaughter with Peter had shown him a vision of the sort of life Grace should be living. Tomorrow when they went for a ride in her beautiful coach, ostensibly to see the countryside, it would in fact be for a very different reason. The country was still in an icy grip after Christmas but despite the weather Algernon pressed on with his plan.

Chapter Twelve

Saint Bridget's Home for Women

The house was in a place called Streatham and was half an hour away by coach, hidden by trees and what appeared to be a small farm. Next to it was a larger building, which Algernon pointed out to Consuelo.

'That is the convent of Our Lady of the Holy Innocents,' he said as they drove up the narrow road leading to St Bridget's. The convent bell was pealing the Angelus to summon the nuns to prayer and Consuelo crossed herself. Algernon took this opportunity to tell her that St Bridget's was not a religious establishment, despite its connections with the convent which was an open order that helped with the running of the home.

'These girls have often been hoodwinked by the bawds who go trawling for new arrivals fresh from the countryside,' he explained. 'These madams are often demurely dressed, even holding a copy of the bible, and they convince the poor girls they can offer them a decent home with respectable employment.'

'Now you come to mention it, I have often seen such women in the city where all the coaches come in, I thought they were missionaries,' said Consuelo.

'And so do these poor creatures,' said Algernon. 'This is why, when we offer the girls refuge here, we let them find the peace of God themselves. You would be amazed how many of them, once they hear the bell tolling and see the sisters rushing to worship, and when they have cleansed their minds of the vile trade that has brought them to this, join the sisters in the convent for worship. All of them turn to God because they are beyond practical help but they go to their maker resolved and loved and pure of spirit.'

As Algernon spoke, Consuelo was so greatly moved that she reached for his hand, and although they were separated by the exquisite leather that clothed her delicate fingers, she moved them softly and he knew she was the only woman of high birth he had ever met who could really understand what he was doing.

The first thing that struck Consuelo as they entered the large hall was the quiet order. There was a table in the middle on which was an enormous pewter container full of sweet smelling winter greenery. Opposite the door, a splendid fire burned in a polished grate. In the distance she could hear a mixture of voices. Some babies were crying and there was a low murmur of women talking and, somewhere, singing. A sweeping staircase led to a gallery, off which were several doors.

A nun with a highly starched wimple came to them almost at once. Smiling sweetly but with lowered eyes, she took their cloaks and disappeared with a slight bow. A second later, another, older nun appeared. She was less formal and was wearing a voluminous white bibbed apron.

She held out a warm hand to Consuelo and then clasped Algernon's outstretched hand affectionately.

'Doctor Lively, you have come on a busy day,' said the nun, smiling expansively at Consuelo. 'Three girls came today; one is delivering her child as we speak and I fear she will have a hard time of it. The poor girl can only be about thirteen.'

'Well, may I present the Lady Consuelo Gonzalez? This is Mother Benedicta, upon whom we all depend for the running of St Bridget's.'

Piercing through the ordered quiet, suddenly there came a long scream from one of the open gallery doors. It was the cry of a child in mortal distress. A young nun came running out and called down to Mother Benedicta.

'Mother, the girl is in a terrible state; you must come; I do not know what to do!' Noticing Algernon standing in the hall, she crossed herself and hastily folded her blood stained apron out of the way.

'The saints in all their wonder be praised! The good doctor is here! Why, it is the only thing that can save her... I must go to the poor soul who is about to depart this life... We are so short of sisters today, it is dire.' Another scream rent the air.

'Find me another apron, Mother. I have birthed many a child, including my own. I did not come here to gawp,' cried Consuelo. As if by magic a nun came with a large starched apron and Consuelo raced up the stairs, following Algernon.

The room was warm and had the sickly smell of blood, a lot of blood. The first thing that Consuelo saw was the shocking sight of a young girl, no more than a child, her face covered in sores and her thin legs splayed in a pool of blood. The frantic young nun rushed to a bowl of water and brought linen to try to cover the girl and mop up some of the carnage. Consuelo immediately called for more clean water and carefully washed her hands in a china bowl brought by the young nun. Algernon recognised a practised hand and silently they began to work together. The child let out another terrible cry and without demure, Algernon drew up a stool and tried to see what obstacle prevented the emergence of the baby.

'She must sit up and then we must turn the mother on her side,' he said quietly to Consuelo.

Talking softly to the girl, Consuelo helped her to sit up but the movement increased her agony. Consuelo helped Algernon to turn the girl on her side and he caught her eye with a despairing look.

'She is too small. She will never get that baby out. She is only a child herself,' whispered Algernon as the girl was riven by another excruciating shot of pain.

'So what is to be done?' asked Consuelo in desperation.

'If I had smaller hands I would get the girl some laudanum and go in and gently ease the child out; if it could be turned a little and the poor mother relaxed, we might be able to save one of them. But the sisters will not do this and it is a difficult technique. I am afraid there is nothing I can do; they will both die.'

'Oh no they won't!' cried Consuelo. 'I have done this myself with the slave girls on the plantation. I was taught by the best of the old women who hardly ever lost a child.'

'Well, let us call for some more hot water to clean your hands and you will have to take that gown off and be in your petticoats. Come, sister,' he said, turning to one of the nuns who had come into the room, 'get the Lady Consuelo one of your grey birthing habits and a clean pinafore and I have the laudanum in my bag so bring it to me quickly. We may get the poor child out yet.'

The nun responded at once and brought the laudanum, which the sister dripped onto the young mother's parched lips. Then Consuelo took control and Algernon could only wonder at her competence and knowledge. The girl fell limp as the drug took effect and stopped resisting the forces of nature. Consuelo sat on a stool and gently rubbed her hands with something the sisters had brought, which smelled of herbs and lavender. She knew the antiseptic qualities of it and trusted the sisters knew what they were doing.

Gradually she eased her hands into the girl, who did not fight and scream but moaned of a vision of the Virgin Mary.

'I have the head,' rasped Consuelo as the sister bathed the mother's damp head and pulled tendrils of hair back from her brow. Algernon soothed her and with a nod of acknowledgement from Consuelo went behind the girl and pressed her abdomen as Consuelo whispered, 'I have the head and shoulders, I am going to slowly twist it round and with God's help get it out.'

Mother Benedicta had slipped into the room, word having got out about the wondrous accouchement that was taking place under the care of their grand visitor, who had looked good for nothing except a polite smile. 'God in his heaven, the angels, Mother Mary, I die!' screamed the girl and with a swoosh the child was in Consuelo's hands as Mother Benedicta stepped into the breach with warm cloths to receive the baby. At first it would make no sound so Consuelo unceremoniously held it up and gave it a slap; it was a little boy. With a loud cry he announced his arrival.

The room fell very silent and Mother Benedicta brushed a tear from her eye. Each birth was of course to her a gift from God, but just sometimes there was one that had something out of the ordinary about it. She was usually hardened to all of this: the wickedness of men and women. It all boiled down to lust, she thought, the desire of man to get their pleasure from women or, as in this case, a little girl. She wondered for a moment what kind of man had fathered this little baby boy.

'Well, our Lord in Heaven will be the only father this poor mite will know,' she murmured under her breath. Consuelo heard and turned to Mother Benedicta, her hands still dripping with blood.

'Yes, Mother,' she said a little sharply, 'but a mother can give a child enough love for two.'

'Unless we have another miracle the child will have neither a father nor a mother,' said Algernon suddenly. 'The girl is losing blood fast and there is no strength in her.'

They looked at the girl as the young nun moved to hand her the crying baby, but she lay ashen and senseless on the bed and more blood trickled onto the white sheets.

'Get her feet right up and let me see the afterbirth,' Algernon went on. 'I think there is more left behind, I must try to press on her abdomen to get it out; it is a rough thing to do but it might be her only chance.'

Together, Consuelo and Algernon worked with quiet efficiency, and within seconds the afterbirth came out.

'Algernon, will you let me do what we did on the plantation in such circumstances?' asked Consuelo.

'Anything! There is little hope of saving her,' he replied in a low voice.

Consuelo raised the girl's legs and bound her lower body tightly. 'If only we had ice I could do more to stop the poor child's bleeding...' Consuelo lamented.

'We have ice in the ice house if it will stop the bleeding! We will get it at once,' shot Mother Benedicta.

With the help of the ice and miraculous good fortune the bleeding had stopped but the poor girl was now shivering to death.

'We must bring her back to life,' said Consuelo. 'Bring some bricks to warm the bed and we must keep her feet up.' Mother Benedicta shook her head slowly; she did not think the girl stood a chance.

Consuelo had seen the look of approaching death many times. It was in the eyes: they seemed to retreat into the head as if they saw another world, a better place and there was little to be done when the soul had seen this. She sat on the bed and chafed the mother's hands but they were cold and her eyes vacant. Slowly a faint smile came on her dry lips and for a moment she looked back at Consuelo. She whispered something and Consuelo leant close to her and heard the words.

'My baby…' Her little hands trembled and Consuelo looked up urgently to Mother Benedicta.

Mother Benedicta gave the baby boy to Consuelo who took it and tenderly tried to help the girl to hold it.

'You will look after him, won't you?' murmured the girl in a barely audible voice. At that moment the baby let out a robust cry and thrashed about with his little hands and Consuelo could see that, against all the odds, he was a sturdy boy. The young mother gave a faint smile and fell back into Consuelo's arms.

'She is gone,' said Mother Benedicta softly crossing herself; the other nun came and took the baby, who was still protesting violently.

Algernon took Consuelo's arm and raised her to her feet. She was overcome with emotion, for the birth had brought back traumatic memories of Pepe's delivery, and she now felt bound to this baby. Many questions flashed through her mind but mostly her worries were about what lay in store for the little boy.

'Oh, Algernon, it is awful,' she wept as she found herself leaning against his chest.

'My dear, you must not take it on so, here this is an everyday occurrence. The poor girl had never known anything but hardship all her life. By the time she came to the sisters she expected nothing. But at least for a little while she had a glimpse of human kindness; she died with a smile on her lips. She had seen a great light and another, better place and she knew that her little boy would have more of a chance in life than she had.'

113

'How can we know that?' cried Consuelo, pulling away from him. 'How can you possibly know such a thing with any certainty?'

'We know such a thing because that is what our life's work is about,' interceded Mother Benedicta quietly. 'We will send the mother to her maker with our prayers and give her a decent burial and, yes, we will care for the baby and find a loving place for him in the world. There are many people who support our work here and God sent us Doctor Lively whose careful stewardship has made all this possible. You must go now, dear lady, and perhaps you can find others who will help us as you have done. It is not only money which assists us in our vocation; it is the messages sent to God and Our Lady who was the fairest of all mothers.'

With the blessings of the sisters, and having said a quick farewell to the baby, now sleeping peacefully in the young nun's arms, Consuelo turned to leave. But then a thought came to her.

'How will the child feed?' she asked.

'Ah well, the Lord takes, but he also gives. We have another mother whose baby died today and she will take the orphan to her and feed him as if he were her own; this is what we do here. With God's help we always find a solution.'

Consuelo and Algernon travelled back Holly Farm in silence. But Consuelo had made up her mind on two things: firstly that she would give a substantial sum to the St Bridget's and secondly that she would look more carefully at what the future should hold for Grace.

CHAPTER THIRTEEN

GEORGE FREDERIC HANDEL'S HOUSE, BROOK STREET, LONDON

The first snowdrops had appeared in the garden at St James's Square and Grace definitely felt that the long winter was coming to an end. She had seen a lot of Peter at court and nothing had dimmed her feelings towards him. Tonight was to be a very special occasion, an evening at Mr Handel's home.

When they arrived Grace looked around in surprise at the cosy intimacy of the small London house. It was in a charming street in a fashionable part of town. Mr Handel's neighbours were members of parliament and lawyers, most of whom also had houses in the country to which they repaired often, according to the seasons. These periods were precious to him as he was prone to become irritated by the constant comings and goings in the busy street, with its noise of coaches and horses and bustling servants. He himself owned a handsome coach with room for two horses in a charming little coach house attached to the side of the building. This was his greatest concession to luxury. Despite his growing wealth he did not consider himself a rich man, partly because he gave so much away to charitable causes. His latest gift had been to the Coram Foundling Home. This was a venture conceived by a worthy gentleman called Thomas Coram who had become increasingly appalled by the sight of pregnant prostitutes begging in the street, and the scandal of murdered babies either left to die or farmed out to dissolute nurses who let them die, and continued to take money from the hapless mothers for their upkeep.

Algernon had told Consuelo about this institution, which had been built at vast expense. It had become a fashionable cause for people in smart London society, keen to smooth their path to heaven when the time came. They would be taken on tours to see the result of the good work, rather as if it were an afternoon's entertainment. Algernon had told her in no uncertain terms that it was for this very reason that his work at St Bridget's was to be kept quiet. The doors of the Foundling Home had been open to all comers and as a result the whole endeavour was a disaster, where seventy percent of the occupants died within weeks or days. 'It is a scandal,' he had said to her. 'It is better to save the few we know are likely to reform and lead a good life and whose children we can care for properly.'

All this was locked into Consuelo's mind as she entered the house, and she ruminated upon the confusion that seemed to reign in this great country of which George Anson was a product.

They were welcomed by a rustic looking manservant and divested of their cloaks by a smiling young girl. Although Consuelo had felt unwell, she had insisted on coming with Grace. She knew what an honour it was to receive an invitation to the great man's home. It would be a very select gathering and the idea was to make music together. This was a supreme opportunity for Grace.

There was a puff of warm air coming from the first floor and the studious murmur of conversation. The young female attendant preceded them up the narrow creaking stairway and Grace saw with relief that Consuelo, with her usual aptitude, had been right to suggest that they wear their simpler dresses; their great hooped skirts would not have fitted in the intimate space where Mr Handel's divine music was written. They were shown to the music room, at the end of a little landing, where there were several rows of chairs facing an elegant harpsichord at which none other than Peter Zuliekom was playing some of the composer's most recent music. Grace met his glance and went in as he played. He smiled at her, without interruption to the rhythm, the candelabra on the instrument casting a voluptuous light over his hands. He did not so much play the fine instrument as stroke it. Grace stood momentarily still and felt almost faint. She supposed this was love. It was clear that he felt this too and the joy of this look was not lost upon Consuelo; indeed, she felt a kind of envy for the two lovers. She had never experienced young love so fresh and unencumbered; her love for George Anson was different, it was born of many other things, which she hoped with all her might that the two young people would never know. Her own journey had been along a savage and rough path to a kind of order, when everything had seemed lost. But for these two it all seemed deceptively simple, although not at all what she originally had in mind for Grace. But what could possibly impede the rosy path that was opening up before them? Grace had found her love: they shared a common interest and he fitted perfectly into the background at Holly Farm. They would marry, find a little house in town, pursue their music together, start a family, and oh yes there would be a delightful country wedding, after which Consuelo would hold a soiree for them at St James's Square. Above all they would never lose their roots; she wisely concluded that she would have to accept it.

The chatter stopped for a minute as Mr Handel made his way into the music room, where he saw the three of them together. It struck him how beautifully innocent Grace appeared. He looked forward to sharing with her and Peter the music that flowed through him in an unstoppable stream.

Here were two that had not been corrupted by the miasma of the court. As the two women gave him a deep curtsey another person entered the room and Mr Handel felt a cold draft. He shivered involuntarily. The newcomer's voice cut through the happy scene like a knife.

'My lady, and with your delightful ward, I did not expect to see you here, but what an exquisite surprise,' he said, with an affected bow. It was of course, none other than Sir Hartley Slinkwell.

Consuelo was at once struck again by his rudeness. It was not for him to interrupt their host's welcome in his own home. She bridled inwardly, and had English been her mother tongue she would have come out with a cutting reply. But she was spared that trouble.

'Sir, it is me who is surprised! Yes indeed. I have no recollection of inviting you here tonight,' said the normally benign host. 'But as you are here and a gentleman is ever courteous to those people who come to his home,' he went on, 'may I ask you to introduce yourself to the elderly lady seated in the other room and attend to her every need for the rest of the time that you are present. She is hard of hearing and has a large appetite and likes to be served individually. Would you be so kind as to sit with her in the other room? The poor lady has no private coach, so I bequeath you the task of conveying her to her house in Grosvenor Square when she has eaten and is desirous of departing. Good evening, sir,' Mr Handel finished with a flourish and turned his back on the imposter, who melted away leaving a heavy atmosphere.

'The best thing we can do is to continue our evening at once,' announced Mr Handel after what was a rather satisfied silence. There was not a man or woman in the room who was not delighted to see Sir Hartley cut down to size and by a man so beyond reproach as Mr Handel.

'This has been a reminder my dears that Satan is never far away,' the great man continued. 'What we are doing here is creating beauty from the chaos that people bring about. Let us cleanse ourselves by returning to our purpose.' He walked purposefully towards the harpsichord and ran his hand over it, beckoning to Peter to continue as if the evening had not been disturbed at all.

'Music is a great leveller,' murmured Consuelo as she took the seat next to him.

'Yes indeed it is,' agreed Mr Handel.

'But I am not a little puzzled by the English,' said Consuelo.

'Why so?' he asked. 'You can speak freely to me dear lady because as you know I am not a Englishman, although I do think I become more so by the day.'

'How is it that a man so good as the King can have such people as that Slinkwell monster about him?' asked Consuelo.

'I often ask myself that question,' replied Mr Handel. 'I think such a thing did not flourish when the Queen was alive, her demise has seen the rise of sycophants and scoundrels. The Queen cut through them. She would very much have approved of the young musician who has fallen in love with your beautiful ward. Such a match will be a happy one I am sure. It is a joy to see them together, you can write all the music you like but it is the execution which brings it alive, and now those two are in perfect harmony... It is rare,' he said thoughtfully, gripping her hand.

The singing finished and Mr Handel retired to his sleeping quarters on the next floor, as was his custom. It was well known that he sometimes kept unconventional hours, a result of the fact that ideas for music were streaming through him at all times, day and night, which meant he must grasp at rest when he could. His loyal servants and friends were patient and long suffering. It was understood that his guests would then seat themselves wherever they could and be served some refreshments. It was already dark but there was definitely a feeling of spring in the air. Some hopeful blackcaps could be heard outside the window, lamenting the darkness and belying the season with their chirping.

'This is the first moment in my life when I have experienced sublime happiness,' said Peter suddenly to Grace. They were sitting side by side on a small love seat, and until that moment there had been no need for words as their complicit and contented silence spoke more eloquently than any conversation could ever do. Now Peter saw that they might be attracting comment. He was unaware, of course, that all the world loves a lover and just how their unspoken joy nourished this intelligent and sensitive gathering from which Sir Hartley had been so firmly and elegantly banished by Mr Handel.

'I have something to tell you,' Peter said quietly

'What is it, I hope I will be pleased,' said Grace, turning towards him, her heart leaping as she gazed into his clear eyes.

'Well, it is this, Grace. I had never imagined that my work, which is a reward in itself, could bring with it enough money to do something for my beloved family, and restore to them all that they lost when my father made some unwise decisions and our circumstances were greatly reduced. In short,' he went on excitedly, 'I have purchased a beautiful little manor house with a small farm near a place called Chichester which has a fine cathedral with an exemplary musical tradition. It is in the middle of rolling downs and has views to the sea. You see, I require the peace of the countryside because to continue my work I have taken to a little composing and I need inspiration.'

'Oh, my dear Peter,' said Grace with a look of disappointment on her face, 'what shall I do without the friend I have found?'

'Grace, my love, my dear, first and only love,' whispered Peter in a barely audible voice. 'Can you think that any plan I made would not be with the hope in my heart that you will be part of it?'

This did not come as a complete surprise to Grace. She had dared to let herself have fantasies about a life with Peter, a life quite different to the one Consuelo had shown to her. She did not quite know what to say, but when Peter's hand searched for hers in the folds of her dress she did not withdraw it as a coy young girl might do, but caressed his hand in return, feeling the calluses on his fingers and loving each small blemish as if she had always owned it. 'Is there something you wish to ask me, something which would bring me a happiness I had not dared to hope for?' she asked boldly.

This took Peter rather unawares, and he smiled at her. 'Oh, Grace, you know there is, and now I know that your answer would render me the luckiest man in the world, there are formalities I must honour. I cannot ask your father for his permission, but may I ask Doctor Algernon and your mother?'

A dark shadow had come into Grace's mind. Of course it was not possible to ask her father; he was somewhere on the vast ocean and there had been no word for many weeks and even then only by third party. She knew he would be away for a long time. She had also faced the fact that he might never return and even if he did he would be a very different man. She had no idea how to face these implications and felt only despair.

'Yes, by all means, you must talk to them,' she said finally. 'We are going to be so happy,' she added bravely. Nonetheless, in Grace's mind there rested an awful feeling of uncertainty about what she was doing. She feared that her father's absence at this momentous time was more than she could bear.

And so it was decided. Peter was blissfully unaware of the hazards that can sometimes await those who choose to pursue an apparently simple path. Later he would tell himself that he should have known life was not so straightforward. But perhaps he thought that because he had faced such hardship and danger, fate now owed him a life unencumbered by cares, and it was this that gave him the sense that all would be well.

CHAPTER FOURTEEN

THE *CENTURION*, STRAIT OF LE MAIRE, GATEWAY TO THE PACIFIC, 17 MARCH 1741

'Commodore, we have the first case of scurvy. I have long been expecting it; only if God in his mercy gives us a sighting of land will we be saved.' The surgeon looked grey and brought with him the dank stench from the men below. The ship, already weakened, groaned as it plummeted, and the cabin darkened as a huge thirty-foot wave built above them.

The Commodore could not allow himself the luxury of processing this disastrous news.

'I fear even God and a miracle cannot give us that,' he said despondently. 'We have so few men left, and it will hit us all in a matter of days. I have a small supply of the vitriol left … if we had been better prepared… What good is salt beef to us now? What with the seasickness …'

The Commodore had lost his senior surgeon to typhus shortly after they had sailed from Madeira and his replacement was a younger, less experienced fellow. He was a good man but nothing had prepared him for the horrors they were encountering, and indeed George Anson himself could not have envisioned so many disasters. He had known of course that if they attempted the rounding of the Horn when the equinox was at is most ferocious, things would be difficult, but nothing had prepared him for the reality. The supplies had been just another disaster, the assumption that fresh produce would be acquired wherever they put into port had proved fatal. And as for the rest: these seas, the worst he had ever known, lashed the ships to pieces and nothing remained dry. The men were drenched in their bunks; the stoves could not be lit; the dry produce was soaked and reduced to foul smelling grey slime. He knew the salt beef should be turfed over board along with the corpses that floated about the decks, stiff with an eerie life of their own, but no men could summon the energy. They were helpless.

'I am going below to see for myself. Will you tell Captain Lively that he must continue to hold the ship?' said the Commodore suddenly. He struggled into his old felt coat, which weighed him down, and froze immediately as he slithered onto the deck just as the ship healed over again in a mountainous sea. Two stalwart men who were struggling aloft were dipped into the icy ocean as the masts plunged into the water.

As the Commodore disappeared from sight, two men were left in his quarters; all other able bodied hands were on deck or trying their best to keep the ship afloat. Luckily both men had overcome the horrors of seasickness, even though the ship bucked and dipped like a wild animal. The portholes kept darkening with the weight of water as the vessel went into a trough, yet above the noise of crashing seas and groaning timbers they sustained a conversation, each trying to disguise the fear they had that the *Centurion* was doomed.

Pascoe Thomas, aged twenty-four, had joined the *Centurion* as the ship's tutor; his job was to teach illiterate sailors to read and write and to educate the young midshipmen in mathematics, navigation and the skills which would eventually equip them to become officers.

The other in the cabin was the Reverend Richard Walter, aged twenty-two, a Cambridge graduate who took a somewhat dispassionate view of this appallingly misadvised adventure.

Unlike Reverend Walter, Pascoe Thomas fulminated almost constantly. 'It is a hard fact, Richard,' said Pascoe, 'that, of the forty sick invalids who were not weeded out by the Commodore before we sailed and the sixty-seven unskilled men who were pressed onto this ship, all of the invalids have perished and only ten of the pressed survive. And those remaining will be the first to go when the scurvy takes hold. The men below, well most of them, only came because of the prize money.'

'It was ever thus,' replied the young reverend cautiously, talk like this could be regarded as seditious. Of course as the horror unfolded, he saw the final outcome for all these souls. He didn't like to admit that all of this had come about because of man's greed: the greed of the Admiralty who dispatched these injured heroes to a certain death in order to cease paying their pensions, and the greed of all who sought the prize money. 'Argh well,' he said under his breath, believing that riches are only to be found in heaven. But the road to it ... now that was another matter.

Pascoe was not to be stopped, even though he detected the note of deference in Thomas's voice. 'You see, as I teach navigation I have a more realistic view of these things. Sometimes, as I see understanding dawn in a young boy's face, I see also fear, because young men are quick to learn, you know. One of them asked me when we left St Catherine's if the Commodore knew that Pizarro was lurking somewhere in the mist. Our mission was no secret, he said, and then he went on to ask why we tarried so long in Portsmouth while the Spanish were able to gather their intelligence and we had lost our element of surprise. The same lad also told me confidentially that he did not think we would be in a fit condition, if we survived at all, to take on the great Pizarro when we had attempted the Horn at the worst time of year in the full equinox.' He paused for a moment. 'If this is knowledge, perhaps it is sometimes better not to know, but to do your duty in bovine ignorance.'

'Even the untutored amongst these men are not as ignorant as you think, Pascoe. Most of them know what their chances are now; they can only trust in divine intervention and the skills of the greatest and truest sailor in the navy: our Commodore.'

'That is all well and good, but another lad worked out just how badly supplied we are because of the hard winter. It is the worst for a century. Most of the country is starving, and the promise of two meals a day and a rum ration is beyond the wildest dreams of nearly anybody. The ship's cooks had told him the supplies were such as you would not feed to animals, the meat rotten and weevils and stones in the sacks of grain.'

'All this is true, and it was an ill wind that took us to St Catherine's. The sick should have recovered in the field hospital set up on the beaches. We even had bread ovens working, but nobody could have known about those infernal mosquitoes. But I will say the men did a miraculous job cleaning the ship and some of the invalids fell to praying in gratitude when they came back on board … but…'

As he searched for the words to complete the sentence, there was a great roar of wind and the sound of splintering and cracking wood as the ship climbed a great, mountainous wave and poised for a fleeting moment while the Reverend held onto the table and prayed loudly.

Pascoe did not pray. He seized a bottle of the Commodore's rum, which was still in its gimbals, and drank as much as he could in one swallow. He sank to the floor and thought of China, the reason he had come on this voyage. He had dreamed of sailing the world to navigate the South Seas and return via China to take the *Covadonga* galleon. He had dreamed of seeing the whole world instead of the Dorset parsonage where his family now waited for news of him. What use was it, he asked himself, teaching shivering boys the skills of navigation when … suddenly his thoughts were interrupted as the ship fell down into a cavernous depression and he felt wildness and despair. This must surely be the end; they were prow down, set to dive headlong to the bottom of the raging, unforgiving ocean.

But it was not the last moment. Men vomited, they cried, they shivered. They had starved, their teeth had fallen out, their gums had gone black, their hair had fallen out of their heads in chunks, and now their insides turned to jelly; but they fought, they protected the young smooth-faced midshipmen – just little, frightened, disillusioned lads. They obeyed, they went on doing whatever was necessary as the days turned into weeks and there was no let up.

CHAPTER FIFTEEN

MADONNA'S COURT, SUSSEX, MAY 1741

The house was built of soft red brick, some of it in a hatching pattern, with exposed timber, and here and there some ornate decorations carved in stone. It nestled in a cleft of hills and they approached by a long avenue of limes in their prime, reflecting vivid, fresh light, enhanced with a glow that is only to be found where the sea is close by. It was late afternoon, the journey from Clapham had taken longer than expected owing to a violent rainstorm and the air still hung heavy with the damp aftermath. The horses quickened in the way they do when they are near their destination. The precious cargo in the coach comprised of no less than four women, as well as Pepe and Peter.

He did not know it then but Peter was destined always to be leading a flock of females. Had he known it, it would not have bothered him: he liked the way they all chatted so comfortably with each other. At this moment he also loved the way Pepe sat amongst his mistress's voluminous, rich skirts, his eyes rolling attentively from one woman to another as they spoke; but most of all he loved Grace. She looked back at him from time to time, exchanging the quiet empathy that only lovers can do. The fulsome gaze they exchanged and the subtle smile they shared, followed by a faint blush on Grace's cheeks, told Consuelo all she needed to know.

'Look, everyone,' cried Grace as they travelled down the long avenue towards the house. 'Two rainbows right over the house.'

There were indeed two of them soaring up and across the lowering clouds, the first one a myriad of intense colour set against the golden light of the late afternoon sun; the second one as a replica but further away in the distant valley, blurred at the edges with a misty grey. Grace wanted to reach out and touch them, to seal the picture forever and hold it in her hand, giving it substance and permanence.

'My dears, could you have a better portent than that?' exclaimed Consuelo. The magnificence and mystery of nature had somehow detracted from the reality of the arrival at the place where Grace was to settle.

The house, built in perfect symmetry, with leaded windows, spoke of an earlier age. There was a sweeping round of gravel, in the centre of which was a bed planted with herbs and lilies of all kinds and a sundial marked with medieval writing, which Grace was later to find out was a poem to the Lady Madonna. Just as they were about to go into the house, the rainbows began to fade theatrically.

'I wanted you to see it now, all of you,' said Peter with an expansive gesture of his arm, 'before anything has been done to it.' He sought Grace's hand and someone from inside opened the old studded door releasing a rush of cool air out into the warm summer evening.

'Sir, Your Ladyships,' said a figure from the shadows. As Grace's eyes focused in the dim interior, she saw it was a very well dressed man in country clothes, with shining brass buttons, spotless white stockings and clunky black buckled shoes, polished to within an inch of their life.

'This is Thomas,' explained Peter, putting an affectionate arm about the man's shoulders. 'He comes with the house,' he laughed, 'and puts quite a value on it.'

The man gave a slight bow, looked fiercely at Grace and gave a little, near imperceptible nod, as if to say, 'She will do nicely.'

Consuelo looked equally intently at the servant, noting his bright blue eyes, and thought how many a woman's head must have been turned by him in his time.

As for Margaret, she saw none of this, just the sense of ordered contentment the house exuded. No one has been unhappy here she thought, it has guarded the occupants and remained constant however much the world outside roared and changed. The house was, she concluded, Elizabethan. Admittedly, she saw at once that it needed what she would call a thorough clean; it lacked a woman's touch.

Grace felt something brush her skirt. She gave a slight start, and, looking down, saw there were, to her delight, two pairs of brown eyes looking back at her. She knelt down to pet two little King Charles spaniels, one black and white, the other a russet splashed with white. Every move they made seemed to be synchronised: their tails moving a small pile of leaves blown through the door backwards and forwards in a sweeping plume.

'Semele and Cleopatra,' explained Peter, leaning down to give them a pat.

'Oh they are so sweet!' enthused Margaret.

'They are, madam,' said Thomas, 'and very well born. They are descended from the royal dogs owned by His late Majesty King Charles I. That's a long way back of course, but His Majesty had a lovely little spaniel called Rogue. He went to the scaffold with him and was torn apart by the crowd.'

'Not before he had done his duty, it would seem,' replied Consuelo sharply. She was still rather uncomfortable with the familiarity her new family enjoyed with servants. But as on many previous occasions she had to remind herself that there was no long ancestry of servant–master here. Grace and Peter would marry and breed a new aristocracy based on something hard for her to fathom, but looking around at their future abode she envied their uncomplicated exchanges.

'That's enough of your stories, Thomas,' interrupted Peter. 'Their Ladyships are tired and we want refreshments quickly.'

'I have built a fire in the long room, young master, and the ladies' chambers are prepared as best I could,' said Thomas with a slight note of apology.

He led the way, his heels clacking on a highly polished flagged floor. He turned a big brass latch and the door swung open to reveal a long panelled room, sparsely furnished with some comfortable but simple objects, the exception being, of course, a magnificent harpsichord at the end of the room, standing in an evening shard of light. Despite the season, a merry log fire flickered and reflected in the shining marquetry case. Grace rushed to the instrument and swept her hands along the keys before examining it further. She gasped when she saw the motif along the case engraved with a cypher and the initials 'G' and 'P'.

'Where is Pepe?' cried Consuelo suddenly; she was so used to his presence that his sudden absence felt as if she had lost a limb.

'I think if Your Ladyship looks out of the window you will see the young gentleman,' replied Thomas with a smile.

There, bobbing in and out of the box hedges, was Pepe's mop of black hair; he was hotly pursued by two yapping little spaniels. Consuelo had never seen him so happy and she felt Margaret's hand in hers.

'It's lovely to hear him laughing like that, like a child should. It's taken a long time,' Consuelo said gently.

Since Grace had fallen in love she had come alive. It was as if a part of her brain had been asleep and now worked in glorious colour.

She understood so much now: more about her parents and the unhappiness of her mother during the long absences when her father was at sea. And what of her grandfather Algernon? He had been invited to come with them on the trip but she had seen the way he had smiled intimately at Consuelo and then said that he thought this was a woman's thing. She had thought it strange; after all he was her grandfather and in the absence of her own father, seeing Peter's house was important. But then he had explained. 'Lady Consuelo will be a most useful person to have with you, and I know your mother would like to be with her ... so I will come another time ... and it is good for little Pepe to feel part of the family.'

Grace pondered how families are formed and evolve. Her own father had very little sense of family and although her mother tried bravely, she was a simple woman and she needed someone more sophisticated to steer her three vibrant, clever children. And now Consuelo had appeared. Perhaps she was just what the family needed. Grace and the two boys, Rupert and Samuel, were all very different. One of the boys was destined for a scholarly life at Mercers' School and the other showed an interest in medicine. Perhaps he would follow in the distinguished footsteps of his grandfather.

Grace returned her thoughts to Consuelo and Algernon. They had been spending a lot of time together and for all their difference in age, perhaps twenty years or so, they cut a pleasing pair when they were together. They exuded a calm order, a rightness, something Grace's own parents had never done. Margaret was always struggling to make ends meet but her husband never really doubted that, however tired she looked, she would always manage. She had of course raised three fine children but they had now grown beyond her. Consuelo had tried to show her the way to realise her own worth, to get off her knees and let Alice and the boy do some of the hard work for her.

And now here they were, Margaret looking a trifle ill at ease, but Consuelo tall and dignified with Peter deferentially looking to her for comment and approbation. Curiously it was Thomas the servant who bonded with Margaret and asked her if she would like to see the kitchens and vegetable gardens. She did not take this amiss and agreed enthusiastically, whereas Consuelo had no more interest in the kitchens than the blacksmith's forge in the village. Peter caught Grace's eye and she gave a nod as Margaret bustled off with the old servant.

'Before you go, Mother,' said Grace, 'I have been meaning to ask you, Thomas, what is the origin of the name of the house?'

'The house was built at the time of the great Queen Elizabeth,' answered Thomas at once. 'The owners were wealthy people and they were very loyal to the Queen. She rewarded them well because the husband worked to get vitals for the Queen's great navy and he were a good man. He had this one daughter because all his family had died of the sweating sickness. The daughter fell for a young man who was a Catholic and the father would have none of it, despite the fact the Queen herself stepped in and gave the match her blessing. It is said that the girl became devout rather than take on another match. She had a vision, you see – the sweet mother of Jesus, the Madonna, came to her. She called her to do God's work and so the girl covered herself and her beauty and devoted her life to the service of others – fallen young ladies and such … begging your pardon… When her father died she renamed the house Madonna's Court for, she said, the Holy Mother worked with her in this place and came to her each day… I tell you, ladies, she was loved for miles around and this house is a holy place where nothing

133

but good can happen... The Madonna is about often still.' Thomas paused for a moment while his enraptured audience listened.

'What do you mean?' asked Grace sharply.

'Perhaps she were running with your little fellow. I fancy I saw a quick darting robe in the garden a minute back...' He stopped quickly as Peter made a gesture. Grace realised that this was not the time for any questions; there was an air of restlessness in the group.

'Come, let us proceed to the rest of the house,' said Peter. 'Mrs Lively is in good hands with old Thomas; he takes great pride in his kitchens and you can take your mother round the house later.

They ascended a creaky old staircase lined with more fine oak panelling. It seemed to have suffered greatly though the ages, through endless comings and goings. There were places on the walls where large pictures had once hung, but no longer did portraits watch over the occupants with a still and steady gaze. The evening light was dimming as the sun dipped outside a long casement window and shadows cast by the old leads made a dancing pattern on the group like confetti.

'As you will see, I have not yet acquired any furnishings to speak of, and that is where your advice and help will be so appreciated, Lady Consuelo,' said Peter as he showed them into a large bedchamber, in which the only furniture was a rickety curtained bed, a wash stand and a couple of large leather trunks.

Grace eyed the bed and her body shivered, not with fear but with something quite different. Consuelo tactfully admired the view from a charming window with an inviting window seat.

'This is a nice room, Peter, and where is the guest chamber?' Consuelo asked, beginning to feel the effects of the journey.

'I will take you there at once,' answered Peter apologetically, 'it is on the other side of the staircase, facing the afternoon sun, which I know is most unpopular. However this house has been occupied by simple country people for a long time and they value the sun as the guardian of their wellbeing. They like to take advantage of the warmth, to store it for the cold nights. Luckily we are very protected from the sea winds by the downs but nonetheless, I am told to expect harsh winters, or at least that is what Doctor Algernon told me.'

'What? Do you mean Grandfather has seen this house,' asked Grace in a puzzled voice.

Consuelo tilted her head, looking intently at Peter. He flushed and looked confused; there was a silence while he obviously worked out how to answer.

'Well yes,' he said tentatively while Consuelo sat down quickly in the window seat, the last of the sun warming her back. There was a rustling of skirts and shrieks of joyful abandon and suddenly Pepe could be heard calling for them as he crashed up the stairs, the sound of his little feet slithering on the polished wood.

He burst into the room, providing a welcome diversion for Peter. The boy rushed to Consuelo who enfolded him in her usual uninhibited way, a bright smile on her face, and at that moment Peter saw it as well: this was the smile of a mother. He had a flashing image of the old rocking cradle his own mother had treasured more than her life and on an impulse he put his arm around Grace's shoulders. She did not pull away as he feared she might do, but looked up at him expectantly.

'Doctor Algernon knew the house and he also knew that I wanted to acquire a home for all the reasons I explained to you, Grace,' he said simply.

'So that is the reason he did not come today,' Consuelo said slowly.

'I don't understand. Why should you not tell us that Grandfather found the house for us?' asked Grace.

Peter noticed the use of 'us' and felt a pang of relief.

'Quite simply he did not want your opinion to be coloured. He thought you might think him interfering … but you do love the house, don't you, Grace, my love?' he asked shakily.

'Yes, as a matter of fact I do,' replied Grace, 'and what is more I can see how Grandfather was thinking.'

'This is a great relief for me,' said Peter. 'There was so much waiting for your approval, not least my parents. I have not told them of this yet, but there is a small farm that comes with the estate and a charming house, which would suit them well; and my little sister Beth will love to be there with the animals. Their circumstances have been very cramped, and they have made many sacrifices to help me. It is my turn to pay them back.'

At this moment Margaret appeared. She was in time to pick up the last snippet of conversation.

'Do you mean to say that father helped you find this house and we did not know and neither did your mother and father, Peter?' she asked incredulously.

'Yes, he did,' replied Peter without a trace of apology, 'he did me a great service and I did not want him to tell you because it is so wonderful a thing and I wanted to see in your eyes, Grace, my dearest love, that it pleases you as it does me.'

'It pleases me greatly, Peter, and especially for your family,' replied Grace.

'But I still want to know how my father-in-law knew of this house,' Margaret persisted.

'I think Thomas, who is just outside the door, can explain better than I can,' suggested Peter.

Sure enough there was Thomas again. He came quietly into the room, where all eyes were upon him.

'It was like this, Your Ladyships,' he began. 'I have been with the family who owned it all my life and my mother before me. My father was a sailor on the ship where the good doctor was the surgeon and when my father lay dying the good and blessed Doctor Algernon found my mother, God rest her soul, and brought her to this place, where I was born. They were a good family who wanted a healthy young woman and regarded a little baby as a bonus, as indeed I hope I have proved to be.'

'That you have been, Thomas, I am sure, and hopefully you will be here to watch over us until God gathers you, as he must us all,' said Peter fulsomely.

'Well, my dears,' began Consuelo, 'it seems the doctor is a man of many parts; I find there is more to him every day. It is so often the way that a family will find the characters it needs for its protection. It is something like the chain that nature has made for itself. Ah yes, it is all the protesting against the divine order which causes the trouble and misery mankind inflicts upon itself...' The room fell silent; it was seldom that Consuelo allowed such free rein to her own opinions, except when roused, as Grace had seen her with Sir Hartley Slinkwell. Grace remembered this now as Consuelo continued while the room stood hushed. 'Take the lady who gave herself to the Holy Mother after her father rejected the man she loved, because of his Catholic faith... You see the Almighty wanted her. He was not so fastidious. He has his ways.' She left the words hanging in the air.

But Thomas could not stand a silence. It was against his principles, as they would all find out. 'My late master and mistress died within a week of each other,' he told them. 'They were so devoted but the Lord did not choose to give them little ones. They were simple folk and they accepted it. The master, God bless him, used to say to me 'the Lord will find a young couple who will fill this old place with children.

Doctor Lively, he said, he'll know just the thing and he were right, he were right about the clock too…'

'What clock,' asked Margaret suspiciously, 'do you mean one which was stolen?'

'No, My Ladyship, I mean the clock which should be on the ship on which Your Ladyship's husband is now sailing. The want of the longitude clock will cost lives. If God is kind, some of them will come back, but men will perish and all for the greed of the old men at the Admiralty who are, begging your pardon, not fit for purpose.'

There was a perceptible shiver in the room as the three women, all of whom had part of their heart on the ships in the Pacific far away from this happy place, listened to this well-meaning man, who spoke simply, unimpeded as he was by too much education and the deference it brings to the common truth.

Madonna's Court was a house full of voices, not all of them present, and, as if to make comment, at that moment an old clock on the staircase sonorously chimed six o'clock. Consuelo thought about the men so far away and of George. Who knew what the day would bring for them? She drew her shawl around her, sensing something she would rather not think about.

'Enough, dear Thomas; we will make good of what we have now for in that we are creating the future,' she said as Peter offered his arm to Grace. The party left the room quietly.

CHAPTER SIXTEEN

KENSINGTON PALACE, LONDON

The one thing Sir Hartley could not abide was other people's happiness but he was drawn to it like a fly to a piece of fresh meat. He had a compelling desire to contaminate it and to watch its destruction. Only then did the people involved become as one with him, for he had observed that latently in all human beings is a resentment when things do not go according to plan which can dissipate the soul and create a space for Satan to enter and destroy.

He saw Grace and Peter now across the room. They were with Consuelo and the King had invited them forward to converse with him. Whatever news they had imparted to him occasioned him to smile benignly at them in an attitude of congratulations and Grace was blushing sweetly. It was then, as he watched the innocent smile and the indulgent, admiring looks of the people around them, that he formed his plan.

The key was separation. He must occupy the young harpsichord maker with some sort of musical event and then lure the unsuspecting Grace to a place where he could spoil her. She would probably be easy prey for she had none of the cynicism that protected people in the hot house surrounding the monarch. She was, in a word, naïve. She was too great a prize for that ridiculous young man, he thought. He would have her himself but first she must be compromised, her innocent credentials altered to put her outside the world of the young, perfect, beautiful love he found so repellent. The King had moved away and he saw his chance.

'My Lady Consuelo, Miss Lively and of course the young musician,' he said with a tiny sneer as he addressed Peter. Consuelo, who was wise to the world, noted this rudeness and replied instantly.

'The young musician, as you call him, is my ward's betrothed and His Majesty has just congratulated the young couple in a most gracious manner, which you would do well to observe, Your Lordship.'

'My dear lady, I had no wish to offend in any way,' said Sir Hartley, noting the discomfort felt by Grace and Peter. In fact this was precisely what he wanted. The ridiculous musician blushed a little and Sir Hartley knew full well that had they not been in the confines of the court he would have received a punch on the nose. But then gentlemen fought duals with exotic swords and firearms, fists were for village louts and members of the lower classes.

'Sir,' interrupted Peter suddenly whilst moving closer to the insulter. 'You may think that you address an ignorant fool of a boy, who does not appreciate the offensive nature of the manner in which you address Miss Lively and myself, but this "musician", as you call me, has favour with His Majesty. Music is the finest of arts and is to be perfected only after years of careful, talented study; it breeds nature's gentlemen and women. Since this is a world in which Your Lordship would be most uncomfortable, may I suggest you move to another group of people more suited to Your Lordship.'

A stunned silence descended about the group, Consuelo deciding this time to add nothing to the exchange. She saw that Peter had come of age – but he had entered dangerous territory. She could not let Grace out of her sight. She beckoned to Pepe, who was always close at hand. She was beginning to feel unwell and knew that she would soon have to retire. What was she to do?

'Pepe,' she whispered in his ear, 'I shall have to return to St James's Square and must leave the palace; you are to stay close to Miss Lively. She is with her maid but should Mr Zuliekom be distracted and asked to play for the King, as I think he will be, there are gentlemen here who would wish to lead her astray and she may be in danger. Here is my small pearl dagger. Keep it close. It is deadly sharp and should you need it, one strike between the ribs will kill. May God forgive me for even suggesting such a thing but I have a strong feeling of impending evil here. Sir Hartley has a plan, I can sense it. I will leave Jane here and she too will watch over Miss Lively. The carriage will be waiting to bring you all home and the footman will come for you as the clock strikes nine.'

Peter was not the only one who had come of age that night, Pepe also felt the weight of responsibility on his small shoulders. Something from his inherited genes had armed him with a deadly and ruthless streak and he knew in his heart that he could kill a man. But the gentle nature handed to him by his mother tempered him and the combination would, Consuelo knew, make a fine man of him. The boy looked long and hard at her for a moment and in the soft light of the glittering candles something passed between them. Consuelo's spine tingled and a voice she only half heard in the back of her mind asked her if he knew. It can happen in fleeting moments such as this that a child can look like the man or woman he or she will become … and Consuelo had a flashing image of Pepe as a noble figure in a court such as this, holding a position of power, a man with elegance and poise, comfortable in his skin, whatever its colour. As if taking part in this glimpse of the future, the boy dipped into a graceful bow, took her hand and kissed it, as lightly as a courtier might kiss a Queen. She wanted at that moment to enfold him in front of all these people and declare him as hers and she knew that one day the world would be a better place because he had lived in it.

Sir Hartley's voice cut through the moment, dragging her to the threatening present.

'So, my lady, I see that you are about to withdraw. You do indeed look very pale, but do not worry, Miss Lively's young man is to be well occupied. I have a composition created by a rival of the great maestro Mr Handel. His Majesty will have no other but the young harpsichordist perform it this very evening.'

When she thought back on it Consuelo realised that to have left Grace there in the circumstances was one of the most catastrophic decisions she could have made, but at the time she felt unwell and unable to do more, so home she went. As she sat muffled in fur in the carriage, she consoled herself that Grace was not alone; she had Jane and Pepe and, of course, Peter.

What Consuelo had not calculated was what an effective diversion the performance in front of His Majesty would prove. And as for Sir Hartley's mendacity, even she had not quite realised the depths of his evil nature.

'So, my dear, we shall sit here at the back – because even one brief glimpse of your lovely eyes meeting his might put your betrothed off balance and this is such an important opportunity for him. We would not want it to go awry would we?' soothed Sir Hartley. He had a soft hand on Grace's elbow as he guided her to her seat. She looked up at him and his eyes seemed kind, almost avuncular, so she sat obediently, smoothing her skirts, and soon a footman came with a tray of tall, delicate glasses, bowing as he offered them. Sir Hartley took one and tasted it, as an over-painted lady next to him followed suit and they nodded in mutual appreciation.

'Oh I am so sorry, my dear,' he said, looking at Grace. 'I know your guardian would not like you to drink wines but may I ask the footman to bring some other concoction, some fruit juice or a little cordial?'

Jane had been quietly observing all this and managed to catch Grace's eye. A specially ordered drink, she thought, now that *would* be an invitation to disaster. Better to drink a little of the one they were all having. She signed to Grace to take one from the tray.

'No, I will have one like yours, Sir Hartley,' Grace blushed, feeling rather stupid. She did not of course see how the footman nudged one particular glass towards her on the tray.

The music started, but unfortunately Grace had a rather restricted view. They were near the door at the back of the magnificent room and a perceptible draught caught the back of her neck, but it was not only that which made her feel very strange; her head began to spin and she tried desperately to recover herself.

What she did not know was that Pepe was not in the room any more. A few minutes before, a strong, rough hand had pressed against his mouth and he had been bundled into a small closet, his mouth bound with a kerchief and his small feet and hands tied together.

Sir Hartley watched his victim closely and the lady next to him nodded at him once more as Grace began to slump forward. Together they got her out of the door, attracting very little attention – after all it was not unusual for young ladies to suffer the vapours at these events. Jane saw all this with horror but in the crush she was unable to get to Grace quickly enough and by the time she got to the door all sign of her and Sir Hartley had vanished.

Jane's heart was beating so fast she thought her breast might explode; she started to sweat. The room was enraptured as Peter played on; the King leant forward, his elbow on his knee, his portly frame straining on his rich silk waistcoat. The ladies who would normally be flapping their fans like trapped butterflies also sat still; everyone was transported into another world, lit by hundreds of glittering candles, their light dancing in the crystal chandeliers. Yet in the real world Jane's beloved mistress had been spirited away into some dark and dangerous place. Thoughts raced through loyal Jane's heart; if she cried out, who would care about the young Miss Lively? Court servants would be summoned; she would also be quietly removed, maybe imprisoned in some cupboard, punished for disturbing the royal presence. Her mouth was dry, but she steeled herself; what did it matter if these people were disturbed in their mindless seeking of pleasure when it was at someone else's expense?

There was one person in the room who had them all in his sway and that was Peter. He would care, he would rise to his feet, he would abandon everything if he thought Grace was in danger. He would think nothing of disturbing the royal presence, and how could she, Jane, do nothing – she could not save her mistress on her own!

She took a deep breath and launched herself; a gilt chair went clattering onto the polished wooden floor as Peter lifted his head and looked toward her. She cried out as she ran towards him, pushing through the outraged throng, treading on skirts, bumping at shoulders. Someone's wig fell off. 'This is disgraceful,' bellowed a large, bellicose lady, followed by another cry of, 'This must be a mad woman.'

Jane arrived at the harpsichord and fell towards Peter who had got up, hands outspread in alarm.

'Jane, what on earth is the matter?' he shouted.

'It's Miss Lively,' Jane gasped, 'she has been taken by Sir Hartley ... they put something in her drink to make her insensible.'

There was a titter of laughter in the room, whilst the King, always slow to react, momentarily closed his eyes in thought.

'Miss Lively?' the King said ponderously.

'Miss Disgrace more like,' exclaimed one of the ladies.

There was another disturbance near the door as a small figure came though like a sprite.

'They take Miss Lively,' the child called. 'They kill her, she dead. They carry her to big coach. I try to follow but they beat the horses.'

'Who has taken her, Pepe?' bellowed Peter.

'The bad man, Slinkwell, Lordship!' screeched Pepe.

'Yes, Sir Hartley!' screamed Jane.

'Sir Hartley has murdered someone?' rasped the King in bewilderment.

The King had a habit of alternating his two mistresses and on this occasion it was Mary Howard Countess of Deloraine who was present. Keenly aware of the subservient role of most women of the time, she had much enjoyed seeing the true young lovers. It was a breath of fresh air in the stagnant court and she now took a furious stance about the affair.

'Are you all just going to sit there?' Lady Deloraine roared in cut glass tones. 'Is there not a man amongst you?' she went on. 'It is that vile Hartley; he is a spoiler of women, he should get his desserts … he has abducted a young girl … I am to my carriage, I will search him out, do you hear?… You, the young player, you will come with me and, the little mulatto too, you know a thing or two. We must ask the postilions outside. They know everything that goes on. Someone fetch my cloak and, girl,' she called to a maid who was standing nervously beside her, 'my purse; the men must be bribed, they are all for sale. They will know.'

'Yes, for sale like everything round here,' muttered one of the ladies.

The court fell silent, nervously awaiting a response from His Majesty. After all, the reference to the lack of manhood must surely have included the King. They waited and the King stared; he was ever slow to get to the point about things and when he did he could be very unpredictable.

'Yes, my lady, you are quite right. I will not have such things taking place here. Listen to Lady Deloraine. I could not have put it better myself.'

The court murmured a mixture of surprise and approval, but most of all relief from the tedium. Even Lady Deloraine was surprised by her own audacity.

Peter saw his chance and took it. 'I have no coach, so, madam, I thank you from the bottom of my heart. We must go with all haste,' he cried.

Lady Deloraine could see that the young man was shaking and then she remembered that he was indeed the future husband of the girl. 'She will not be dead, young man, I can assure you of that. She is of no use dead, but we must find them before that wicked man has his way. I dare say he is not alone in this. The court is a breeding ground for such people and the King, may God bless him, is kept ignorant of all this. After all, who would have the courage to tell him about the court over which he presides?'

'Madam, I know more than you think,' said the King. 'For a young girl to be abducted under my nose is an insult. You, madam, shall have all the support you require and you, young harpsichordist, my stewards will come with you and there will be retribution for the blaggard. Who has dared such a thing in my court ... no, my home?' There were tears in the King's pale, bloodshot eyes and his accent was distinctly Hanoverian, as always happened when he became emotional.

The room had now warmed to this adventure, having been at first characteristically sceptical. Jane noticed the red wheals on Pepe's wrists as he stretched his hands urgently towards her.

'Why, you poor fellow; what did they do to you?' she asked.

'They lock me in Jane, but they not know what a boy can do. I came out take scarf off my head. I have it.'

He pulled the gossamer scarf from his jacket and waved it at Jane. She looked at it closely. It was delicate silk and there was an extraordinary pattern of peacocks and parrots on it, amidst garlands of roses. The colours were what struck her most though: blues and greens, all threaded with gold. She had seen the scarf before on the bonnet of a lady getting into a coach in the city where Jane often took the carriage to shop for food. It had stuck in her mind because of the beauty of it. The coachman had seen her looking and commented on it as well.

'Look at her thinking she is above us with her fine scarves, but believe me, Jane, that house is a whore house,' he had said. 'There is many a fine gentleman who goes there and risks the pox; they sometimes pretend they are quite respectable, with musicians and fine gowns, all furbelowed, but any lady who goes in there may go in with her pride but she will leave her soul behind.'

Jane had looked carefully at the elegant building, which for all the world could have been the home of a most respectable member of the gentry. She had never forgotten the house or the scarf because for her they stood for the cautionary tale which could so easily have been her own, if it had not been for her new family, whom she loved with all her awakened heart.

'I know where he has taken her,' she cried. With an extraordinary revelatory flash, she had seen the house in her mind's eye, even the picture of her beloved mistress being conveyed inside it, insensible.

'How can you know such a thing?' came Peter's distraught voice. He was clutching Jane's shoulder in desperation.

'It is the scarf! I know the woman who wears that scarf like a banner to her whoredom. I saw her wearing it once coming out of a fine house in Spittlefields, I can direct you there,' gasped Jane, her breath casting a fine mist on the freezing night air.

'I somehow think the girl knows what she is talking about,' said Lady Deloraine, her voice rising with excitement. She had never cared for Slinkwell and disliked the way her benign lover, His Majesty, only saw what he wanted to see and refused to deal with the Slinkwells of this world who would inevitably circle the royal presence like basking sharks.

'In you all go and I will come with you. I cannot wait to see this villain get his just desserts,' said Lady Deloraine firmly. 'Take your orders from the young lady,' she called to the driver as two footmen packed them all into the coach with deft hands folding in the ladies' skirts and velvet cloaks. Little Pepe infiltrated the mass of bodies unnoticed except by Jane who's hand reached for his as she gave instructions to the driver and the footmen through a tiny levered window. The night air streamed in and Her Ladyship called to him to whip up the horses. There was no time to be lost.

The big coach wallowed and swayed, clattering down the silent streets where most good people had retired to sleep; leaving it to the gentry to spend money on candles and the like and play and dance when the lord would have them doing as he suggested.

Sensing the importance of the mission, the skilful driver, one of the best to be had since Lady Deloraine was a perfectionist and would accept no less, pressed on as quickly as the streets would allow. The coach came to a grinding halt when Jane shrieked through the window that they had arrived at the house.

It was not hard to spot in the relatively quiet street. The windows were ablaze with light and silhouetted figures showed women's headdresses bobbing back and forth like butterflies and racing couples dancing, only to suddenly dip from view. The onlookers could only guess at why. Loud music and laughter mingled with shrill drunken shrieks and men's lewd shouting. Pepe made to leap from the coach to take the law into his own hands but Jane quickly restrained him.

'Wait, Pepe, this has to be carefully done,' she commanded. Lady Deloraine had meanwhile instructed the coach to pull forward beyond the house lest they be apprehended. Surprise was the element needed here and Lady Deloraine was also reticent about revealing her own role in the affair, fearing embarrassment for the King. But she was most definitely in command.

'Now you, young harpsichordist, my three men here will be with you and when the time comes you must rush in and take them by surprise; but first you, my dear loyal girl, must gain access to the house. Use your wiles; say you are a young woman from the country seeking work and you have been given this address. One look at your pretty, innocent face should do it; it is quite perfect for the evil doings of these scoundrels and bawds. Meanwhile you, you wonderful little menace, will take advantage of this and slip in unnoticed and find Miss Lively.'

'Then I will kill Sir Lord Slinkwell,' shot Pepe eagerly, feeling for the pearl handled knife.

'No you will not; we have other plans for him, little man,' Lady Deloraine answered briskly. 'You will call out and alert my men outside and they will come in and retrieve the young lady at once, and if Sir Slinkwell decides to leave in a hurry you will mark his path for us. When Mr Harpsichordist's betrothed is safely away this entire disgraceful thing will be unravelled and His Majesty will be very pleased.

Despite the confident tone in her voice, Lady Deloraine was not really sure about any of this; but she calculated that speed was of the essence and she would use the tools at her disposal. One thing was certain: she wanted Slinkwell alive. She had born a grudge for a long time following a casually delivered insult and she smelled the delicious aroma of justice and revenge.

There were many with similar feelings. One thing Sir Hartley had not learned was that the fate of hostages to fortune gathers compound interest and, whatever the outcome of this present escapade, much villainy would be laid at his feet once the floodgates opened. He had insulted His Majesty in his own home and that could and would not go unpunished. This was precisely the chance many people had been waiting for.

Jane shivered, mostly out of fear; this was indeed a bold plan, but Pepe nestled in her skirts and Lady Deloraine had lent her a thick cloak, which she wore inside-out lest it not look the part of a poor country girl down on her luck.

Pepe, for his part, felt a surge of bravado from within the rich ermine. Together they mounted the steps and rang the heavy rope, which worked a loud clanging bell.

The door was opened at once by a smart young footman who enquired of her business. Behind the footman a whirl of activity was taking place.

Jane blurted out her story, which was evidently heard by a bawdy woman in the background who advanced immediately.

'Come on in, young lady, it is much too cold for such a pretty one to be out.' As she stretched out a hand to take Jane's arm the rush of men who had been waiting outside in the shadows came forward. Pepe was through in a second and instinctively darted up the stairway. He ran at the speed of light, calling as he went in a shrill high-pitched voice that he had learned as a child; it pierced the cacophony of shrieks and screams as the King's stewards and Peter with the drivers and footmen began a thorough search of the downstairs apartments.

Suddenly Pepe's voice echoed through the fetid air and down the staircase.

'He has found her!' Peter shouted. Like lightning, he was up the stairs to where the sound came from. There, the door to one of the apartments was open revealing a scene of awful debauchery. In the middle was an enormous rumpled four-poster bed, the curtains carelessly and lasciviously spread, as were the legs of two plump scantily clothed bawds. Peter's heart missed a beat until he saw the redemptive vision of Grace, still mercifully clothed, protected by a ferocious spitting Pepe, who was extending a small pearl handled knife. She was sobbing hysterically, and when she saw Peter and the company, some of them with drawn swords, she ran to him and he held her shaking body in his arms.

'Oh, my darling,' he muttered into her dishevelled hair. 'Did he touch you?'

'But for you and my little angel here he would have done,' she replied tremulously. She looked about for Pepe but he was nowhere to be seen.

Pepe, meanwhile, had set off in pursuit of the villainous Sir Hartley. He was like a small bloodhound and indeed he had a taste for revenge. He knew that Sir Hartley would be making for his own bed to try to convince his accusers that he was not guilty of attempting to compromise Grace's virginity. In fact he would probably say that he had tried to save her. Off the little fellow went into the night.

Sure enough he caught up with Sir Hartley, heavily cloaked and making his way towards his house. Pepe guessed that he had not taken his customary sedan chair because he did not want any witnesses to his movements that night. Pepe's blood was up and, small though he was, he felt a rush of confidence. He wanted to have his say with this villain and deduced that nobody could know anything about his whereabouts. The street was completely deserted as he came up behind the hurrying figure, who appeared to be more than a little unsteady on his feet. He jumped before the man, blocking his path, and stood his ground. Sir Hartley almost collided with him.

'Out of my way,' Sir Hartley bellowed furiously, reaching for his sword and he would gladly have severed the boy's head. But, unwisely, he decided to laugh instead and remove one of Pepe's long black curls with the weapon's tip. That was enough for Pepe. Out came the little silver knife. There was, as the boy saw it, no issue at all here. This was now a matter of self-defence, should there be any witnesses. In went the knife, just below the rib, nearly but not quite to the hilt. Sir Hartley let out a gasp and doubled up, falling to the ground while conveniently removing his body from the knife, which was still in Pepe's dogged grasp.

Pepe ran, as fast as his agile little feet would carry him. He was convinced that he had avenged the beloved Grace for Sir Hartley's crime, but he would tell nobody. The assailant would never be found. The boy was proud but at the same time fearful; the noose was a terrible way to die and to think of the grief it would cause his most precious lady Consuelo and all the family who now loved him as their own. No, he said to himself, this is perfect justice and I will take pride in carrying it with me for a long and honourable life.

So there it was. And still the turmoil in the bawdy house raged: constables came, neighbours woke from their sleep and joined the peering crowd. The madam was arrested for kidnapping and some of the women were taken to Newgate prison, while Grace was taken home to St James's Square. And the hunt was on for the wanted man, Sir Hartley Slinkwell.

Chapter Seventeen

Back at court

The King had said very little after the commotion. He maintained his normal pose: a formal upright stance with a straightened back and projecting stomach tightly upholstered in one of the unusual waistcoats of which he was extremely proud. He had now remained so for a few minutes while the court fussed and gossiped, animated by the relief from the normal tedium at Kensington palace. Most of them thought enviously of the rival court, set up by the heir Freddie and his Queen Augusta to whom the King did not speak. Sir Robert Walpole maintained that this impasse was affecting the entire country, making it rotten from the top.

It was on occasions such as this that the King missed Caroline most. Since her death, the country, and, mostly, the chattering classes, had begun to tire of the quarrel, especially as it was a situation that replicated the hatred that George's father had for George himself, his own son. The King had few harmonious memories, the bitterness rankled and he escaped it by hiding behind a stuffy routine about which he was obsessed. The young harpsichordist had brought a breath of fresh air and the young love played out to such a melodious backdrop had lifted the mood of even the most jaded of courtiers. The King's protuberant pale eyes had even watered at one point as he thought of the woman he had lost. He had never known such sentiments until he fell in love with his wife Caroline, and her vivacious personality had made her adored by all except her own son. But even Caroline had become tainted by the curse of the Hanoverian kings. Her hatred of her son almost outdid her husband's. She had found herself perpetuating the pernicious atmosphere that the King's subjects were by and large unable to comprehend. Indeed the quarrel had become tedious in the extreme.

The false sense of calm that was maintained by ritual and court life was fragile and an event such as this destabilised the volatile King, who was easily riled.

Suddenly he called for for Sir John Hervey who came at once.

'We will adjourn,' the King announced, his face flushing and his forehead breaking into a sweat under his elaborate wig. 'But the court is not dismissed,' he added to the dismay of the assembled company who wanted nothing more than to return to their own drawing rooms to gossip about this riveting escapade.

The King retired to his own apartments with John Hervey in attendance, and for some reason all his pent up emotion overwhelmed him. John Hervey looked on, helplessly wondering whom to summon. Placid, plump Amalie Von Wallmoden had been supplanted for the evening's game of cards by the now absent Henrietta Deloraine.

'Your Majesty, shall I summon Amalie?' he asked tentatively. The King had a foul temper that was quick to flare and while usually he recovered quite quickly, this was something different. Sir John was confused; he could not understand why this unfortunate incident had affected the King so deeply.

'No, my dear fellow,' the King replied in a wavery voice. 'I keep an ordered life around me, the court is testament to that. This has thrown it all into disarray and the truth is that under the surface it is full of wickedness. That such a thing could have gone on under my very nose…' The King sought a kerchief and sat despondently with his head in his hands.

'Your Majesty, none of this can be laid at your door. Since the Queen died there are many factions who have taken advantage of her absence and indeed, sir, your own grief,' soothed Sir John. He had removed his wig and now ran his hands through his thinning fair hair and the King saw how old he looked without it.

'There is trouble everywhere I look,' gasped the King. 'Sir Robert councils war with Spain… We harry their ships… Europe is all strife. We cannot afford this. I remember nothing but betrayal: my own father stole my daughters and it broke the Queen's heart; she never recovered. But for this, I believe she would be here today; she hid the facts of her illness in the same way people use masks here in the court when it is rotten at the core. These two young people should have been under my protection and yet this young woman has been abused and despoiled by the vipers that lurk in our midst.'

In truth, Sir John could not but agree. It was time the King came to his senses and proved himself a force to be reckoned with.

'I believe, sir, that when a man lies with dogs he will get up with fleas. Sir Hartley Slinkwell is an impudent villain; an example should be made of him. When he is found he must be sent to the tower for what he has done under Your Majesty's nose. It is treason, no more no less.'

The King looked up. Behind Sir John's head several candles burned, casting an orb of light. It was an important moment for the King.

'You are right, my dear old friend,' said His Majesty slowly. 'I cannot hide behind the cloak of grief anymore. Assemble the court again; they will be informed of the action I must take. Sir Hartley will be made to pay for this insult. And the young couple must be protected... The girl ... she is such a beauty ... she must be found ... do you hear? Found!' The King got up and straightened his wig while Sir John sent for his stewards and hurried back to the salon with his instructions.

The hunt was on for Sir Hartley. The streets were scoured by groups of constables with lamps, but there was no trace of the man; neither was there any sign of him in his run-down house in the city. A slatternly servant announced that Sir Hartley rarely shared his plans with his retainers and was often absent for days at a time. Eventually the hunt was abandoned, but the King was furious. He had been severely disturbed by the commotion and was just beginning to enter into the spirit of the thing. It was not until daylight that the discovery was made. The King had retired long before and dozed fitfully, greatly troubled by his haemorrhoids, a condition heavily veiled in secrecy – in much the same way that his late wife's hernia had been concealed, even from her own husband. In fact it was such secrecy that had ultimately claimed her life in the cruellest way possible.

This drama with the two young lovers, taking place as it had under his own roof, had opened a kind of floodgate for the King, and many deeply buried horrors had begun to dance about his fretful sleep, including regret about his treatment of his own son. He knew it was irrational, but then he had left the boy as a child, deserted him and left him in Hanover to be reared by strangers, lonely and unloved. But it was not just his own intransigence; his beloved Caroline had shared the aversion. They had fed upon it as couples do, stacked up the bonfire of small irritations until it became an inferno. They had eventually summoned the young man, no longer able to resist the constitutional necessity of having the heir to the throne in the country over which one day he would rule. The hatred continued even now though...

How could all this have happened? he often asked himself. As the fingers of dawn light came through the royal shutters and diffused around the edge of the thick floral curtains, the King twitched himself into reality, but first he searched in his mind for some kind of positivity. He reassured himself that he had been a forward thinking King: there were many ventures he had supported and he had tried to do his duty. He had a vague recollection now of something he had been told about the girl who had been abducted. Of course, his mind flashed ... her father was one of the officers on George Anson's great expedition... Of course! That was it! He could not ignore the plight of this young woman for many reasons, but not least because her father was on the high seas risking his life for king and country and it was he, George, King of England, who had pushed this venture through. The least he could do was to protect the daughter of one of his own officers.

There was a gentle tap at the door and two of his footman came in with a tray of the hot milky chocolate he never failed to enjoy. But on this occasion there was another more untimely visitor.

John Hervey was about the only person who could gain access to the King at such an hour and it was up to him to make a judgement in these circumstances; it was only a matter of grave importance that would allow such an intrusion into the royal presence. The King did not look his best in the mornings, before he was primped and powdered. He was a messy sleeper, tossing about most of the night, waking up intermittently at the noise of his own snoring. He had taken to wearing powder in his latter years and without it his face was red and flushed. His eyes however remained his most striking feature, even though they bulged rather too obviously.

Lord Hervey cleared his throat nervously several times. As was the custom, well-born persons slept in an upright position, supported by many cushions and pillows, in the belief that death, when it came, would be more likely to gather its grim harvest from people already in a recumbent posture. It was this which made the perfunctory awakening of His Majesty less of an intrusion. But all the same Lord Hervey began perspiring profusely; what if the King did not think this a sufficiently sensational matter? What then? Being a royal confidant, indeed the most intimate friend, if there could be such a thing, to the King was a heavy responsibility and His Lordship knew only too well that he could be cast into oblivion on a mere whim. The prospect was unthinkable, but fortunately the King opened one protruding eye and spoke.

'Lord John,' he said huskily but without a trace of anger. 'You have news?' He reached for the large tasselled bell-pull that clanged into the crowded anteroom, which was already full of eager servants, stewards and foot men, all with the accoutrements of their various tasks, preparing for the royal wakening.

Before Lord Hervey could reply, some of them came quickly into the room. The first to approach the bed was a steward with a heavily embroidered dressing gown which he held up judiciously as the King swung his legs around the bed and placed himself into the garment, nightgown and all. As if by magic, a pretty young female servant knelt at his feet with a pair of velvet slippers, the toes upturned like those of an eastern sorcerer. Another man came with a bright red velvet hat with a long tassel attached, and it was only then that His Lordship felt it wise to disclose the reason for the interruption.

'Yes, sir,' he began. 'Sir Hartley has evaded us all I am afraid,' he said mischievously, his earlier nervousness replaced by his moment of glory.

'What do you mean? The devil he has,' exploded the King, as a young footman, new to the position, jumped and spilled some of the warm fragrant water he held in an exquisite Meissen bowl, ready for the royal hand washing.

'Be careful, boy,' the King shouted, 'that bowl was my mother's, and it is precious beyond rubies... Who has given its charge to this callow youth?' he went on, looking angrily about the room.

Lord Hervey never ceased to be amazed by the King's obsession with domestic trivia. Even during discussions with the prime minister, Lord Walpole, he could be diverted by some ridiculous issue like a badly sown button on his waist-coat. But he had learned the way of it and the trick was to keep the King focussed and plough on regardless. It was a lack of concentration that his wife Caroline had always handled with skill and without her this cerebral fragmentation was now much more in evidence, and hampered the work of government.

'If I may, Your Majesty,' said Lord Hervey, adopting the more formal address since he now had a much larger audience. The room was silent and the King stared at him lugubriously. 'Sir Hartley has been dragged out of the river, and his remains are now still on the embankment, laid unceremoniously for the necessary formalities.' He announced this in his most sensational voice, one which made great use of the pause and a certain tremulous emotion.

'You mean he is dead?' said the King stupidly. One of the servants tittered.

'Yes, Your Majesty, murdered like the dog he was,' replied Lord Hervey, lowering his head.

'Murdered by whom?' asked the King incredulously.

'We do not know. It appears there was a small and expertly delivered knife wound just below his ribs,' said Lord Hervey.

'Ah, so the assailant wished to be quite sure in the matter,' said the King, undecided as to how to react to the outcome of this sorry tale, but harbouring not a little disappointment that he had been denied the satisfaction of delivering the sentence on the man who had flaunted the rules so flagrantly.

This whole affair, especially now with its dark denouement, had brought many things back to him and he suddenly recalled another drowning, the floating body of his mother's lover. His crime also had been to insult the King, but in very different circumstances.

'So we are to be deprived of being judge and jury, are we?' considered the King. 'This man had many enemies and such a man should not walk alone at night. I will see him. I want nobody to touch the man until I have seen for myself, but before I do this, tell me, Lord Hervey, what of the girl? I want to see her as well; I need to be assured and I want the young couple to be vindicated... Do you know, by the way, whether or not the young harpsichordist remained with the girl for the night?' The words hung in the air. It was not a question to be answered; it was a dangerous territory. But of this Lord Hervey was sure, it was the King's way of telling him to make matters quite clear with regards to the whereabouts of the young man.

CHAPTER EIGHTEEN

The house in St James's Square was quiet at last. Grace slept fitfully; Consuelo had summoned her physician who had administered a mild sedative. Peter insisted on remaining with them. Jane had prepared the great bed in what had been the Captain's bedchamber. It had needed airing but now the fire was lit and copious warming pans put between the fine embroidered sheets and comforters.

Peter posted a young servant outside the door and left strict instructions that should anyone come with news of Sir Hartley he was to be woken. The young porter nodded off occasionally in his high backed chair, grateful for the protection of its design in the shape of an upturned boat; it was a godsend as the drafts came whistling through the large house, funnelling up the wide rounded stairs like a chimney. Without good shelter, many a poor soul succumbed to horrific winter chills and colds, which often left them weak in the lungs. Consuelo's enormous hunting dog sat on the porter's feet, glad of the warmth, while the young man wound himself into a fur rug kindly provided by the Lady Consuelo. Other men of a similar position were amazed by the comforts that were presented to them, as they had seen nothing so luxurious before in all their lives.

The crier in the street called out four o'clock and at the same time, the porter heard a vague swish coming down the staircase. Instantly alert, he poked his head out of his wooden refuge; there was the lady Consuelo white as a sheet. He gave an involuntary start. At first he thought it was a ghost, the thing that worried him most in his lonely vigil.

She held up a lamp and spoke. Reassured, he got to his feet and asked how he could be of service.

'Have you seen Pepe?' she whispered hoarsely.

'No, my lady,' the young man answered swiftly. 'I haven't left my post since the house retired to bed and I have the keys here to all the doors, which the housekeeper and head man always give to me for the night – in case of fire or such like.'

'So nobody could have come in without you knowing?' said Consuelo, growing ever paler.

'No, my lady, not a living soul,' he assured her.

Consuelo shuddered. She knew something was amiss; Pepe had never been away from her for a night since the day he was born. She had been told of how Pepe had bravely protected Grace and set off in a foolhardy way to pursue the villainous Sir Hartley.

She asked for a lamp and instructed the porter to unlock the door to a cosy downstairs room where the embers of the fire would still be flaring. She needed to think. It was nearly dawn and the city would be coming to life. She asked him to stoke up the fire and then penned a note in her large ornate hand to none other than His Majesty. She begged of him to send word, if he had any, as to the whereabouts of the man who had terrified her ward and left her so distressed. Of course she dressed the note up in flowery terms, which might appeal to the King's chivalrous side. She sealed it with an enormous crested coat of arms from her own Portuguese family, with two long red satin ribbons secured in the hot wax.

She rang a little silver bell and the young porter came at once.

'Send for one of the coaches and have this note sent at once to the palace,' she said firmly, 'and tell the messenger to wait for a reply for as long as is necessary.'

Consuelo retired to her bedchamber. She knew the King would reply at once; even if he did not reply in person, there would certainly be a response.

She willed herself to turn her mind elsewhere. Grace had eventually calmed down, and Consuelo had tactfully left her with Peter, who could do nothing else but hold her quietly in his arms. She had decided that the young lovers must set their own parameters and after recent events the sooner they married and set up home the better. The whole purpose of bringing Grace out of obscurity and presenting her at court had, of course, been realised by an outcome where she would most certainly find happiness – although perhaps not quite in the way Consuelo had imagined. Peter was clever and had a certain future; he had proven himself to be a brave and incorruptible protector and, truth be told, since she had been back at court without George Anson by her side, Consuelo had felt vulnerable there. She thought more often of the simple life out in Clapham, from which she had removed the innocent Grace. As Consuelo's health was not quite what it had been, this whole affair had shaken her. She had never seen how simple people lived until she met the Lively family and then she had wanted to take Grace away. Perhaps God was watching and had carefully taken Grace's future into his own hands. But what of Pepe? She began to weep uncontrollably. What if some harm had come to him? It would break her heart and all for what? Nobody would care about a little mulatto child; they would not realise that he was the most precious jewel in her life. She fell to her knees and prayed.

In Grace's bedchamber the atmosphere was rather different. It was not that they had forgotten about Pepe;

Grace was quite sure he would be back and she knew the household was on alert, but for the moment at least the reassuring warmth of the room and lying in Peter's arms on her own bed was the nearest thing she had been to heaven. She had never really liked the reality of being at court; it had seemed like a wonderful idea at first and of course, she reminded herself, had it not been for that brave venture she would never have met Peter again and they would not now be embarking on their life together. Grace had been reared in a family that took things in its stride, by and large. Adversity was to be expected. Naval families were adept at dealing with calamities. The horror of the abduction had shaken her profoundly, but she had an indomitable quality to her; these vicissitudes were there to show her a path. One thing she was sure of was that she did not ever want to go back to court. All she wanted was to go to the country and live a happy life with Peter.

What she had seen was unadulterated evil, a desire to destroy something pure and good. Now, in the warmth and safety of her room, Peter said: 'I want to hold you, my darling Grace, but nothing more until we are husband and wife.'

He knew how easy it would be for them both to take advantage of this wonderful moment, but then he would be no better than some of the feckless men at court. Grace stirred in his arms, and pressed her face to his.

'I want the same,' she whispered. 'I want to go to Madonna's Court and live there with you.'

'Then we shall,' said Peter, 'there is the cathedral, the music there is excellent and I can make my harpsichords there, I have already planned it. It is only a day's journey away from your mother and Holly Farm, so what is to stop us?' he asked.

There was something of course. Life is never that simple. Grace knew this, and Peter should have done, but since that fateful moment when Grace had put her scarf under his head and he had run for his life, all had gone well for him – even the reunion with the angel who had saved him – and now he had saved her, so they were even in the lottery of life.

'My father,' Grace said, pulling away from him.

'Your father?' he asked abruptly.

'Yes, Peter, we cannot marry until he is back; it would break his heart, it would be a betrayal.'

Peter drew away, considering what Grace had said. Most musicians have a mathematical facility and he was no exception, seeing life in a logical manner. Now, many things flashed through his mind: he had a hazy picture of Grace's father, but in his opinion a man who had other options in life should not set about making a family only to desert them for indefinite periods without any real knowledge of what the outcome would be. Grace's father might be away for years and the odds were that he would not come back at all. So he asked himself how could the fate of this father, who had left his family to fend and graft for themselves, take priority in Grace's plans?

'But surely he would not want to stand in your way, Grace. You might wait for years and who knows what might happen in that time?' he asked slowly.

He knew the words were a mistake the moment they left his mouth. But once in the ether they could not be retracted. This was to be their first quarrel.

'Stand in my way? What do you mean?' asked Grace, flaring up in a way that she later realised was unjustified. 'My father is the most precious thing in my life,' she cried, leaping from the bed, her hair flying wispily around her.

'Yes, but he was not here to protect you, Grace, was he?' Peter shot back.

'How could you say that? He has always come back to us, always, do you hear, and he will again!'

Peter did not have a great deal of experience with women. He had no idea, for instance, that in the same way a man must cut the cord that connects him to his mother, a daughter must also do this with her father. Grace saw Captain Lively in a very different light from that which Peter had deduced.

It was only then that Peter began to see that the collateral damage caused by people like Sir Hartley was enormous and far reaching. He decided he would say no more, but absent himself from his beloved for the moment. It was nearly morning and obviously Grace was overwrought. He regretted deeply that he had made such assumptions about her; it was a lesson he would not forget. He had thought he knew this girl, that their hearts beat to the same rhythm, that they dreamed together as one. He had thought there was no need for discussion between them, and that she had no secrets. He left the room when he heard her breathing fall into the deep pattern of sleep, Grace retreating into her own private world of dreams. It was a hard lesson for him, one of the hardest he had ever known.

As he made his way along the passage his intention was to slip to the room that Jane had prepared for him, but there Jane was, standing in front of him, her face red and angry.

'So, you are just like all the rest!' she said bitterly. 'My poor innocent lady, you have done what that venomous pig would have done. I thought better of you, Mr Peter, I really did.'

She had been carrying a brass pitcher of rose water that she was going to put on the griddle of Grace's fire. She put it angrily on the floor and it made a clanging noise, which echoed down the passage. Consuelo heard it and came at once to her door. She saw the two and perceived an angry exchange.

'What is going on?' she said in a quiet, puzzled voice.

'You had better ask him,' said Jane sullenly.

'You must not address Mr Peter in that way, Jane. It is disrespectful,' Consuelo reproved.

'Respect is as respect does, my lady,' said Jane, nudging the brass pitcher with her foot and sending water spilling onto the floor.

'My lady, Jane thinks I have dishonoured Miss Lively... It is true I have only just left her chamber and that we quarrelled. But dishonoured her? No, that I have not. In a way it is I who am dishonoured here.'

Peter had become icy cool. He felt piqued. It had all seemed so simple to him and all the time Grace had had it in the back of her mind that a marriage could be years away. No, this was ridiculous. Love or no love, he had a very practical side to his nature. He had done everything he could: he had acquired a wonderful home for them and even taken the whole family to see it. He had behaved immaculately towards Grace where many would not have been so forbearing. Indeed no, he would not have his life turned into a waiting game in which there was absolutely no certainty.

Consuelo saw the expression on his face and felt her stomach constrict. She had seen that look in a man's eyes before; she knew that to a woman love is her whole life, but to a man it is a thing apart. Grace might lose this man, he might well just walk away, that was the nature of the beast.

But she could not face this now; it would all have to wait and Grace would have to start being more realistic. First there was something far worse than Grace's naivety.

Consuelo gripped Peter's arm. 'Pepe is missing,' she cried frantically.

Peter was considering this information when suddenly there was a loud clanging at the door. He went at once to find Consuelo's head coachman with an important looking envelope, upon which could be seen the royal seal.

Consuelo was down the stairs in a flash, her velvet morning robe flying behind her. She snatched the letter and tore it open, hands trembling like jelly as she read it. Peter had closed the door to the freezing morning air, but Consuelo continued to shiver and her face drained of colour. She started to sway. Peter was at her side in an instant and almost carried her to the small library, where he carefully deposited her on a settee near the glowing fire. Jane was there at once with hot chocolate and a wrap. She took Consuelo's clammy hand and held it tightly.

'Peter, read it please,' Consuelo muttered in a frightened voice.

He drew up a chair and read; it was in the King's own hand and came straight to the point. Sir Hartley was dead.

Peter lowered the paper and met Consuelo's gaze. 'And Pepe is missing,' she said quietly. She was of course thinking about the small pearl handled knife. Her mind raced. What if Pepe was the murderer? It was by all accounts too much of a coincidence that Pepe had set off in pursuit and now the man was dead.

'Sir Hartley had many enemies, Lady Consuelo,' said Peter carefully, watching her face intently. 'It is perhaps not really the greatest of surprises that his life has finally caught up with him. In many ways this will be a relief to Grace, although she will not say so. It is strange though that the King does not say how he died,' he added.

In fact, they were about to find out how he had died. There was a loud banging and clanging of the bell as someone attempted to gain access quickly. Peter ran out into the passage and shouted, his voice echoing up the stairwell.

'Do not open the door, young man, until we have assembled some of the male servants and we know who it is,' Peter ordered.

'It is the constables!' cried the porter, in a shaky voice.

'Do not let them in until I am down myself,' yelled Peter.

He ran to his room, dressed as quickly as he could, and was in the hall, very much the man of the house, by the time the great door was opened. Consuelo was not far behind, now in a thick black velvet day gown.

There were two well-built constables on the steps and they were about to push past in a manner that did not bode well; that is until Consuelo came out from behind Peter and asked them what their business was at such an uncivilised hour.

'A very serious matter,' said the larger of the men roughly.

'It must be,' replied Consuelo in her most imperious voice.

The two men were slightly less confident now; one of them nervously removed his hat and nudged the other one who reluctantly did the same.

'It is very cold with this door open,' said Consuelo politely. 'I would be obliged if you would clean your boots, gentlemen, and my servant will escort you to the library and bring you some refreshment. This may put you at your ease so you can state your "important" business in a manner we will all understand.'

Consuelo was being very careful not to give anything away. The men could not know anything about Pepe's absence; indeed they would not even know Pepe existed. 'So how may we help you? Why is this business, as you call it, of any concern to us?' she asked in a level voice.

'It is about a gentleman called Sir Hartley Slinkwell,' explained one of the men hesitantly. 'My lady, we know that there was an incident at the palace concerning a young lady who is your ward, and that Sir Hartley was guilty of abducting the young lady.'

'Of course we know that,' shot back Consuelo impatiently.

'Well, the gentleman, if you could call him that, has been murdered,' announced the man dramatically, pausing for

169

effect. Consuelo had left the message from the King on a table beside her. The King's cipher was clearly visible and now she stretched out a delicate hand and picked up the envelope, holding it close to her chest.

This did not escape the attention of the men.

'We do know the details of this terrible affair. As you see, the news came to us in the early hours,' said Consuelo.

There was a confused silence in the room until one of the men turned to Peter and asked him if he was the young lady's betrothed and whether he could account for his whereabouts the previous night.

'The gentleman was here all night,' broke in Consuelo swiftly.

'Was he now?' said the constable with a slightly supercilious look.

CHAPTER NINETEEN

Surprisingly, Grace had fallen into a deep but troubled sleep and heard nothing of the disturbances below. She dreamt she was in a garden, one she had made herself, and had been wandering through a sunlight orchard; there were artfully arranged wild flowers at her feet, and at the end of a long grassy path was a house bathed in light. It was of course Madonna's Court and there was the sound of laughter drifting from a walled courtyard, a glimpse of which was visible through an ornate open wrought iron gate with initials on it scrolled in an elaborate setting of flowers. She approached the gate; she could see flashes of white, children's clothes catching the morning sun, but she could not get closer to the vision and the more she tried the further away it went. She called out to the children but they did not hear her. She knew this was a vision of her happiness but she was outside it and these people were in another life, she was not part of it. She wept in her sleep and then the figure of a man came to the wide door into the house and the children ran to him. Did she imagine it or did he look up for a fraction of a second before they went inside and he closed the entrance behind them?

She woke with a start as the fingers of the present snatched her from that tantalising moment and there she was in her bed, her heart thumping.

Peter had been in the bed beside her... She extended an arm. Was he there? The space was cold and empty, something had happened. It was not just the awful recollection of the abduction which broke into her mind; no, it was the harsh words she had spoken to the man who would be the font of her happiness – and then it came flooding back: the dream, the garden, the future. She had just broken the indomitable trust that she had had with Peter, into whose life she had thought herself indelibly woven.

Perhaps she would never be able to restore what they had once had. She had seen a facet to Peter's character she had not known. He was a proud man and could not endure being put aside. And how stupid of her not to see that the man she had always idolised, her father, had not put her first; no, she was second or even third to his own dream. They had not had news of him for more than three months, since he had arrived in Madeira. She'd dented Peter's loyal and confident love for her. She had to find him at once and regain it! Grace leapt out of bed and Jane came immediately, but did not tell her about the visit of the constables.

'Miss Lively, what can you be thinking of? You should have called me,' Jane fussed. 'It is a bitter morning in more ways than one, but at least you are safe, and Mr Peter ... I regret now my suspicions, it's a rare thing in this life, a man like that.' Jane thought about the perfect vision the young couple made; Grace with her thick auburn hair and slim figure, Peter tall and well built, but not roughly fashioned like the folk in Jane's own family ... how could her young mistress let him slip? Grace looked at her for a moment and burst into tears.

'Oh, Jane, I am so stupid! I have offended him deeply, I could see it in his eyes; it was much more than that even, he looked cold and unforgiving. I have never seen him with such a look.'

172

'Miss Lively, what did you say?' asked Jane, sitting on the bed, a thing she would never have done in another circumstance, but all pretence of etiquette was gone as she knew at once that this was serious. This was about friendship, two women whose lives were interdependent. Grace had come to depend upon Jane, and she knew that in the established order of things, her own happiness was Jane's happiness. Jane was as pleased as anyone could be about the prospect of a life in the country with a young master and mistress. They had even discussed how it might be after the two were wed. And to think of the excitement, all the preparations, and after it was over Jane would have a position, she would be in charge of other young men and women!

Jane had come to know her mistress's ways as nobody else could, and she could sense trouble. The wicked, depraved Sir Hartley had sown the seeds of evil in the most fertile ground: the young, unsuspecting hearts of two people in love, who assumed all was well with the world. This was a time for simple, down to earth common sense. Whatever it was, Jane was sure it could be resolved. There was such affection between Grace and Peter, and help from the God who created them.

'Oh, Jane, I told him we could not wed until my father came back, however long it took,' Grace said quietly.

'What possessed you?' cried Jane. 'Surely you know that a sailor's life has no certainty; you might wait for years. Don't you think that if, and it's a big if, your father comes back he would rather find a happily married lady with a bevy of grandchildren for him to bounce on his one good knee than a sour old maid – for that is what you will be, my girl. Really, you have raised me, Miss Lively, and for that I am grateful, but you set no example to a girl such as myself who has had to learn and live on their wits. I saw how you improved your own life and I came with you… As dear to me as a sister you are … but this? Well, I have no patience with you! Get up and dry your eyes, my fine lady, and repair the damage. Tell him you must be wed as quickly as is decent and drop your foolish thoughts of your father, who abandoned you all without a glance – as all men who yearn for the sea do. It is a lonely grave for most of them. And your father was not driven by need and hunger, he came from respectable folk, and he left your poor mother to work her fingers to the bone to keep you all and provide an education to better yourselves…' Jane put her head in her hands for a brief moment while Grace picked herself up from the onslaught, recognising startling similarities between what Jane had just said and the thoughts that had come from Peter himself.

She pulled Jane towards her and hugged her, breathing in the scent of good, sensible clean linen and simplicity. 'You are my dearest friend, Jane. Whatever the show we may have to put on to please the people around us, never forget how we are like sisters. You saved me, I know that and I was feeble minded or I would have stayed close to Peter instead of allowing myself to be isolated at Sir Hartley Slinkwell's mercy. I will be there if you need me, Jane. Meanwhile, please help me to compose myself and look my good fortune squarely in the face.'

The household was beginning to stir. The maids were bustling round with their buckets and black lead for the grates, which had to shine like gold before the mistress rose. The rugs and cushions needed to be beaten, the kitchen ranges stoked up and the pots and pans simmering as the cook went through the meals for the day. The first thing Jane always did was box the kitchen boy's ears. He had thought of ways to avoid this, but even getting up earlier made no difference. Today she forgot this ritual because the word had filtered below stairs of the comings and goings in the night, and now the head man had caught her attention to tell her that the mistress was in the library; she had been there since dawn and none of the maids had been able to get in and see to the fires and the cleaning.

But the most worrying news was that the old priest, Father Benedict, had come in the early hours and was now deep in prayer with Her Ladyship. Inside the room Consuelo knelt on her prayer stool while the priest heard her confession. What she told him was indeed startling, even for him who had been privy to so many secrets.

He thought carefully about what the poor woman had told him. So the little mulatto boy was hers; this was something he found hard to accept, but when she told him the circumstances he placed a firm hand on her head. It was not a hand of admonishment.

'My child, this is not your sin. It is the sin of the world and you have borne it,' he said in a low voice. 'You have given the child your love with no expectation of recognition. God will love you for the courage you have shown.'

'But he can never be mine, he can never know, and now he is gone,' she sobbed, 'lost in a world which will give no quarter and it is all my fault.'

'We will pray, my dear. All things are in the process of change: you yourself are learning from the vicissitudes of life. You are a good woman, this I know ... and I know you have more to tell me – things you must unburden from your heart. But these things are undergoing a great transformation and you will find a different way. It will be revealed to you.'

'But, Father, the knife ... the knife... I gave it to him for his own protection. I encouraged him to use it if needs be and now I have made him into a murderer, which is why he has hidden himself. He knows what will happen if he is caught... What have I done?' she sobbed.

The old priest had kept his hand on Consuelo's head and he did not move it as he heard this. He knew about the horrible events of the previous night. He was a stranger to the

175

protestant court and, along with many devout Catholics, he thought it was mired with mindless vanity and the feckless abandonment of basic moral codes. This was the reason for the current state of affairs.

Consuelo's mind was racing. She had been born and raised a Catholic, and now she had the chance for confession; she needed to be forgiven. Her relationship with George Anson was never one that could proceed with God's blessing. She needed to reveal the contents of her heart to Father Benedict and he would give her forgiveness. This he did; but he finished with the words: 'Go in peace, my daughter, and sin no more.'

Having unburdened herself, Consuelo began to feel very unwell and Jane came quickly to her aid, with Grace on her heels. The old priest was also concerned and the three of them helped Consuelo to a chaise longue. It was at that moment that Peter made an instant decision: this was no place for him. He turned quietly and left the house, emerging into the morning air without a backwards glance. He needed somewhere he could reconsider his choices.

'Who is Her Ladyship's medical attendant?' the priest asked anxiously. 'She needs rest. I have seen this condition before and I believe she has a fever that has recurred for many years, which is affecting her lungs. Someone must be summoned at once or I fear I will be recalled for a very different reason.' His face was full of concern, and he could not be ignored.

Jane, who had found herself very much in control, thought at once of Doctor Algernon. Word must be sent to him straight away, he could be with them within the day if the horses went without break.

'Miss Lively, enough of all this nonsense; we must send for your grandfather. He is a fine physician; he will come with all haste and see what can be done. The Lady Consuelo is very sick. I have known this for a long time. Indeed Doctor Lively confided as much to me.'

'But, Jane, she will never rest until Pepe is found,' said Grace.

'I realise this is all because Her Ladyship thinks the boy was the one who killed that villain Sir Hartley,' Jane said. 'With respect, Miss Lively, the stable lad has already told me the manner of the man's death. It is all over the town. He was bound and thrown in the river, but not before he was strangled with hands as big as a giant's... Now, I ask you, how could a slip of a boy do that?'

Grace knew that the situation was now spiralling out of control and looked around frantically for Peter.

'Where is Mr Peter,' she cried out.

Jane ran out and confronted the hall boy, who was still doggedly attending to the comings and goings.

'Mr Peter left a while ago,' he replied.

'Did he say where he was going?' asked Jane, sensing that this did not bode well.

'No, miss,' said the boy. 'But he looked very put out.'

Jane guessed immediately that this was not good news for her mistress. But she decided to make light of it all. She must focus on Consuelo and take control; she would send for Doctor Algernon immediately, after settling the Lady Consuelo in her chamber with some laudanum to help her sleep.

About an hour had passed when a letter arrived. It came from none other than Peter and it was, of course, addressed to Grace.

After what Jane judged to be a suitable amount of time, she went to Grace, who had read the letter in the empty library. Her mistress sat staring out of the window, watching the grey morning through a thin veil of snow.

Jane ran to her and Grace held out the letter.

'Read it, Jane. It is as you feared – I have lost everything,' said Grace flatly.

Jane sat down and digested the contents.

So Peter was leaving; he had already decided to go to Hanover and compose for the distant court.

Jane knew the world rather better than Grace and she could detect from the tone of the letter that something had changed profoundly for Peter. She knew there was a latent danger with all men: the issue of pride. A man could distance himself coolly from a situation that had caused him pain and without a backwards glance engage in a new life. She had noticed that women had a tendency to damage the male ego. When they returned to the injured prey of their own volition they usually discovered that the door had been closed. The love, of which the woman had been so confident, was real enough but young men were eager to heal their wounded hearts with new adventures. She did not share all this with Grace at once because, after all, she might well be mistaken.

Chapter Twenty

The *Centurion*. The coast of South America, off Juan Fernandez, June 1741

The once proud ship was now a desperate rotting hulk, home to desperate men. Two thirds of those who had embarked with such high hopes had already perished as the *Centurion* laboured aimlessly through the cruel ocean, turning back on itself for many months. Only the rats dined like kings, gnawing on the rotting corpses below. It was too much effort for the few weak, desperate men who were left to heave their former comrades up to the deck, and sew them into the white bags, putting a needle through their noses to make sure they were dead, before consigning them to the ocean. So the rats did their job for them and the dying watched with hollow eyes and empty bellies and innards turned to black jelly by the scurvy.

The Commodore never slept – though he kept himself fed, for he knew, as did the men, that without him there was no chance of survival. His ears pricked up, that fateful day, when he suddenly heard a boy's cry, girlish and shrill on the nagging wind. He was at the boy's side in seconds, grabbing the telescope, and there it was, Juan Fernandez!

But now he faced the impossible task of getting the great, stricken vessel into the narrow inlet. There was hardly a man left to manage the sails, but man them they must. He called the most able-bodied lads to his aid and even the soft-handed tutor seemed to have toughened up and did more than his share. After what seemed an eternity beating against a treacherous wind, there was nothing but sheer rock to meet them. The men's hopes were dashed. It was only the Commodore's superb seamanship which, after days of struggle, nudged the exhausted ship into a safe anchorage. Sadly, there was not another ship in sight, so all hope of a rendezvous with the remaining fleet seemed to be lost. The Commodore felt utterly bereft; all his high, gallant hopes were at an end, they were gone. He clutched his precious crucifix and prayed for the other men on the sister ships fearing that they might be consigned to a watery grave.

Finally, on 21 June, after the sick had been conveyed ashore, the promise of woods, grassy valleys and cascades of fresh fruit and water was fulfilled. The men even found recently abandoned cooking utensils – although this was not a good omen since it was evidence that the Spaniards had been there recently and had then disappeared. Old stories about Shelvocke's *Speedwell*, a large vessel that was wrecked on the island and waited six months for rescue, began to surface. The men knew that others before them had been marooned there for many years.

The surgeon Richard Walter was mystified by the powers of recovery exhibited by some of the sailors, especially the young boys. He knew that if the survivors did not get fresh fruit within hours all would be lost – but he could not understand why some men died at once, just as help was at hand, while others were cured and restored within a matter of days. Later, he was to remind himself just how quickly some of the sailors returned to health. It was like a miracle. One day, he said to himself, he would make a more careful study of this. On that terrible day when they arrived at Juan Fernandez, however, he was one of the very few who indulged in thoughts of relief from this unendurable hell. One day, after the Commodore had finally given up all hope of making a rendezvous with the rest of the fleet, someone spied a sail. And there they were: two of the three missing ships, the *Gloucester* and the *Tryal*. The Commodore sent a sloop to bring back news of their condition and try to aid them, but what they found was worse than they could imagine.

The Captain of one of the godforsaken vessels was barely able to raise himself in his bunk and the dead and dying festered below, riven with starvation and scurvy. The six boys and the few officers who were left standing were not strong enough to raise sufficient sail to conduct the ship through the delicate manoeuvres needed to reach safe anchorage.

George Anson was a man of conscience and all this, taking place only a few months into his noble plan, was an ever-increasing burden for him. He thought often of the families left behind, of the hopes and dreams lost to the endlessly cruel ocean. Mostly, he did not reveal the pain he endured to anyone, but he did confide in one of his officers. Lieutenant Saumarez was a bright young man from Guernsey. He was always there when he was needed and kept a cool head. On this particular day, he suggested some of the few now recuperated men attempt to row out to the helpless *Gloucester* but as the hapless sailors approached the stricken ship, the poor men in the rescue vessel collapsed. Shortly afterwards the ship caught an ill wind, lost its anchorage and disappeared over the horizon.

George Anson prayed and felt that somehow he knew the ship would be back. He would concentrate his efforts on repairing the *Centurion* and *Tryal* and caring for his men. When the *Gloucester* miraculously returned he would be there with a useful force.

That night they fell with relish upon succulent seal meat that had been brought back by two enterprising men, along with armfuls of wood for the cooks, but the men were silent, only muttering among themselves. They glanced at the Commodore and his officers, who, with scrupulous adherence to naval etiquette, ate from a formally laid table with items brought ashore. They drank the red liquor despised by the men, who preferred extra rum – those, at least who still had the stomach for it. There always seemed to be a supply despite the most extreme of sufferings. It was this formality that kept the order and respect that made these men so implacable. But the secret of the blind loyalty given to George Anson and his officers was that the Commodore would never shirk from any task expected of his men; he would be up there aloft with them in the fiercest of storms and when a young lad was sick to his stomach he would lash himself together with the boy until he overcame his fear.

When the wine had lifted their spirits a little, Saumarez asked the Commodore what he might anticipate as the greatest joy when, if they were spared, they returned to England. The older man turned to him with a wide and frank expression, and a steady gaze that suggested a carefully considered reply, which was very typical of the man.

'I had a life very dear to me as you know, Saumarez. It came to me when I was not searching for it. Although I do not like the thought of a quiet domestic fireside – and indeed it would be a very unfortunate person who would live such a life with me – nonetheless, love, that is to say real love for a woman, my dear fellow, that is to be treasured. You know, of course, of what I speak?'

'I think I do, sir,' replied Saumarez cautiously, not wanting to move too closely into the Commodore's very private life, which might damage the disciplined nature of their relationship. 'I was with one of the men when he died, sir,' he answered slowly. 'I knew the man quite well and he often spoke of his family at home; he had three children and spoke proudly of his hopes for them. He was going to give me a letter to keep for them if he should not return, but he never did, and he wept for them as he breathed his last. He mentioned their names, but I have forgotten, God help me.'

'You will remember,' said the Commodore, 'when your mind is freed to recall the names. That reminds me, may I ask the same of you if I should perish and you should be spared as a messenger?'

'Of course, sir,' said Saumarez.

'And you? Do you have a family?' said the Commodore.

'Only my mother and father, but if God spares me I decided before I came on this voyage that I would not wed or be promised until I was a rich man and had answered the call of adventure and could settle as a country squire where nobody would ask me about how I came to be so settled. It is my journey, nobody else's.'

The Commodore looked at him and slowly nodded his head.

Chapter Twenty-one

Holly Farm,
EARLY SUMMER

Consuelo was still sick. Where should she go? Home of course – and for Consuelo her true home was now with Grace and the Lively family. She had come to belong in Clapham and all the more so because she had developed a comforting and enduring relationship with Dr Algernon.

Although he was so much older than her, he had led a healthy life and was still a handsome man, comfortable in his skin and fulfilled by the choices he had made. He remained engaged with the world around him, and many were dependent on his vigour and knowledge. Consuelo had come into his life when he least expected to find love.

The arrival of Consuelo had been overwhelming at first. He had fallen under her spell immediately, but she was so far from anything he had experienced. She was a strange bird of paradise and he had amazed himself when, the first time he had even seen her as she came into the dining room at Holly Farm on that September evening, he had wanted to put his lips to her splendid neck – just at the back where her coiled hair rested like a massive sleeping bird. And then, before he could stop himself, his thoughts had travelled to the magnificent, voluptuous bosom shimmering in the lamplight and framed by delicate black lace, which contrasted with the white alabaster skin that was so warm, so inviting. He had felt young and vigorous; he wanted to plunge his mouth into the secret crevasses leading to the tight bodice.

Nobody at the table would have guessed that such things were racing through his mind. He did not feel in the least ashamed but all this had remained sealed in his heart. Then something strange had started to happen. They had become close in other ways. For him a robust kind of love had quietly grown, but for her it had been more delicate, the winding of many strands. His age meant nothing to her. George Anson had been older than her, a kind of father figure, their relationship rather formal. George knew her secrets and he had given her his protection as he watched her become more confident, a figure in her own right in this new country where things were so different. Nonetheless, Consuelo had remained an enigma to Anson.

But not to Algernon. He had an unusual understanding of women. The death of his wife in childbirth at the tender age of nineteen had led him to leave the navy, where he had learned only of men and boys, and dedicate his life to the care of the poorest and most destitute women in the city, at St Bridget's. And now the cruellest of things was that Consuelo was ill. She was sick and ailing and Algernon had been given the responsibility of caring for her. She had submitted without protest. The bond between them had grown even closer; he had of course never touched her in the way he had desired when he first met her but now, ironically, he had to explore her ravishingly beautiful body with a gentle physician's hands. This took place under the ever watchful gaze of Jane, standing with water and soap, the room silent and hushed.

'My dearest lady, does this pain you?' he asked her now as he pressed softly with the flat of his hand on her marble belly.

Consuelo winced, and Algernon came to a decision.

'Dear Lady Consuelo, with your permission I would like to summon Mother Benedicta from St Bridget's so that she may examine you in a way which I would not feel appropriate doing myself, as we are, if I may be so bold, very close friends.' He replaced the covers and turned to Jane.

'Jane, faithful servant that you are, Her Ladyship has a fever and we must continue to keep her cool and provided with refreshing sips of water. It is my opinion that she may have contracted this sickness many years ago in South America and for some reason it has flared up again.'

'Oh, Doctor, let us hope it is a simple explanation like that! I will mix some cranberries up with the water; it is an old recipe and works wonders for the fever and keeps the insides clean, if you will forgive me. And I will get some water of witch hazel to bathe her brow. I have cured many a fever in my time.'

Consuelo stretched out a hand to Jane and muttered weakly, 'If only Pepe were here, Jane; it is the worry of it which is making me so ill. I can think of nothing else.'

'Mercy, it is as if he were her own child,' Jane whispered to Algernon. It was then that he decided Jane should know the truth, in fact they should all know the truth. This continuing charade could only bring more complications. Besides which, he had spent his whole life trying to deal with the stigma of children born out of wedlock in circumstances which were no fault of their own. Even the boy must not be kept in the dark any longer. They would all live with the truth from now on; this was his mission. But exactly how this revelation was to be approached he had still not quite decided.

It was agreed that he should fetch Mother Benedicta at once. When he announced this to the family waiting for him below they looked at each other in puzzlement. Of course Margaret knew that her father-in-law had a medical interest in the convent a few mile away but she was a contained sort of woman and didn't, what she would call, 'pass remarks'. Besides, she had a vague notion that the establishment provided for that unmentionable subject, fallen women. She had been bred to be terrified of such things; to fall from respectability was worse than death itself. She had even named her own daughter Grace to imbue her with the very essence of purity.

But Grace was cut from a different cloth. 'I will have none of this, Grandfather. There is something going on here. I like none of it; nobody here speaks the truth any more. I hate that wretched court. I hate the way there are secrets. I am sure this is what drove Peter away. He will only come back to a simple life. I want no more of it, do you hear, no more! What is the matter with Consuelo? And why is everyone being so strange about Pepe? He is just a child and why did Consuelo bring him here? Who are his parents? I don't understand any of it!' Grace grew in stature and faced her grandfather while her mother dissembled behind her apron.

'Hush up, child, I forbid you to speak in such a tone to your grandfather,' she implored. Grace's brothers Samuel and Rupert had joined them. In fact the whole household was now in the large kitchen, even Alice and the kitchen boy.

'I cannot answer all of this at the moment,' Algernon told them. 'There are two things of importance here: the first is that we try to find Pepe. I have an instinct that he will be somewhere close to here. I don't know why but he loves the Lady Consuelo like a mother and he is, after all, only a child. It would not surprise me to learn that someone knows where he is. He may be frightened after the terrible business with the death of Sir Hartley, but he needs to know that the unfortunate man died at the hands of several large men who had the strength to overcome him and consign his remains to the Thames. The child is in no way implicated.'

187

This was, of course, a coded message and Algernon watched closely to see if there was any subliminal response from any of them. But there was none that he could see, except from Grace, who had a tight expression as if she were working something out.

After what seemed like a long silence, Grace spoke in a voice which was both quiet and ripe with meaning and, as is so often the case when someone speaks quietly and with authority, the room remained silent, in rapt attention so as not to miss a word of what she was saying.

'Grandfather, I have had a revelation. I believe that Pepe is Consuelo's child. This explains it all, why didn't we all guess? I can see why she has been so secretive, because a half-breed child would be very hard to explain. But the poor boy, it is not his fault and he is being made to live a lie for all his life. No wonder he has gone missing; he will end up in the gutter and we will have been complicit in putting him there. Why after all these months couldn't she tell us the truth? I will tell you why,' Grace answered her own question, 'because we are all playing the game of deception, each one of us in our own way.' Grace did not waver; she did not burst into tears when she had made her own declamatory, life-affirming statement. Instead she challenged the room to confront their own truths.

'You are right, Grace, and of course I have known for a long time, but Consuelo had her own reasons for the deception. You must not think ill of her, she is a noble woman,' said Algernon gravely.

'Why should you think I feel ill towards her, Grandfather?' asked Grace.

'Well I feel something about this,' chimed in Margaret with uncharacteristic candour. 'If I had known I would have stripped him of those ridiculous clothes and he would have been welcome to be here as one of our own. I have always

188

had a soft spot for the boy. He is a little tinker. But he is sharp and not workshy.'

'And, you boys, what do you think of all this, since you have been let into a secret of the most profound nature?' Algernon asked, turning to Rupert and Samuel.

'We are as brothers,' said Rupert rather hastily. 'When he first came we pledged our friendship in blood; he said it is what people did where he came from, and we have never regretted it.'

'So ...' Algernon considered, 'if he had a secret you would not divulge it under any circumstances unless he wanted you to?'

'No,' said both boys in unison.

Algernon was a wise man to say the least and he knew better than to try to break the loyalties forged by young boys. He sensed that they knew more about Pepe than they would ever say and at that moment Algernon was sure that he was for now still alive. But Pepe was no more than a child and his dark looks would make him stand out from all the other displaced rag boys who roamed the streets, deprived of childhood and a full stomach. Sometimes a very life was poised on that terrible dilemma of conscience, which can make hypocrites of us all. He decided to say nothing more to his family about this and concentrate on the priority.

'The most important thing at the moment is to find out what is wrong with the Lady Consuelo,' he said in a professional voice, removing his small steel glasses and wiping them with a flourish on a dashing silk kerchief.

Soon they heard steps coming down the staircase announcing the return of Mother Benedicta, who had swept quietly upstairs to her charge on her arrival when she saw that the Livelys and their servants were deep in some sort of conference. As she came into the room, she brought with her a feeling of quiet control. Lady Consuelo was sleeping quietly, she informed them.

'You can leave her be now, doctor,' she said with a fleeting smile. 'Our sister will be quite safe – but I would like the young lady to stay.' She nodded in Jane's direction.

Margaret and Alice waited with Algernon in the kitchen.

'Could I speak to you and the doctor alone?' Mother Benedicta asked Margaret, her eyes lowered.

'We must go to the parlour,' said Margaret quickly.

Algernon led the way. The only sound to be heard was their footsteps and Mother Benedicta's robes sweeping on the stone flagged floor. They sat down on two of Margaret's best chairs as the midday sun slanted through the open window and sparrows cheeped in the holly tree outside; the faint aroma of autumn wafted in.

'Dr Algernon,' Mother Benedicta began hesitantly, 'Lady Consuelo is very ill. She has an infection in her womb, which is of long standing. This of course came as a surprise to me, but there was no mistaking it, I have seen it so often. These things can be masked for many years, as is the case with her, and then for some reason the infection breaks out and travels fast to other organs and death comes suddenly.'

This was grim news and Algernon was prepared for more to come as his suspicions were confirmed.

'So it is childbed fever,' he said, 'which has lain in her womb for all these years. What can we do, Mother? This infection will never abate and I do not have the skills to do what I have heard can be done… I do not know how she will recover.' He put his head in his hands despairingly.

'Doctor, I have very tiny hands as you can see. Over the years I have learned many skills which are hitherto untried in the male dominated world of medicine. I have examined Her Ladyship thoroughly and I know where the infected tissue is. I am prepared to give the lady as much laudanum as she can take and I can attempt to painstakingly remove this matter and then nurse her afterwards, making sure the source of her infection is under control. I saw the scars of what must have been the most agonising birth possible, conducted by ignorant butchers. I cannot promise anything but without this the lady will most assuredly die. And may I offer you some guidance, dear doctor?' she asked.

Algernon nodded and she continued. 'It is the right of all human beings, who are, after all, given the gift of words, to be told the truth about their parentage, however unusual it is. The little boy must be told that Lady Consuelo is his mother; it is only the hiding of his beginnings that make them outside the normal. There are no secrets hidden from God, and if only his creatures would all do as he does, then life would be so much easier, would it not?'

'I have already told the family,' said Algernon quickly, 'and I have a feeling that the child may be close at hand and that Grace's brothers will be the first to hear anything if he chooses to make himself known.'

'That maybe so if God is kind,' said Mother Benedicta carefully. 'But they must be told not to tell the child about who his mother is; this is a thing which must be done with the utmost care. He might develop a resentment; after all he has had no real childhood.'

'For once I do not agree with you, reverent mother. I suspect the child may well have guessed already. He obviously loves the Lady Consuelo and she him. He is wise beyond his years and children have a gift for locking things away in their hearts while they get on with the business of growing up; it is the way of things. But I agree it is only his own mother who can tell him, and we must make her well so that she can.'

It was agreed that Consuelo would stay at Holly Farm and that the nuns would turn her bedchamber into a safe environment for the risky procedure, to avoid sepsis. Consuelo had made a will and confided all her wishes to Algernon. Grace helped the nuns with the preparations for the operation; the room was scrubbed, the bed was substituted for one more suited to the ordeal and the boys were detailed to provide a continuous supply of ice from the ice house.

The operation had been completed and Jane was giving hourly bulletins. The laudanum had made Consuelo very sick but she had felt no pain and now lay still and white, her feet elevated as the nuns worked silently, conferring in hushed voices outside the room, the doorway to which had been covered in a sheet soaked in lyre to keep the risk of new infection down.

'Doctor Algernon,' Mother Benedicta finally confided, 'I found a mass of infection, which I have removed. Such a procedure would never be undertaken by conventional surgeons because the risks of bleeding and further infection are so great. But the fever is declining and we have stopped the bleeding. We will stay here until I am satisfied that Her Ladyship will recover, but I am convinced that if we had not done this she would undoubtedly have died. She must have been suffering greatly for many years. Still, the next few days are crucial, we must continue to pray.'

Grace sat beside Consuelo and held her hand softly. Sometimes Consuelo whispered something, usually about Pepe, and she often asked for Algernon.

'My dearest Consuelo,' murmured Algernon when he decided it appropriate to visit her. To his surprise she grasped his hands in hers and levered herself slightly towards him. He lent beside her and called to Jane for yet another pillow. As Jane positioned it gently, she smoothed Consuelo's coil of dark, lustrous hair, just as an anxious mother would do.

Consuelo smiled a thank you to her and Jane melted back into the corner of the room. To Algernon, Consuelo had never looked more beautiful and with his physician's eye he saw that the thin moisture of fever had left her brow and there was a faint glow to her cheeks. He dared to hope in his heart and he began to believe that she would survive. After all, she had not yet seen her thirtieth year; she might even bear another child – although Mother Benedicta had indicated that such a thing should be avoided for many months, and perhaps forever. As the woman had told him this, Algernon realised that she had assumed that Consuelo and Algernon were closely involved with each other. This had come as a shock to him, despite the fact that he had known for some time that he was deeply in love with Consuelo.

He would never regret the spontaneous action he now took. 'There is something I must tell you, dearest Consuelo,' he said softly, his lips very close to her face. 'I am in love with you and if you were to give me the slightest encouragement I would ask you to become my wife in the eyes of God. I want to care for you and offer you all that I can give. But if you cannot answer yes, our friendship will remain the same and I will never mention it again.' He did not mention the difference in their ages: a good twenty years.

She gazed steadily into his eyes, her own welling with tears. She did not see what he thought she saw. Instead she saw a handsome man graced with a strong face, with a fine, aristocratic nose and vibrant eyes, his hands beautiful and manicured as befits a man of medicine. His hair was still thick and vibrant and sprang up from a noble forehead.

'Oh, Algernon,' she whispered, 'dear Algernon.' He sought to pull his hand away, expecting a rebuff. 'No,' she cried, taking back his hands. Jane had quietly left the room, sensing a dramatic moment. 'Algernon, my dearest Algernon,' Consuelo breathed, looking steadfastly at him, 'I would be so honoured to be your wife.'

She paused … he caught his breath, and then a miracle happened. Consuelo sat forward and, holding onto Algernon's shoulder, she swung her feet out of the bed and stood up. He steadied her and there she was, standing in front of him. She reached out her arms and put them round his neck, carefully laying her head against him. He could smell the faint waft of her perfume and as he put his arms about her, he could feel her body melting into his. Just for a moment he was in heaven.

'Yes,' she breathed. 'Some things are so natural, my dearest. This is almost the first time something has happened to me which is so simple, uncomplicated and obvious. I feel completely at peace, safe, and yes, my dearest, happy, quietly happy, except…' she paused, 'that Pepe, my child, is not here. Sometimes I think I have given up hope but still in my heart there is a feeling that he will walk through the door.' Algernon gripped her hand. 'But never fear, Algernon my dear, we do not have much time in this world and it is better we take what comfort we can. Our union will help me accept whatever will come, but hope will never leave me. I will go on searching and we will find him, please, God let us find him.'

For Consuelo there had been no decision. Her life had always evolved, events dictating how she lived. George Anson had sailed into an uncertain future, this time without her, and she had no way of knowing when or if he would return; they had not even spoken of it, though it was tacitly understood.

Algernon shook with emotion. Her words touched on something deep in his heart and he felt that he might have waited all his life for this moment of resolution. They were two people so very different and yet so perfectly matched. Yes, together they would never give up hope.

And there they were when Jane, who, of course, had listened at the door, her heart beating with vicarious joy, came back in. She stood very still on the threshold and then they both turned to her, a look of sublime contentment on their faces, and she knew that Consuelo would regain her health, that all might be well. She hardly knew what to say, so she just smiled. They motioned to her and Consuelo broke from Algernon and embraced her joyful servant.

'It is fitting, dear Jane, that you are the first to know our joyful news, for you have nursed me so well. We both owe you a debt of gratitude which, if ever we are able, we will repay to you, but for now our love must suffice.'

'Oh, My Ladyship, this wonder must be shared with the family! We have had so little cause for celebration recently and this will set a new pattern. But none of us will rest in our beds until we find the little lad.'

'Yes Jane and I will put on one of my country gowns without adornment and you will gather them in the big kitchen, not in the parlour. I will be the wife of a country doctor and be done with all the finery that has been a false idol.' She looked fondly up at her future husband and he left the room as a man walking among the stars.

CHAPTER TWENTY-TWO

LEINE PALACE,
HANOVER

Robert Walpole was not accustomed to being kept waiting and he did not care for the palace in Hanover. He had reservations about the ornate décor. And most particularly the creaky wooden floors. He was a big man and had put on a fair amount of weight; consequently he liked to shift about on his feet or his gout troubled him. The floor bent as he stood impatiently for the King, producing an embarrassing sound effect which reflected his annoyance at this unnecessary wild goose chase. For that was just it: they were only there because the King was chasing Amalie von Wallmoden, and she was a goose indeed – but not fit for the King's table. Walpole thought about the many other ladies who might have caught the King's elderly eye after his wife's untimely demise; none of them would have enticed him to this dreary backwater.

The worst part was the political fallout that Walpole had to deal with while the King dallied with the German woman, playing cribbage to while away the time as London fermented in the exhausting late summer heat. There were riots in the streets on occasion and the Prince of Wales was losing no time in using his father's absence to his own advantage. If the King was not more mindful of his decreasing popularity during these long absences, things could turn very sour. Walpole was a pragmatist and his foreign policy was quite simple really. He avoided confrontation for he knew that war on any level meant increased taxes and selling that to the people was the big problem.

Of course, Sir Robert himself was rather astute at feathering his own nest. He had built the largest and most lavish house possible while remaining seemly within the unwritten laws of society – his family was not well born and ideas above their station would be frowned upon. And then there was the public money that he had cleverly siphoned off into his own grandiose household embellishments. 'What happened to all the mahogany revenue?' the King had enquired when he had heard about it. He had questioned Sir Robert, because, after all, they were friends... The answer had been resolute. 'A man cannot work for free,' Sir Robert had replied, 'and it is for one year only. I give my whole life to Your Majesty's service and it is proper that Your Majesty's most loyal supporters and advisors should be seen in the surroundings of gentlemen... How else can the game be played?'

'What game?' the King had shot back.

Sir Robert thought about that now as he fidgeted irascibly. Yes, he ruminated, it was all a game. And then, most unexpectedly, the eerie silence was interrupted by the distant strains of music. He could not quite work out where it was coming from. The trouble with these pretentious German palaces was that each room had many ornate double doors and one never knew which one would open. Added to which there were these blasted mirrors everywhere. He expected one or other of them to open suddenly and so it did, but before anyone came through it the sound of music wafted through the air, a sound which was unusually charming and of a high calibre, which he found surprising in this distant enclave. It was most definitely Handel, one of the harpsichord suites, probably the second one. But the touch on the keys, it was masterly and singular. He had heard such playing once before. Sir Robert liked fine music and had an ear for it which was astute and accurate, as it was for many other things, particularly inaccuracies with the truth.

Before he could work out the familiar hand of the musician, Amalie von Wallmoden came into the room with a flourish.

Her agreeable character always lifted the mood. Although she was rather short, her pleasingly curvaceous figure, fiery dark eyes and vivacious, lively countenance, worked their magic. On this occasion she was wearing an informal gown of sprigged silk with no train and a frothy shawl around her neck. Sir Robert was not unaware of attractive women and she struck him as most charming. Now he could quite see why the King liked his retreat in Hanover, away from the dreary routines of the English court.

Truthfully, Sir Robert was also tired of the life in many ways: the burdens of politics and the endless backbiting and conflict between the rival courts in London were wearing him down. It would be hard to persuade the King that he must return and take up the yoke of responsibility instead of remaining in the dreamy confines of the Hanoverian court.

'Sir Robert,' Amalie said sweetly, with a most elegant curtsy, 'it must indeed be important business which brings you here to our humble court in Hanover.'

'Yes, madam, these are momentous times and His Gracious Majesty is sorely missed by his people.' Sir Robert let the remark hang in the air, observing Amelie's dark, intelligent eyes as she digested the direct message. She hated England, but she had thrown her lot in with George. Her dreary magistrate husband had put up no resistance to his wife's position as the King of England's favourite and most important mistress. In fact he had welcomed it. Their two children, Franz and Johann, also basked in a certain reflected glory. This royal connection had been established by Amalie's grandmother, who had been one of George I's early mistresses in Hanover. This gave the liaison a respectable veneer in Germany but not so in London where Amalie was not considered quite the thing by smart circles, despite the fact that her portrait hung at the end of the royal bed.

So of course Amalie liked to be in her home country with her lover, because there she reigned supreme. In London she had been allocated unsatisfactory apartments in Kensington Palace, previously occupied by Lady Deloraine. They were both damp and dingy, despite the piecemeal gesture of new and expensive wallpaper. She had no view of the gardens. When asked how she felt about this she had been typically self-effacing, saying *'pas pour moi'*, in French rather than English, which she spoke very badly. Since the Queen's death the palace had become a lifeless place and Amalie loved the lightness of Leine, with its long walks and sparkling fountains, ever bathed in sunlight. A return to London was inevitable but she did not look forward to it.

Thus, Sir Robert had a difficult mission, but it could not be left unaccomplished.

'Madam,' he ventured, 'I am glad we have an opportunity to speak before we are joined by His Majesty.'

'Of course, Sir Robert,' Amalie said lightly. 'But would you not like to hear the wonderful music? We could venture into the next room where the young man is playing. He plays in the mornings and then he walks. He is suffering from a broken heart, you see, and he finds the country here very restorative.'

'A broken heart, you say,' said Sir Robert pensively. He had never indulged in the luxury of a broken heart himself; he was a pragmatist. This is what he could not quite understand: how the aging King allowed himself to be governed to the exclusion of caution by matters of love.

But, yes, it would be very agreeable to listen to some music, even if it was not in his schedule. And Amalie, recently elevated by the King to Duchess of Yarmouth, was a delightful companion.

'Your Grace,' he said, offering her his arm and, mindful that he had overlooked her ducal preferment on his arrival, he made quite a show of escorting her into the large salon where the young man was playing. The room was decorated in a pale effervescent blue and the harpsichord was heavily inlaid with ornate, halcyon pastoral scenes. Sir Robert had the vague impression that the scantily clad figures depicted were engaged in activities not entirely proper for the royal music room. He decided to blank this out of his mind, reminding himself that this was, after all, Hanover.

The young musician was simply dressed in a very loose shirt, which gave full movement to his arms while he played. In fact his entire body was so engrossed that he had not even noticed the arrivals in the room. Sir Robert and the Duchess stood very quietly, both giving way to a rapturous pleasure.

The piece finished and there was silence while the young man closed his eyes for a minute, paying homage to the great composer who had given this joy to the world.

Without demur, the Duchess flung herself across the room. The young man tried to get up to offer her the correct formal acknowledgement but she was having none of it. She spread out her plump arms and embraced him with genuine affection.

'You see, Sir Robert,' she exclaimed, turning to him with a broad smile, 'we are all so happy here – just like a family – and with Peter to bring such beauty into our lives it is indeed an idyll.'

'Yes, Your Grace, I can see that,' replied Sir Robert indulgently, because in spite of himself he could see that Amalie was a delightful creature. For a second he almost envied the King being able to live in a fantasy.

Suddenly there was the sound of brisk footfall on the polished floor and there was His Majesty himself. But, unlike his mistress and the court musician, he was, as was his custom, formally bewigged and attired.

Sir Robert bowed deeply to the King. They had developed a very close friendship over the years and Sir Robert was one of the few people who really understood His Majesty. Usually the King listened to him and although he might not indicate agreement at once, he would think about it for a day and then come back with a positive answer. Never once had the King rebuffed Sir Robert. To be dismissed would be a serious impediment to his ambitions and he hated the thought of joining the club of those who had lost favour. Pettifogging minor recipients of the Royal dismissal had to suffer alone without consolation.

'Do you think, sir, that we might retire to discuss the reason for my visit, as I have to return to England as quickly as possible. Things are not as they should be and there has been simmering of discontent among the people,' said Sir Robert in a perfunctory way.

The King, rather unnervingly, did not respond at once as would have been expected. He stared steadily at the harbinger of this bad news, guessing at once that Sir Robert was about to suggest that he cut short his stay in this summer paradise and return to an ominous autumn in England, where the winter would come with all its damp palaces and dreary routine and the continual neighbour war with his hated son Frederik. The King's eyes bulged in the forbidding silence. At best they could be said to protrude a trifle and this feature was accompanied by a rheumy look, which meant he was ever patting them dry with a silk handkerchief. On this occasion, however, he held the handkerchief in front of his face for some time, as if he could not bear to face the situation that was unfolding.

Amalie did what she usually did when this happened. She burst into nervous and rather inconsequential conversation.

'Your Majesty,' she twittered, using the full title as she did when in public, 'Sir Robert may have disagreeable news but everything is going to be all right with him in control.' She reached out a delicate hand to Sir Robert's sleeve and squeezed it affectionately. 'After all,' she went on, 'this is the man who solved the bubbling south sea problem.'

The King winced and withdrew the handkerchief. He hated it when Amalie appeared frivolous and stupid. She was not stupid – in fact she had a firm grip on political affairs. She was astute and also tactful and reticent. But sometimes she made stupid remarks. He knew it was probably due to her poor command of English but he was nevertheless mildly embarrassed. He saw Sir Robert's face harden a little and assume the inscrutable look that had served him so well in his political career.

People on the whole underrated the King and those who knew him well also knew that without his beloved Caroline, upon whom he had depended so profoundly, he found life very challenging – especially negotiating Parliament – so it was Sir Robert who managed everything. It was Caroline who had taken a liking to Sir Robert and advanced him to this great and powerful position. He was the first all powerful prime minister of England. But as Caroline's influence waned following her death, Sir Robert had begun to face the fact that all political careers end unsuccessfully. The thing to concentrate on was feathering your nest so that when the day came you were a man of great wealth and through that, you still had power and position. The 'South Sea Bubble' was the scam that had almost ruined the country's economy and brought many honest people to penury. But not Sir Robert. He'd had advanced warning of the mad investment that had bewitched a nation and was built on nothing more than a pack of lies, and as it rose to fever pitch he got out at the top and made a vast fortune. But his real stroke of genius had been to be in the seat of power at the same time, and to effect a rescue operation for which he took all the credit. Thus, the first government bond was invented and he emerged the hero. Even the King himself had become enmeshed, falling for the promise of an easy fortune to embellish the distinctly distressed royal coffers.

Sir Robert had cunningly managed to get close to the King following the Queen's death and they were friends, yes, definitely friends, thought the King now. But he knew that his friend had come to take him back to England, much as a parent might bring back a wayward son from the colonies, to take on the mantle of responsibility.

Now, Sir Robert decided to take advantage of the King's mistress' mistake like the genius he was. 'Your Grace,' he said admiringly to Amalie, 'such an amusing way of describing it! You are so witty – and in a language which is not your mother tongue… There are many politicians who could do well to learn from you.'

Amalie bridled but, after a brief moment of thought, she concluded that there was no irony in Sir Robert's remarks whatsoever and this was confirmed by the artless way he smiled at her. The King on the other hand was not quite sure; he knew Sir Robert too well.

Eventually the King was forthcoming with a plan and suggested that Sir Robert join them for the big meal of the day, which, in contrast to such an occasion at court in London, was consumed in the full glare of the court and all the hangers-on.

'But first,' he announced, 'we will make our way to the music room and listen to some more of the fine playing you have already heard from my personal protégé. Yes, young Peter, he came with a broken heart and what better place to recover than here in Hanover?' asked the King, casting an affectionate look at Amalie.

The King walked purposefully towards the double doors from which the music had come. Two flunkies hurried to open them and the party sailed through. The young harpsichordist appeared to be carefully studying a score but in reality his thoughts were many miles away. He was thinking about a place called Holly Farm, far from Hanover. At the precise moment the King, his mistress and the prime minister came into the room, Peter had been considering the reasons for his flight to take up the King's offer of patronage. Mr Handel had advised caution:

'Yes, of course any young musician would be flattered at such an offer,' he had said. 'But then you have carved out a reputation here in England. And there is more to this, young man. There are affairs of the heart to consider,' Mr Handel had added with one of his severe looks. The great man had gone on to give young Peter a piece of advice, which of course Peter had disregarded: 'When confronted with an angry woman, my boy, grovel, yes grovel. It is the only way.'

'Thank you, sir,' said Sir Robert quietly, when they had taken their seats and Amalie had nodded to the young man to play for them. 'Where have I seen this young man before? He has the most singular looks. They could break many a young girl's heart.'

There was a great deal about Leine Palace which Sir Robert found attractive, and so, despite his original plan to make the visit to Hanover as quick as possible, he found himself instructing the official messenger to announce a delayed return. The packet coach had set off speedily earlier in the day and now Sir Robert sat with the King and Amalie in a cosy dining room where a painted porcelain stove exuded a therapeutic warmth, and many candles flickered in Meissen holders adorned with elaborate shepherds and shepherdesses attended by garlands of delicately painted flowers. It was the embodiment of one of Mr Handel's most celebrated arias. Robert sat back comfortably in his richly upholstered chair with his two equally well upholstered companions. Laconically, he held an ornate glass up to the candlelight. The contents were the colour of a fragrant weak afternoon tea. He anticipated the joy of the first sip and it lived up to his expectations and beyond.

The King watched Sir Robert like a large Cheshire cat.

'So, Sir Robert, what do you think?' he smiled smugly. Impressing Sir Robert was a hard thing to do, but it was, he reminded himself, ever so with arriviste families like the Walpoles. They got to the top of the mountain and they forgot how hard they had grafted to get there and how many people they had stepped on, and how many disgruntled rivals lay plotting in the wings. Power should not be given to those who seek it, the King sighed to himself now. As for himself, he mused, he did not particularly want it but it had been thrust upon his reluctant father. It was a poisoned chalice, which blighted the lives of fathers and sons.

'A most excellent wine,' agreed Sir Robert. But, as always with him, there was a sting in the tail. He went on to suggest it was not from one of the great and most sought after vine-yards, and then to proselytise the virtues of economy. This irritated the King and he began to regret that he had shown Sir Robert such a friendly welcome. His eyes bulged more than usual and he delivered a sharp response. He had decided that Sir Robert, although they were good friends, had risen too high for his own good.

'We,' said the King sharply, using the royal we, 'have not noticed Sir Robert practising even the most rudimentary signs of economy in his domestic affairs. Indeed we are often told that Lady Walpole is not averse to exorbitant bouts of expenditure. The Queen, God bless her, used to try to settle these matters for Her Ladyship with the desperate tradespeople who found it difficult to obtain settlement.'

Sir Robert was piqued, although he was now on dangerous territory, and wished he had not made such unguarded remarks about the wine. But here was a man who had cleverly learnt to avoid confrontation. It never did to get personal with royal persons; he should have known this, so he plumped for benign avoidance. He wriggled a bit like a fish and then extracted himself from this line of conversation by turning it to his advantage. Everyone knew that Sir Robert could manage the King very well and now he had to lead the King into feelings of responsibility. His Majesty was disengaged from his royal duties and had to be brought back into line. All the rest was semantics.

'Your Majesty,' said Sir Robert, using the more formal mode of address to delineate the lines of engagement. 'I will come to the point.'

'When did you ever not?' asked the King. 'But then point or not, you might as well enjoy the doing of it, is that not so, Lady Yarmouth?' he added, catching Amalie's eye with a meaningful look which did not escape Sir Robert.

'Well then, sir, my mission is simple. England cannot manage without their King, and these are hazardous times. War is all people can think of when there are difficulties, but it is not the way, sir, no not the way. Nobody ever really wins a war. You defend what you have, yes, of course, but the rest...'

The King cut Sir Robert short with a laugh. 'Sir Robert, spare yourself this agony. Well before your arrival I had recognised the necessity of a return, but I did want to discuss the manner of it with you. It will be a great deal easier because I will not be alone.'

They set to discussing a date and Sir Robert agreed that the King's return should be conducted as if he had never been away; little should be made of his absence and there would be a carefully orchestrated series of dinners leading up to Christmas... Perhaps Mr Handel could compose a new work to be played at the Palace... No acknowledgement should be given to rival entertainments planned by the Prince and Princess of Wales.

'You will see, Sir Robert,' said the King, 'there is much to be said for a little absence. Naturally people will wish to attend my own court and see what fresh winds blow through its corridors.'

Amalie looked at the King affectionately and he in turn indicated that she could add something to the plan if she wished.

'Sir Robert, this is all splendid and we must bring the young musician back with us. We have had many visitors this summer, including the great Mr Handel himself, who admired him.'

'Oh yes,' replied Sir Robert thoughtfully. He remembered, now, why the young man seemed familiar.

'Yes, the musician,' replied the King. 'That business with the scandal and that rogue Slinkwell, I felt responsible you know, Robert.'

'Why?' enquired Sir Robert in a puzzled voice.

'Well, the girl's father is one of Anson's men on the great voyage. She is the ward of the beautiful Lady Consuelo who brought her to court, where she encountered the young man who was Mr Handel's protégé. It was a natural romance – an unusual event these days,' the King said, casting an affectionate and conspiratorial look at Amalie who plucked suggestively at her lace collar.

'Then why is he here and not with her?' replied Sir Robert reasonably.

'I understand,' the King explained, 'it was some business about the girl's father who is somewhere on the high seas with Anson, although it is any fool's guess as to where. The girl would not name a day, and told the boy he must wait until her father returned.'

'This confirms my view, sir. All this expense harrying the Spanish, and to what end? The loss of fine men, that's all. Mark my word, that young couple are a prime example. The voyage will end in disaster and the father should not be considered. If a man chooses to throw his lot in with buccaneers and leave his family unprotected they must do what is best for themselves...'

Sir Robert was becoming emotional; he reached for a kerchief in his pocket and dabbed his eyes. At first the King could not think why he should be so affected by the young man's story. Sir Robert's antipathy to war was of course familiar to the King, it was part of his foreign policy. The mere mention of the widely celebrated John Churchill, whose battles had won him glory and bankrupted the nation, sent him into frenzy. But Anson's voyage had inspired the King, it was so much more than keeping those confounded Spaniards in check; the man would bring back maps of uncharted territories, make discoveries. He had convinced the Admiralty himself about the merits, and now yet again Sir Robert was damning it. Besides, there was the prize money, he thought to himself.

'It is not the voyage so much as the thought of the girl,' breathed Sir Robert. 'My own dear child has been so long with the angels... I would never have deserted her, never. A daughter is a prize to be treasured, a gift from the Gods.'

The King thought about his own silly daughters and truthfully he would not be much bothered if he never saw them again. He tried momentarily to empathise with Sir Robert, who sat there in complacent confidence, his person exuding success and prosperity, and could not quite see this more sensitive aspect of the prime minister, so he did what he did well and changed the direction of the conversation.

'So, Sir Robert, how goes your great house in Norfolk?' He was referring to Walpole's magnificent family seat, Houghton Hall, of which he was justifiably proud. 'I hear the refurbishments are a sight to behold. It is quite far from London though – but, there, you and I have much in common... They tell me you and Her Ladyship spent many weeks there this summer enjoying the country air. But I gather London was a dangerous place to be in that very hot weather. Some of my advisors suggest that your government should be in the House of Commons for a longer period. But then who am I to talk? I say it for you, Sir Robert, yes, I say it for you. I have dallied too long here. It is delayed grieving, you know; my beloved Caroline was the power behind the throne and I am not ashamed to admit it.'

Sir Robert looked uncomfortably at Amalie. It seemed indelicate of the King to speak thus in front of his mistress.

'Oh, but Amalie is my great consolation,' reassured the King hastily, with a fond gesture towards Amalie, who nodded amiably. Sir Robert began to understand for the first time how simple a man the King was. He just wanted the support of a 'good woman', in a sense a motherly figure who resembled that which his own mother might have been.

Sir Robert felt reassured after this brief time with the King. He knew his own star was beginning to wane. He must return with the King as his trophy. He decided to play the game more tactfully. To this end, he did what he did rather well: he flattered and cajoled.

'Sir,' he said, dissembling unashamedly, 'Your Majesty, Your Grace, the delicious wine has gone to my head so forgive me in advance if I speak to you as a dear friend in whose presence one revels … You see, happiness is contagious. I feel inspired with a certainty I did not enjoy when I decided to come here, yes a certainty that when you return it will be the start of a golden period. A happy monarch is a happy country, but it is hard to achieve it without the companion who gives you wisdom and support. Dare I venture to say that your present circumstances in that respect would have pleased the Queen. She wanted nothing but Your Majesty's happiness and I can see it for myself.' Sir Robert finished with a flourish, signing the footman to replenish his glass. With the passage of time it would be hard for either man to know just who was manipulating whom.

CHAPTER TWENTY-THREE

MADONNA'S COURT,
AUTUMN 1741

Peter stood in the middle of the old rose walk. It had been a mild autumn and now very suddenly it felt like winter was coming. Leaves still hung doggedly to the branches but a fine hoar frost covered it all with delicate lace, which glistened in the late afternoon light. An insipid sunshine during the day had left it alone, respectfully dipping behind banks of dark cloud. But they had cleared now and Peter had decided to leave his practice and have a walk around the gardens. A cheerful robin peeped constantly, making plans already for a partner with whom to raise a family in the spring. The bird hopped beside Peter as he walked from tree to tree, as if it wanted to share its world with this sad, lonely human.

The place seemed soulless and empty. True, his parents now lived in the farmhouse, but they were missing their old ties and had made the move in anticipation of Peter being there with his own family. They hardly dared ask what had happened with Grace and it had been difficult when Peter suddenly disappeared, but at least they had forged a great friendship with Thomas, the old servant.

'I hope I am not disturbing you, sir,' he asked tentatively. He was worried about his young master. The time had come when he thought it would be unnatural if he did not express some of his concern.

'Thomas, of course you are not, I love this time of day, and I would like some company for an evening stroll,' answered Peter, putting an arm about the old man's shoulder.

The two men proceeded in silence and Peter noticed that Thomas had developed a gait which suggested that he had a painful hip.

'Forgive me, Thomas, but how old are you?' he asked.

'I am the same age your father, sir, and we often walk together and grumble as old men do,' Thomas replied.

'My father had a hard life Thomas. As you know, he was a carpenter and taught me all I know about wood and such like. It is a living thing and understanding it is the secret to my craft. It is something you have to touch and feel. When you begin to work on a new instrument, you have to know which way it will bend and how it will eventually resonate.'

'Yes, sir, like a woman – if you will pardon me.'

Peter was rather startled by the frankness of the remark but it was so natural and down to earth that he did not change the theme.

'Yes, Thomas, and I may have a way with a harpsichord,' said Peter ruefully, 'but with women I think not. I simply do not understand them, except for my mother, of course.'

'Would you think it a great impertinence, sir, if I asked you about Miss Lively?' ventured Thomas quietly.

Peter stopped walking and turned his face towards Thomas. His own father had tried to broach the subject of this calamity and he had been abruptly rebuffed. He had gone back to Peter's mother and told her their son had clammed up and that perhaps it was something to do with the death of the terrible Sir Hartley.

Peter decided to unburden himself to the faithful Thomas. 'I was tactless,' he answered slowly. 'I did not realise how difficult it is for a daughter to accept that her father might not come back from the kind of naval expedition that Mr Lively has embarked upon. And so I assumed that we could make our wedding plans; there was no doubt in my mind. It was arrogant of me but it all seemed so very simple at the time.'

'That is one thing a woman cannot abide, sir. They call it taking them for granted. But in the end they are the most powerful... If things come right, you will not be doing that again in a hurry, sir.'

'It was not only that,' Peter went on. 'The shock of what happened under the King's nose and when her guardian the Lady Consuelo was unwell, must have had a lasting effect, and then the little fellow disappeared and he has not returned. I fear he could have been murdered by Sir Hartley's henchmen.'

'Pardon me, sir, but I do not think the lad is dead. He is a clever little fellow but there was talk at the time that the lad thought he had been responsible for the murder of that wicked man. Have you thought he might be in hiding and afraid to reveal himself? Whatever way you look at it, it is a nasty business.'

This *had* occurred to Peter, but since he had returned he had not given himself time to untangle the web of events. He nodded to Thomas and told him to continue.

'There are types of ladies, sir, and some are their father's daughters and I think Miss Lively, if you will forgive me, may be one of those. Think how the absence of a father would have preyed on her mind when she was so cruelly abused.'

'I would have given my life for her, Thomas; she must have known that, and when it came to it, the little fellow would have done the same. We all saved her. She was not harmed, and now she is with her family and I dare not go there. I am fearful of being sent away. If I could find little Pepe I could return with at least something to offer her.'

'Sir, do not underestimate yourself. I have been told something of your history; your mother has told me. Grace's life and yours are bound, you see. When a person has given a man a chance of life they are bound forever, like it or not. You must go to her quietly – soon, before the winter. She needs to accept you as the strong man you are, not the boy to whom she said 'run'. It was fate that brought you together, but fate is a funny thing. It usually has a sting in the tail. The trick is to see it for what it is, a challenge if you like. The young lady is lucky there are many father figures in her life: Doctor Algernon for one; he is the man you should see and ask him to advise. Miss Lively is very headstrong. I could see that in an instant.'

Peter was amazed that Thomas had observed so much about it all, and indeed that he had the wit to explain it so clearly.

The two men made their way back to the house as darkness began to fall and all was welcoming and warm. Peter's mother had come to supervise the house and a young woman from the village had moved in. The floors shone in the light of many well-stocked fires; the table was set for three in the cosy parlour because Peter's parents were going to join him. Their two dogs – a shaggy breed that had no name – had come in advance and lay stretched out on a rug in front of the fire.

It was a comfortable scene, made all the more poignant when Peter heard his mother and father talking as they came from the kitchen, his mother pulling off her apron and exclaiming, 'When will the boy pull himself together and just go and get her? It is all so ridiculous! This living like the gentry is all very well, but with no wife to fill the house with little ones and make a life with him, what is it all worth?' She clicked her tongue disapprovingly.

Peter heard, of course, but he made no comment; he had made up his mind. His father saw at once that this was the case, so he caught his eye and lightened the atmosphere.

'Well, Peter, as you will soon find out, at least our young Mollie will fill your house with the patter of feet; she always comes back here, you know, however much we try to keep her at home.' Peter's gaze turned to the dog who, hearing her name, looked up expectantly, and he suddenly realised how loving and faithful everyone had been. He owed them something in return. All their hopes were bound up and invested in him. He must not let them down; he might even have to compromise on something ... but what?

Chapter Twenty-four

The Coast of Mexico,
spring 1742

It was the beginning of March and the debilitated fleet hovered off the coast, in sight of the harbour in Acapulco. They waited for their prey, the great *Manila Galleon*, but after days and weeks of searing, humid heat, the men began to sicken again. They had lost the appetite for the waiting game and thoughts of the great prize were superseded by rumours that the voyage home would not retrace the outward journey down the coast of South America, but veer into the North Pacific, looking for the trade winds, and go via China, making for Canton where they would pick up supplies and undertake vital repairs. The men were by and large alarmed by the plan. Horrible tales were circulated of the strange and alien people in that far flung place, where a warm welcome would be unlikely.

And then there was the matter of the prize ships they had already taken. What was the Commodore planning? There were not enough men left to man the *Gloucester* and the *Centurion* and there was no sign of the cutter, which had gone missing weeks before. Many of the men were supernumeraries from other ships that had been scuppered and the prize money, which should have been enjoyed by the original crew, might not now be shared equally as it would be apportioned to newcomers as well.

In the Commodore's quarters the officers were assembled to hear what he had in mind. The new men were restless, while the invalids and marines languished below, dependent on the exhausted crew for meagre rations and small sips of sour water. It was necessary to keep the men informed and the Commodore had taken some difficult decisions, for which the officers were only too pleased to let him take responsibility.

'So I think it is best for the safety of His Majesty's subjects, and for the security of both His Majesty's ships the *Centurion* and the *Gloucester*, to destroy His Majesty's ship the *Tryal* and allocate the remaining men to the remaining ships – and the same with the Indian prisoners,' he said quietly.

There was a silence. They all knew the Commodore had made a brave decision. The *Tryal* was a magnificent ship, one that any man would be proud to serve upon, but it had no fighting capacity and was a luxury the dwindling men could ill afford.

'Sir, this is going to be a difficult plan to accomplish; it will break the men's hearts to fire a good ship. They have respect for such things,' said Matthew Lively awkwardly.

'And what if we do find the *Manila Galleon*? Are we to take her back or are we to load her contents onto our ships and weigh them down whilst the Spanish hunt us to regain what, after all, they see as rightfully theirs?' added one of the young officers.

'I must remind you,' replied the Commodore with uncustomary ferocity, 'that we are at war with the Spanish. War is never a pretty thing and scruples do not enter into the equation. The navy is a noble force, which plays its part in the security of our country. Supremacy on the seas is the future for England, and it is what makes us great. We are an island race and must be feared. I have seen many atrocities carried out by the Spanish and have you asked yourselves about the provenance of the prize on board the galleon? It was not obtained by gentle and honourable barter. No, gentlemen, it represents intolerable cruelty and oppression. They will be in no state to pursue us. We will take no prisoners!'

The men sat very still. George Anson was showing them exactly where honour began. They thought of the numerous magnanimous gestures they had witnessed and indeed benefited from when retracing the Commodore's steps on their arrival in South America. Anson's reputation had often afforded them lifesaving assistance.

'I speak for us all, Commodore, when I say we respect without question your decision and will carry out our duty and convince the men. Although it would be easier if we could realistically have a hope of capturing the illusive *Manila Galleon*,' said the first officer.

The Commodore passed round the flagon of port he saved for such occasions, for he had bad news for them. 'I think the Spanish have got wind of our presence, and it is becoming clear to me that the *Manila Galleon* will not sail this year. I come to these conclusions because I know how Pizarro thinks and I try to think as he does.'

For the weary men this was one of those rare moments when the camaraderie of life at sea becomes real. It was not a common occurrence for the Commodore to take time to sit with the port around the captain's table and they all relaxed as much as the stifling heat would allow. All the port holes were open, there was a faint breeze, and the young midshipmen took it in turns to wave a large piece of thick paper, fanning the officers. Some of the officers felt uncomfortable with the menial nature of the lads' task but they were assured by the boys themselves that they also benefited and that it was an honour.

'It is important to know your adversary well,' pondered the Commodore, returning to his musings on Pizarro. 'I know that I would like to share a bottle of fine brandy with the man and that he is a formidable seaman, but I also know he would not be magnanimous in victory and sensing defeat he would be ruthless. He has a dangerous quality about him, but he does not know *me* as well as he thinks he does. He is a man who assumes too much.'

'Do you think, sir, it is the galleon or the defeat of His Majesty's ships which matters most to him?' asked Matthew pertinently.

'It is victory, the destruction of the English fleet, which is the prize he wants. He was born to privilege from a long line of aristocrats who were used to wealth and used to the service of those lower in station.'

'So he offers the galleon as bait, assuming you would jeopardise us all for that,' summed up the first officer slowly.

'He does, Captain, he does. And the poor men in my service would follow orders blindly for the want of it, but, no, we will do no such thing. We will put in at Acapulco but only to play cat and mouse. We will replenish our ships. The galleon will be in hiding but we will not declare ourselves and then when we have regained our strength we will slip away at night and he will not be able to understand what the devil we are doing. He will be watching but he will have missed the opportunity to spring the trap.'

After a few moments Anson decided that now was the time to voice aloud his thoughts for the continuation of their voyage, anticipating an easy run across the North Pacific to the coast of China. Cautiously he shared this plan with the other men. It was greeted with complete stunned silence. The rumours were true. Anson had no apprehension about his decision even though the season was too advanced. This route was described by the Italian traveller Careri, who had made the crossing in 1647, as the longest and most dreadful in the world. Matthew Lively had read the account in detail and repeated it now.

The Commodore did not seem to take this well and dismissed it completely.

'But, sir, surely if we drop a few degrees latitude and pick up the northeast trade winds, as the great galleon would, we would run a straight line in smooth seas before the wind.'

'We are not here to have a quick run home. China it is! Other navigators have done it before us...'

'But, sir, the charts we supposedly followed to get us here were entirely incorrect. We chased the trade winds assured us by Sir John Narborough and we never found them. As we all know, this delayed the trip round the Horn and I blame the loss of over half our men on it. We cannot repeat the mistake.'

'We must surely follow the great Dampier who left California in March and followed a steady course. He picked up the easterly winds and made it to Guam in fifty days,' interceded the first officer.

Many conflicting plans were mooted by the men whilst the ships mouldered in the calms, men who had been trapped into the disastrous decisions of the past and would be so once again in the coming months. They talked of latitudes and the magic of them, particularly the latitude of thirteen degrees.

'And all for the want of bloody longitude... Hang the latitude! See where it has got us, months of death and disaster... And with respect, traversing the globe in the year of our Lord 1742, we are like the blind. The Chinese did better with the North Star five hundred years ago,' burst out Matthew.

This was one of the few occasions when Anson showed despair. 'Matthew, you say what we all know. Aye, the mistake was not pressing the Admiralty for Harrison's longitude clock.' He put his head in his hands and spoke through clenched teeth. 'It was 1717 when, as a young captain, I took the first clock to Tangier. It worked perfectly and it did not falter even in a storm of great severity. After the return voyage, it was wrong by only a hundredth of a second. But Their Lordships declared it too big and cumbersome. They said it would reduce the space for the large canon and officers' quarters.'

'Much good the space had done for us! I remember you pleaded for it and the point was well made – that the Centurion could have been the guide for the rest of the squadron, set the course without fail and round the Horn. But instead we spent two months adrift… It does not bear thinking of,' said the young first officer.

One of the most junior officers who had come from the *Gloucester* could no longer restrain himself. 'If God spares me and there is prize money coming to me, I tell you, men, with the Lord as my witness, I will give it to old John Harrison or his son to finish the work on the clock and no man will perish as ours have done for the miserly old men who have deprived so many of our friends of their lives and their families of husbands and fathers.' He hit the table with his fist.

There was not a man among them who did not agree and Anson examined his conscience, wondering if there was any more he could have done to advance the progress of the clock. This was a moment of doubt, but had he not been to the King himself? And had not the King reminded him that the voyage was a controversial matter? The prime minister had been against it all along; he did not see the point of harrying the Spanish any longer, and the Admiralty were grudging from the start.

Sadly, Anson thought again of how the men had been waiting on board for a year already, eating stale bread and becoming more and more impatient. He recalled the splendid autumn morning when the fleet had sailed from Portsmouth.

Morale had been high, restored by their glorious departure, the men jubilant, raring for adventure.

When the officers had gone to their duties and the task of explaining the plan to the men beckoned, most of whom had no idea where China was or what the North Pacific had in store for them, Anson reached for his Bible and prayed for the hundreds of souls that had been lost on this fateful voyage. Suddenly he thought about Matthew Lively, one of the staunchest of his officers. He remembered as if it were yesterday the man's family on the quay at Portsmouth. The wife – he could not remember her name – had a look in her eye, one he recognised: it said that she was out of patience with her husband; she was a capable woman, and Matthew might find something different from blind acceptance on his return...

Next his thoughts turned to Consuelo. She was an exotic beauty and her parlous state would not have gone unnoticed. He knew instinctively that she was not a woman to wait for life to run to her; she would instead run to life. She was young enough perhaps to add to her family... He thought of Pepe and smiled. He had been fond of the boy and loved to ruffle his thick curls.

Of course he wanted to see Consuelo again, but truthfully he was not a family man, and more than that he had become very ambitious. He saw the next stage of his journey as a gift from heaven. He was destined for it. On his ship he was master of all he surveyed.

Anson began to make plans. Saumarez had been at the officers' meeting and, tactfully, had said very little – but he had caught Anson's eye every now and then, marking a point that both men knew would be discussed later. He had a unique knowledge of all the charts and accounts favoured by Anson himself and had indeed been to China as a young midshipman. He had already warned Anson that navigation of Chinese coastal waters would be fraught with difficulty and that the Dutch charts on board the *Centurion* were inaccurate. There was now an air of fatalism on board and Anson knew many of the men had given up all hope of returning home, let alone of acquiring wealth and reputation. But Anson believed differently. He had to.

Chapter Twenty-five

Holly Farm,
April 1743

'We have some news for you, my dears,' announced Doctor Algernon one Sunday morning. 'The Lady Consuelo and I have decided to proceed with our wedding plans. We have waited far too long. I am not young and feel that I do not have time to waste; I need to care for my lady and we have plans to extend and probably rebuild my modest home across the fields.'

Margaret smiled broadly; she loved her father-in-law. Although much of his life had been a mystery to them, he meant everything to the family. And now she also loved Consuelo. She trusted her completely and the idea of their happy household so close to home was a source of great joy. But there were clouds hanging over it all, the biggest being Pepe. There had been no sign of him and now she could see in Consuelo's eyes that she thought the boy was dead. Finding Algernon was at least a blessing to her: she had a chance of a new life away from the flummery of high society. It was as if God had taken something away but replaced it with an enduring consolation. There could be no doubt that she loved Algernon in a way that Margaret had never really loved Matthew.

The other cloud of course was Grace.

Margaret looked at Grace nervously. Her daughter got up from the pretty lace she was making and, placing it with a clatter of bobbins on a small sewing table that Consuelo had given her for Christmas, she went to the couple and embraced them both singly. When she turned back, Margaret saw that there was a tear in her eye that she quickly brushed from her cheek.

Alice had to be summoned, of course, and the stable lad was sent to find Samuel. Rupert was away studying at Mercers' School, which had not been to Samuel's taste. Samuel had announced that he wanted only to be a simple country doctor like his grandfather and had applied, with Algernon's help, to study medicine at a place called Oxford. But for now he was enjoying a few weeks accompanying his grandfather about his work. This had transformed the boy into a very serious young man. The only problem with him was his tendency to speak his mind. When he was told the happy news he offered heartfelt congratulations, but then turned at once to Grace.

'And what do you have to say to that Grace? It is time now that you put away that mopey face. I know that poor Peter has been patiently sending you messages and it is said that he even waits quietly in the lane, hoping for a glimpse of you. And meanwhile you make lace and are destined to be an old maid, when you could be mistress of the beautiful house he got only for you. You make us all unhappy, Grace, by your selfishness. Working with Grandfather I have seen how some women live, and you have it all: a bright future with a man who is good and true, a man whose life you saved when he was a boy... And what do you do? It is for want of a father that you are behaving so, and what does he know of you Grace? Our father has been away for two years and only one letter... Must we all moulder away while you turn your back on God's gifts to you?'

The room was aghast. Nobody could have imagined such words coming from the carefree Samuel; he had said what they all felt but had not dared to express.

225

Grace stood very still, her mouth wide open, and then Algernon spoke. He knew that he must, although he had felt that Grace should decide these things at her own pace, despite the fact that Consuelo had wept in frustration about it all.

Never had the house in St James's Square looked as magnificent as it did on this sunny spring morning. The imposing railings at the front, looking out over the square, were bedecked with blossom and greenery. There was a velvet platform on the pavement, onto which the guests could alight from their sedan chairs or coaches and a thick red carpet went from the street and up the steps. The trees in the square had burst into flower that very week and a thin confetti of petals floated on the breeze. It was a fairy tale scene, as befitted the marriage of Doctor Algernon and the Lady Consuelo, the future Mrs Lively.

Jane had excelled herself in her role, having had a lesson from none other than the late Queen's maid who now worked for an aging countess living in the square. She fussed over her mistress's hair as Grace watched impatiently.

Consuelo had chosen a dove grey gown, having decided that virginal white was not appropriate. It was close fitting and bound with black velvet, with black lace sleeves and gloves. Round her neck were the thick pearls George Anson had given to her before he sailed, but the most elegant thing of all was Jane's arrangement of her hair, which was intricately wound around her head and shone in the soft light. Consuelo also wore a plaited velvet snood studded with pearls, each one in a bed of lily of the valley. On the top of her head was a small diamond coronet, from the centre of which trailed a delicate silk veil which could be thrown back or worn over her face like gossamer. A fragrant bouquet of the lilies hung from a black satin ribbon attached to her wrist.

'This is perfection!' cried Jane, hearing the chatter of the crowds who were already assembled to see the bride depart for St George's, Hanover Square, where the anxious groom had been waiting for over an hour.

Consuelo was not used to this level of happiness. The only thing that could have made it more perfect would have been Pepe being there.

'Yes I think we are both ready,' Consuelo responded, reaching for Grace's hand. 'Nobody ever had such a lovely maid of honour, my dear,' she exclaimed.

Grace was in simple white velvet with a silk bodice decorated with tiny satin bows. Her sleeves were organza, caught at the wrist with pearl bracelets. She wore no gloves as they would impede the deft handling of Consuelo's train.

The party made its way to the grand hallway and the footman slowly opened the double doors to a great cry of delight from the waiting crowd, who would remain there doggedly until evening, not wanting to miss a minute of the spectacle where His Majesty would be a guest. Jane was in peach silk and black gloves and never in her life had she imagined being one of the principal characters in such a scene. Her chest constricted with pride as she was helped into the sedan chair, which was to follow the bride for the short distance to the church.

The church was completely full and a murmur of excitement trembled in the air as the bridal party arrived. Consuelo had decided to walk up the aisle on her own, followed by Grace. There was, after all, nobody to give her away. She had survived and she had found a life where she least expected it and for that she felt some considerable pride. The left front pew was completely filled with the Lively family and on the right with prestigious members of the court and His Majesty with the Countess of Yarmouth.

Of course Algernon was somewhat bemused by all of this; he had imagined a simple ceremony. But such was the wisdom of God that the splendour of the day had turned out to be more than justified.

As he saw Consuelo he felt almost overcome, but it was not only her radiance that made his eyes well up with emotion, it was the picture behind him in the front pew and the thought of the look on his future bride's face when she saw.

The King was smiling broadly in a way that was most unusual and so was Her Grace the Countess. Between them was a small boy in a pale satin suit, white stockings and black buckled shoes.

At first Consuelo did not see him, but as she turned to face the groom she let out a cry. The church erupted in a most unseemly roar of jubilation, for the whispers had taken hold like a forest fire on the morning of the wedding and London liked nothing more than a good romantic story. This was the stuff of fairy tales. The little lost boy whose face had been on posters all over the town and beyond, was there! Of course few knew the real pathos of the situation, but when the King and Her Grace pushed him to the front, and when their shoulders shook as they dabbed their eyes, as did most people on that sunny May morning, there was not much doubt about the truth of it. As for Consuelo, she could not think that one day there would be a heaven to which she might ascend. No – it was here.

There was another drama playing out as Consuelo and Algernon took their vows. Grace could not have failed to recognise that Peter was playing the magnificent organ; she had seen his back in view at once: the sturdy shoulders, the way his hair curled at the back of his neck. And of course he had seen her in his mirror and his playing had faltered.

Grace had felt her heart beating as if her chest were about to explode. She would go to him, she had decided, when the service had finished; she would climb the rickety steps to the organ loft and wait patiently behind him as the bridle couple walked down the aisle into a shower of fresh blossom petals.

But none of this went entirely according to plan. Pepe could not contain himself and broke away from the King and the countess and threw his arms around Consuelo's skirts. He had grown in the months he had been lost to her. The congregation fluttered at this astonishing interruption and nobody quite knew what to do, least of all the confused priest, who had thought from the start that it was very irregular for a Catholic woman to be married in an Anglican church with an Anglican service. In fact Consuelo had renounced her faith, persuaded that there was only one God and that the happiness of many people would be blessed by Him whatever ritual was observed. When all was said and done, religion had never stood in the way of Algernon's work with the holy sisters.

Grace stepped quietly forward and took hold of Pepe's shoulders and ushered him to her side as the service was completed and many delicate handkerchiefs were hastily pulled from velvet bags and secret pockets.

Afterwards, Grace ran as fast as her feet would carry her, round and round the circular staircase and up to the loft. Peter was playing Mr Handel's 'Arrival of the Queen of Sheba', Pepe had taken his place right between the newlyweds, and the royal party stood back and followed the couple into the sunshine.

He saw her reflection, but she did not wait for him to turn around before she put her arms around him and placed her lips on his neck. His playing did not falter this time; he simply watched her in the mirror devotedly as she mouthed the words. The words that all lovers know are the key to the simplest and the greatest of things.

He answered with a single syllable, clearly audible: 'When?' Then he turned to her and seized her.

'As soon as we can, dearest,' she answered, 'I have been a fool! Seeing the happiness of Consuelo and grandfather grasped even when the child was still missing...' She quavered. 'I truly believe that fate had a hand – or ... was it you, Peter? Did you find Pepe? And was this their wedding gift?'

'No, it was the King's men who found him,' murmured Peter, 'but I did offer something for the reward.'

'A reward?' exclaimed Grace.

'Yes, my dearest, such things do not come without an exchange of money – and Mr Handel helped. It is how the world works. But we did it for you all, my darling future wife.'

It was all too much. Grace could not take it in. Suddenly they heard a clatter of feet and there was Pepe. 'You must come! Both of you. The coaches are waiting for us all, my family,' he cried, as if it had always been so.

Chapter Twenty-six

What better place could there be for Consuelo and Algernon to have their honeymoon than Madonna's Court? It had all been arranged. And now, with the news that Grace had finally come to her senses, the newly engaged couple were to join them. Mrs Lively was to accompany them, bringing Pepe with her. It had been difficult to persuade Pepe that Consuelo must be left to her husband on the night of their marriage. For that reason it was also decided that Pepe should not, for now, be told the truth about his mother.

He had told her briefly what had happened to him during the months after his disappearance. 'To think,' mused Consuelo, 'that there are people who will imprison a child like that and that even Pepe, who is wily as a snake, could not escape; it hardly seems credible.'

'Well, every house has chimneys, my dear, and they all need cleaning. None of us think about the poor little wretches who climb them and sweep them. There are many people who do not choose to treat these poor mites well. He was beaten into submission and only fed when he did the job well and then not enough to feed a cat. He had to be kept thin of course.'

'But I still do not quite understand how he was found; nobody has explained this properly to me,' said Consuelo.

'It was Peter who had the idea of the reward, and the King's men have many secret ways of conveying the message. To tell you the truth, Grace's brothers hid him for a while after that fateful night, until one day he just did not return. We all feared then that he had been snatched by one of the gangs who take children for the most terrible reasons. He is lucky not to have suffered an even worse fate. As it is, he is a tough little lad and the scars will heal.'

Consuelo put her head on Algernon's shoulder and they made their way back to the house as Consuelo set to wondering exactly how much money had been found to retrieve her son and why she had not been approached herself. She would, of course, discover eventually, but not now, since Algernon was clearly reluctant to discuss it.

Old Thomas, who kept an eye on everything, opened the door for them when they got back to the house. 'We have it all ready, and the servants have arranged such a spread! At last the house is to have a mistress – not before time,' he added with a cluck of disapproval. 'We low folk think only of the natural rhythm of things: we work when it is light and sleep when the Lord puts the world to sleep. When a man sees the light in a thing he must take it and, pardon me, the same applies to Their Ladyships.' He gave Consuelo a slight bow and she smiled indulgently. She was used to Thomas's homilies now and by and large they were profoundly wise.

It was obvious when the party arrived that they were in a more than celebratory mood. Grace was the first to rush from the carriage, even before the driver had tethered the horse to the rail at the bottom of the steps.

'Wait, Grace, you will do yourself an injury!' called her mother. But Grace would not wait, she bounded to her grandfather with the news which her mother would have preferred to deliver herself.

'Grandfather!' she cried, flinging herself at him. 'Your son is coming home!'

Algernon held her tightly; he could feel her trembling like a small bird.

'Yes, it is true,' added Margaret quietly; she was never one to be overly emotional.

Consuelo felt her stomach lurch; Did this mean George was on his way home? Why was she the last to know? After all, as far as he was concerned she was still languishing in the demimonde of women with no fixed position. But as her mind raced through all the implications there was a voice within her that celebrated the fact that she now had a husband and a position in the world, which left no room for sideways looks and nudges. Money and beauty had protected her, but beauty is an elusive gift that fades quickly, as surely as evening follows a bright day. And as for her money, it had eased her entry into the tinsel court, which even the King found odious, but it could never count for more than the love she had now found.

They bustled into the large room, which served many purposes in the old house. It had been where the Mother Superior had chosen to hold court and it faced southwest, allowing the company to enjoy the warm late afternoon glow which showed them all to advantage. Thomas and one of the servants took their cloaks and hats. The servant, a young village girl of no more than fifteen, was agog at the sight of her soon to be mistress and thought her the prettiest lady she had ever seen. And as for her master, he was transformed. His long composed face seemed to have put itself on quite the opposite way, and he was smiling widely.

Grace could not sit down, she flitted around making plans in her head; there were so many things she would do with the old house. She felt a sigh in the old rafters, as if the house knew that it was to be cared for again and that young lives would race down the stairs and into the gardens; it had been such a silent place for too long. Now her life was complete, a fairy story she could never even have imagined.

It was Peter who had to settle them all and explain the reality of this astonishing news. There was a sting in the tail which had been entirely overlooked and Margaret had asked him to explain, sensing that she might be too emotional to bring the level of gravity such news required.

'Mrs Lively received the news yesterday in a letter delivered from the Admiralty.' Consuelo stared unflinchingly at his face. She saw at once that he had more information, which might be less joyous. Nobody interrupted him and he reached for Grace's hand as he went on. 'It seems Commodore Anson's fleet, having incurred terrible losses, finally arrived in China – Canton to be precise. The voyage into the North Pacific at the wrong time of year had debilitated all the officers and men who survived and not least your father, Grace,' he said slowly. 'He was much weakened by the scurvy. The Commodore deemed he would not survive the tribulations that still awaited the great voyage, which was yet to be completed. An old French Indian packet ship, which makes good speed and was on its way to Portsmouth with a cargo of tea, offered to take some of the very sick men – those who were not thought to be infectious. Captain Lively was one of those men and will, with a good wind and favourable conditions, arrive in Portsmouth in the next three weeks. Word will be sent in time for us to meet him and bring him back to Holly Farm where he can be nursed by Margaret.'

'Ah ... so Matthew agreed to that, did he?' asked Algernon, calculating that his son must have been indeed very sick. Never would the old Matthew have agreed to be invalided onto, of all things, a 'French Indiaman' amongst a hold of tea and slave sailors. He shot an apprehensive glance at the

the group of women who were not prepared for the shock they had in store.

Grace was not going to allow the anticipation of her father's return to be marred by thoughts of doom. She had tasted complete happiness and the greatest joy of all: that her beloved father would be home to see her married. And what was more, insofar as Peter was concerned, she had overcome the priority of putting her absent father first.

As for Margaret, her feelings were well and truly mixed; she knew only too well that George Anson would be continuing his quest for the greatest prize, the *Manila Galleon*. And despite the man's promises, Matthew Lively would more than likely lose all his claims to the prize money. She wondered if any of the other prizes that she had heard about in the rare communications from her husband would be sent home with him. Apart from that, the facts spoke for themselves. She would have a weak man on her hands. He was not young anymore and another voyage would be hard if he did survive. She let her mind wonder at what manner of disease he would bring home with him. The little information she had received from the Admiralty had been vague. Margaret had had a hard life and there were no provisions for a husband who could not work like an ordinary man.

CHAPTER TWENTY-SEVEN

PORTSMOUTH HARBOUR

The docking of a great ship was a laborious business and word had come to the excited crowd that the *Alicia* was entering the harbour with nothing but the barest of sails. It was a blustery day but even so those watching could never imagine the awful, treacherous nature of the sea from which Matthew had been delivered. Some thought only of the prize the adventure might have brought the poor souls who had been on the ocean.

Matthew was slung on deck, cocooned in his hammock like a cadis fly. At last he was heaved up, hammock and all, bumped down the gangplank and dumped unceremoniously on the harbour. He was hanging on to his naval bag, in which was a handsome portion of the prize that had been taken before the *Centurion* had reached China. He had been safe with it on the ship as there was an unwritten law that you never robbed a fellow sailor, but on shore things were less sure. He levered himself up weakly and scanned the sea of faces. He caught site of a likely group and then had to look again. Could this be his family? It was his father he saw first with a handsome lady on his arm and a small dark child nestling in her skirts. His father Algernon was dressed like a very smart gentleman and his beard was clipped. Next to him were two boys. Could they be his sons? He hardly remembered their names, fuddled as he was by fever. Then that must be

Grace, so elegant and composed, startlingly beautiful, even from distance, as she hung on the arm of a tall, imposing young man. Margaret hung back as usual, younger than he remembered, as if her face had been wiped of some of the odious cares that comprised her life. He called out feebly and it was Grace who saw him first and rushed towards him. In a flash he saw the real treasure in his life, which he had neglected for so long and he knew at once that he would never again leave this blessed isle that he called home.

'Father,' Grace sobbed, falling on him with disregard for the pungent smell he gave off. He had been too weak to wash and it had been a long passage. The crew, a motley group of Indians and disenfranchised Spaniards, had been too busy to care for an additional sailor. They were manning the ship and securing the cargo in the fierce storms, ensuring the safety of the china pots that stored the tea, which were protected by straw. Their meagre pay was dependent on the safe delivery of a cargo more valuable than the decrepit Matthew Lively.

There are moments in life when words are merely an intrusion. Nothing could be said which would adequately describe a reunion such as this. Each and everyone had their own sorrows and hopes. Some of the hopes and sorrows were filled with resentment, which made the bearer of that emotion feel guilty. Margaret Lively had very mixed feelings towards the wreck of a man who lay on soiled canvas in such a horrible state. She had discovered her own ability to survive in the two years he had been away. She had raised her children above their station, she had managed the farm, she had found for the first time in her life her own strength as well as a simple beauty that had remained hidden for so many years. Since Matthew had been away she had learned to think only of the present and not to spend her time counting the endless days and weeks leading to an uncertain conclusion. She saw her daughter sobbing with joy as she clung to him, and thought about the unconditional love that exists between parents and children. She resented the way her daughter asked nothing of this man who had left them without a backward glance, taking their mother for granted. As she contemplated the future with this man who was to all intents and purposes a stranger, she felt guilty but at the same time resolved. She would fulfil her obligations – but without love, just because it was her duty.

Margaret went to Grace and pulled her gently away. Matthew saw his wife and also the cool look in her eyes and he felt the distance.

'Husband, I cannot say you look well, but if God is kind we will nurse you back to health. Your sons are here Matthew; I have kept their hopes for your return deep in my heart. Treat them with care, Matthew; they are young men who will look for more from you than you will be able to give.'

Grace heard nothing of the quiet exchange. She had returned to the firm hold of Peter. He too shared the ambivalence of his future mother in law.

Rupert and Samuel stepped forward respectfully and took the thin hand of their father in turn.

'I have letters in my bag from the Commodore and from some of the men,' said Matthew in a ready voice when he was settled in a warm, comfortable bed. Margaret had washed and shaved him and cut his ragged toenails. She had tied his hair back from his face and miraculously some of the ice in her heart had begun to evaporate. He had brought with him a substantial pot of gold but not, as his wife muttered to herself, anything like the portion he might have expected, and she had taken it at once and hidden it in the false bottom of an ancient sea chest.

As the boys drew up chairs by his bed, Matthew began to describe some of the wonders he had encountered. His sons listened with awe and soon had to be removed so as not to tire their father out.

The wedding had to be planned. It would be at Holly Farm but the date had not yet been arrived at. The family had begun the difficult task of reconnecting but while Peter had been accepted by Matthew, the older man tired easily.

One evening Alice decided to talk about this to Margaret. 'Madam, may I speak frankly to you about the captain?' she asked solemnly.

'You may, Alice, when did you not?' Margaret replied.

'The captain will not recover,' Alice said in an even tone.

'I know,' replied Margaret softly.

'It is the wound in his leg; it was an old wound which opened up when he had the scurvy. I have had Doctor Algernon look at it. It is healed over the top but underneath it is festering. He has a fever with it and, I know, much pain.'

'I had suspected as much,' said Margaret, beginning to weep. 'It is a cruel thing, Alice. When he first came back, I hated him… Don't be shocked, Alice, but I did. But slowly I have begun to love him again; this is why I have let you do so much for him – I needed to think of him as the man he was when I loved him as a young girl. But I see it in his eyes. I wish I had more time with him, Alice. What shall we do? Grace will not believe any of this.'

'We must have the wedding as quickly as possible. I will give him some laudanum… It is summer… Let us have the young couple married without further ado and, as God is my witness, Captain Lively will walk his daughter up the aisle and then Madam Grace will have to leave and cleave…'

Margaret had put away her sewing and fell forward into Alice's lap; she cried all the tears she should have cried in the long, lonely separation from her husband. She had held them inside her like captive birds in a cage, but now they flew out.

Just as it had been decided to protect Pepe from the truth for a short while, so it was decided not to tell Grace about her father's dire situation; they would not mar her day, and she would find out soon enough.

Margaret went quietly up the stairs, and found Matthew half asleep. She looked at him in the soft light of the lamp. His face was smooth and his hands lay peacefully on the linen sheets; all was in perfect order. Of this she was proud and as she sat quietly in the chair beside the bed, she thought about forgiveness. She had been to the local priest and confided the anger in her heart and he had calmed her. 'My child, to deny these thoughts is to deny your humanity; they are natural but think only of the opportunity to cleanse these wounds with love.' The old priest had wanted to visit Matthew, but Margaret warned him that this was a man without faith. 'No man is without faith,' the priest had thundered.

As if reading her thoughts, Matthew began to speak. With his eyes still closed, he reached for her hand. 'My dearest wife,' he whispered.

'I am here as I have always been.'

'Yes, you have always been, but I had so wanted to come home to you Margaret and be a proper husband. I know, Margaret, that I have not much time, but in the end I have my wish. I will hand my daughter to another man before I start my journey, and what with the gold I brought back...' He moved his leg with a slight groan. 'I will have done well by you all in the end, but only because I had such a woman and they had such a mother.'

There were tears welling in his eyes and Margaret leaned down to him and put her mouth to his. All the years of resentment fell away and she laid her head on his chest. He was warm, much too warm, but she felt his heart beating, a brave old heart.

Grace came quietly into the room and found them like this. It was the greatest gift she could have asked for. She sat at the other side of the bed and held her father's other hand.

'Father,' she said quietly, 'Peter and I are to be wed next week in the church on the green and we are to have a great celebration. Now that you are home, you will never leave us again. I am so happy! I could not imagine anything that would make my life more perfect.'

Her parents spread their arms and they stayed locked together for a while. Matthew and Margaret would not tell her the truth; she would have her perfect day. In her own way, Margaret had always known things would be alright when all was said and done, but this was a gift for her; it was an epiphany. As the priest had said: 'It is not how your life begins that is the measure of it, it is how it ends.' Her husband would have the best of it because it was her gift to herself to see that it was so.

Chapter Twenty-eight

Holly Farm,
THE DAY BEFORE THE WEDDING

'I told you he would be there, and he will,' assured Alice.

'But how?' asked Margaret. 'He is so frail and the fever is worsening; this could be the final straw that kills him.' She put her head in her hands. Was this right, she wondered? Shouldn't he be left in peace? She said as much to the stalwart Alice.

'No, madam. Thankfully, Miss Lively does not know quite how near the end he is. It is only his determination to give his daughter away which is keeping him alive. Would you deprive him of that?' She was beginning to lose patience, but she knew that a great deal was at stake: Miss Lively would cancel the whole thing if there was whisper of her father being so ill that he could not have his wish.

Alice was a practical woman – planning a wedding was no small thing, and this was to be the loveliest thing Clapham had ever seen. Already the villagers were putting Alice's commands into action: the flags were up, the church was decorated and looked like a garden in full bloom. The feast for over a hundred was to be under a big awning in the orchard. Massive hams and potted meats waited in the larders; marinated fruits and chutneys had been brought from the store cupboard and all manner of breads would be in the oven by dawn. And for afterwards there were cheeses from the farm and possets laced with cider. But the triumph was the cake. Alice and 'her girls' had laboured night and day at such icings as had never been seen before.

The dress hung in the parlour with satin shoes, which had come from the finest shoe maker in London. The maid of honour's dress was still to be finished as they spoke. The dress was for none other than Jane. Alice had clucked a little when she heard, she was mildly jealous of course, but then Jane had served Miss Lively well and, rumour had it, saved her life. Twelve small girls from the village were to be the flower maids. Their mothers had all got together to make the muslin frocks amid a flurry of excitement.

The Lady Consuelo had made a gift of a pearl and diamond necklace, which she had hidden in her skirts when her family home was ransacked. It was Miss Lively's now and would go to one of her own daughters, if God blessed her with some.

'You are right, Alice,' said Margaret. 'He will walk her down the aisle. You are always the voice of common sense.'

'This is so much more than common sense, madam. It is our history. We can make it or break it. Now – away with you to the captain; take him his milk and I will lace it with laudanum… And keep Miss Lively out of there; she will only tire him.'

The day was as fair as any could be. Matthew was calm and peaceful and his sons slowly dressed him with a kind of reverence. Their eyes met, and they knew. Grace was kept out of the way until the moment of departure.

And then it was time. He waited for her in the hall and she stood at the top of the stairs. For her father it was a vision; he knew he would soon say goodbye to this world and pass on to the next but what man could ask for more than this? He faltered a little and the boys quickly supported him. Grace came to him in her own joyous haze. If she had any idea of the truth she did not show it.

It was only a short distance but a little open cart bedecked with flowers and hoops of roses made its way briskly to the packed church through crowds of joyful faces.

The church was heavily scented with the rich perfume of summer flowers and Peter was already a little light-headed. When the music began, to announce the arrival of the bride, he thought he might faint. They joined hands and exchanged a gaze that hung like a balm in the air. Matthew did indeed hand his daughter to Peter and he gave a sigh of disbelief that it had been possible. The whole church was intoxicated with the moment. In future years they would think of it and tell their grandchildren how glad they were to have been there.

The afternoon turned into evening and Grace slipped quietly away from the gathering and went into her father's room. He did not stir so she took his hand. The greatest loss to a young girl is her father and it was going to be all the greater for Grace as she had already lost him so many times; but for the moment, here he was in physical form. On an impulse she leant over and gathered his frail body in her arms. 'Father,' she sobbed deeply, her shoulders shaking, the tears falling over his craggy face and into the runnels of skin weathered by the sea and sun. 'Don't leave me, please don't leave me! I can make you better… I can… I can…' she wept. He was very hot and suddenly the blood seemed to drain from his face.

'Grace, my beloved daughter, I must leave you. I have had a good life but you are the greatest gift I have known and today I give my treasure to another man who will be the fa-

244

ther of your children, a better father than I have been. Today heaven was generous to me. I ask no more. I am tired and I must make my peace.'

Peter had been waiting quietly by the door. He came into the room and put a hand on his wife's heaving shoulders.

Matthew opened his eyes, sighed contentedly and was gone.

EPILOGUE

I am a modest man and my history is shared with the nineteen hundred men and boys who left Spithead with Commodore Anson in September 1740. I am one of the ones who survived; almost fourteen hundred died a cruel death of disease and starvation rounding Cape Horn at the season's worst and lost for the want of longitude. We had gone to find fame and fortune, and capture the great *Manila Galleon*, the Spanish treasure ship, 'The Prize of the Oceans', which sailed from Acapulco each year. In this we succeeded but only by the will of God, the skill of the Commodore, and acts of bravery such as cannot be believed. We lost all the fleet save our sturdy ship the *Centurion*, and I was one of the few to serve on the flagship throughout.

Of course we returned to a hero's welcome but it tasted sour for me. I was not to know in the beginning what the future of the voyage held for me and the men we had to leave behind or that George Anson would be instrumental in reforming the British Navy and be considered the greatest admiral in history.

My share of the prize money has made me rich beyond what I deserved. When I think of the cost in lives better than my own lost, I want to weep. Some men returned to the families they had left behind broken in body, spirit and faith and received a pittance. The fortune was unfairly divided – a great wrong, which is still to be righted. I took my share and vowed to do what was right with it. I sought out the old man John Harrison who had invented the Longitude Clock. The want of it on our voyage cost countless lives and all for the lack of a few thousand pounds, which the Admiralty would not afford him.

He was past his eightieth year and his son received me with gratitude, and joy at the thought that his father's life's work would be completed; truthfully the gratitude was mine.

But there was something else I did. Matthew Lively was an officer on my ship and my dearest friend and inspiration, who had twice saved my life. He was sent home when we got to China as his health was failing, back to the family he talked of in the endless night watches. I found out he had died and as I felt I knew all his family, I vowed to visit his widow and pay my respects.

I was not a married man, and what I found when I met the Livelys was such happiness as no man could have imagined. Margaret Lively, there was a woman! And her fine sons and gentle daughter are as their father described. Grace is in wedded bliss and soon 'my beloved Margaret' is to be a grandmother. It will be the first babe I will hold, and I will think of it as one of my own.

ACKNOWLEDGEMENTS

With deepest thanks to all the people who have made the solitary life of a writer possible. First and foremost Naim Attallah, who had faith in me even in his own darkest hour. Elspeth Sinclair, editor, agent and friend extraordinaire. Anna Stothard and Peter Jacobs for their painstaking editing along with all the team at Quartet. And then there are the many others who have given their support. Steve Dodd at Shugborough Hall, where the long dead voice of my grandfather Francis Anson still resonates. And of course the many recorded accounts of George Anson's epic voyage which are part of the family folk law, particularly the original diaries of the Rev Richard Walter, the chaplain on the Centurion; a graphic account of the journey published in 1748 which inspired me to visit that time and place.

George Anson was a brave but rather dense character and as a novelist I wrote about what is already known, but also what is not. His political life was an important area to explore but, of course, throughout my writing Anson and his story grew in complexity and owes much to imagination. On a personal level thanks go to Joanna Dabkowska and Deike Begg who both restore order from chaos in their own different ways and a very supportive family.